"The third in Harper's Witches o
suspenseful and action-packed as

—*Library Journal* (starred r...)

"This is sure to enchant series fans and new readers alike."

—*Publishers Weekly*

"The delightful lore of charming Thistle Grove continues to grow in this evocatively written story." —*Kirkus Reviews*

"With each book in the series, Harper's characters and community inspire more delight." —*Booklist*

"I am happily and completely under the spell of The Witches of Thistle Grove series."

—Emily Henry, #1 *New York Times* bestselling author of *Book Lovers*

"The only flaw in Lana Harper's magical, whimsical, sexy-as-hell The Witches of Thistle Grove series is that I can't set up shop in Thistle Grove myself right this second! These books truly do cast a spell."

—Erin Sterling, *New York Times* bestselling author of *The Ex Hex*

"Clever, fiery, and so much fun. *From Bad to Cursed* is a sharply written romp with wicked imagination. It's pure magic."

—Rachel Harrison, author of *Cackle*

"These books are intensely queer, honest, and essentially kind. I adore them so."

—Seanan McGuire, *New York Times* bestselling author of *Where the Drowned Girls Go*

TITLES BY LANA HARPER

Payback's a Witch
From Bad to Cursed
Back in a Spell
In Charm's Way

In Charm's Way

Way

LANA HARPER

BERKLEY ROMANCE
NEW YORK

BERKLEY ROMANCE
Published by Berkley
An imprint of Penguin Random House LLC
penguinrandomhouse.com

Library of Congress Cataloging-in-Publication Data

Names: Harper, Lana, author.
Title: In charm's way / Lana Harper.
Description: First edition. | New York : Berkley Romance, 2023. |
Series: The witches of Thistle Grove
Identifiers: LCCN 2022060587 (print) | LCCN 2022060588 (ebook) |
ISBN 9780593637968 (trade paperback) | ISBN 9780593637975 (ebook)
Subjects: LCGFT: Witch fiction. | Romance fiction. | Novels.
Classification: LCC PS3608.A7737 I5 2023 (print) |
LCC PS3608.A7737 (ebook) | DDC 813/.6—dc23/eng/20230104
LC record available at https://lccn.loc.gov/2022060587
LC ebook record available at https://lccn.loc.gov/2022060588

First Edition: August 2023

Printed in the United States of America
1st Printing

Book design by Alison Cnockaert

*To the Delilah devotees who wished
she'd taken center stage in* Payback—
this one's for you.

1

Small Victories

HE VIRIDIAN TEARDROPS *should* have been in bloom by now. That much, at least, I had no trouble remembering.

But I'd been trawling the Hallows Hill woods for almost four hours, walking the forest in as methodical a grid as one could manage on terrain that tended to shift around you like a daydream if you let your attention wander, and I hadn't spotted even a glimmer of the distinctive, iridescent color that gave the flowers their name. A languid twilight had begun to gather above the rustling treetops; a midsummer wash of dusky lavender that dipped the already hushed bower in an almost melancholy light, subdued as a sigh.

If anything, I was more likely to spot one of the elusive flowers now than I had been earlier. Viridians unfurled at dusk, revealing glinting amber centers like fireflies—the stamens that held the magically active pollen I was hunting for.

Six months ago, I wouldn't even have needed to traipse along a grid. I'd been hiking Hallows Hill for pleasure since I was a kid, even when I wasn't on the prowl for floral ingredients for a tincture or brew. Many of the plants that thrived up here were unique, native to Thistle Grove. Exactly which herbs, blooms, lichens, and mosses grew where had once been imprinted on my mind like an intricate schematic, a precise framework crystallized among my synaptic pathways. In the Before the Oblivion times, I'd had a photographic memory; the kind science wasn't convinced existed, even if every other neurodivergent TV detective laid claim to one.

But I'd *really* had one. The ability to recall whole pages of text I'd read only once, to summon up faded illustrations I'd pored over by candlelight, to confidently rattle off lists of ingredients for obscure potions I'd never even prepared. The Delilah Harlow of before hadn't had the first idea just how much she'd taken her keen mind for granted.

In my bleakest moments, I hated her for that smug complacency almost as much as I hated Nina Blackmoore for what she'd done to me.

With an effort, I shook off the creeping angst—in the months since I'd lost and regained most of my memory, I'd developed a maddening tendency to brood over my own misfortune, a waste of productive time if ever there was one—and turned my attention back to the forest floor. Viridian teardrops often grew in little clusters of three, usually around the exposed root balls of deciduous trees. By early July, there should already have been a good crop of them ready for harvest.

But Lady's Lake had been a little tempestuous lately. Nina Blackmoore's discovery of Belisama's statue at its distant bottom seemed to have stirred up the sleeping avatar, jolted the piece of the mysterious goddess that lived in our lake bed into some semi-elevated state of awareness. We now enjoyed the odd lightning storm crackling just above the lake on otherwise perfect days, while balls of Saint Elmo's fire had been spotted drifting down Hallows Hill and through the town below, rolling through walls like ghostly, electrified tumbleweeds and scaring the entire shit out of Thistle Grove normies. (The oblivion glamour cast over the town prevented memory retention of spells directly cast by Thistle Grove's witches, but it was nowhere near broad enough to cover all the other unusual "meteorological phenomena.")

Disturbances like that might have seeped into the forest as well, upset its natural growth rhythms or shifted them.

Just as I was about to cut my losses and call it a day, a flash of amber winked in my peripheral vision. I wheeled toward it, a flush of pure joy searing up my throat.

Sensing my excitement, my raven familiar, Montalban, hopped down from one of the boughs overhead, where she'd been examining intriguing insects and tracking my slow progress below. She landed on my shoulder, talons gently digging in for grip, then nestled her glossy dark head against my cheek and emitted a hoarse, contented caw. She didn't understand exactly what was happening; though familiars were empathically bound to their witches and attuned to magic, they weren't the snarky, anthropomorphized pets you saw in cheesy witch movies. But she could feel how happy it had made me to spot the viridians, that this was something important to me.

If nothing else, familiars excelled at very earnest "I *love* this for you" vibes.

Montalban and I had been bound for only a little less than six months; Ivy had thought that bonding a familiar might be healing for me as I recovered from the glamour, a friendly presence to both ground my mind and facilitate my scattered spellwork. But I already couldn't imagine life without my salty little sweetheart always at my shoulder.

"See?" I whispered triumphantly to her, though I didn't really have to vocalize; Montalban could pick up on the general gist of my thoughts. But I loved talking out loud to her, like the friends we were. "Still got it, my bitch!"

"*Craw!*" she agreed, ruffling her feathers.

It wasn't a typical cluster trio, I saw as I bent to examine the flower. Only a solitary blossom, and on the smallish side as viridians came, growing in a nook just by a slim sycamore's base. But its teardrop petals were plump and glossy with health, a gorgeously vivid bluish green—and nestled within, the stamens quivered with a rich dusting of that precious yellow pollen. If I was meticulous about extracting it, this single flower would be enough to cast a full iteration of Marauder's Misery—one of the anti-theft wards I'd been restoring at Tomes & Omens ever since Nina Fucking Blackmoore undid three centuries' worth of them in her brief and catastrophic rampage as a demigoddess.

Flames and stars, living in this town could be *exhausting.*

I sank down by the tree's base, pebbles and blades of grass pressing imprints into my bare knees. Then I closed my eyes and reached for the flower, cupping my hands around it without grazing the petals.

Sensing the flow of magic, Montalban brought her focus to bear on the spell, too, facilitating my work with it. She couldn't make me stronger than I was; that wasn't how familiars helped. But her added attention was like a lens held to the sun—anything I cast, she rendered finer and more precise.

Like most magically imbued flora, viridians couldn't just be plucked by mundane means. They needed to be harvested with the use of a particular preservation spell, to keep their potency intact. Magical botany was like that; infinitely fascinating and challenging, and also finicky as fuck. Hence, why I loved it. It demanded expertise and finesse, a deep understanding of theories and disciplines that the other Thistle Grove families largely cast aside in favor of relying on their natural talents. Even the Thorns didn't bother with it much, given their affinity for magically coaxing plants into simply doing whatever it was they wanted them to do.

But arcane knowledge, and its practical applications . . . that was where Harlows shone.

Especially *this* Harlow.

I took a slow breath, twitching my fingers into the delicate position called for by the spell, lips parting to speak the incantation. The words floated into my mind's eye in swooping antique copperplate; I could even picture the yellowed page upon which the rhyming couplets had been inked.

Then the entirety of the charm sluiced out of my head like water sliding through a sieve.

All of it, vanished in an instant. The words themselves, the lovely script, the aged grain of the paper. Where the memory had lived, there was now nothing. A cold and empty darkness, a void like a miniature black hole whorling in my head.

The panic that gushed through me was instantaneous, a prickling flood that engulfed me from the crown of my head to the tips of my toes, a flurry of icy pins sinking into my skin. And even worse was the terrible sense of dislocation that accompanied it, as if the entire world had spun wildly on its axis around me before falling back into place subtly misaligned. I'd *known* that spell, only moments ago. Now, I didn't. It was simply gone, lost, as if it had been plucked directly out of my head by some merciless, meticulous set of tweezers.

"Crawwww!" Montalban croaked into my ear, shifting fretfully from foot to foot as my distress seeped into her.

"I'm okay," I managed, through the terrible tightening in my throat. "It's okay."

But it wasn't. It felt nauseatingly like existing in two realities at once. One in which I was the old Delilah, a living library, a vast and unimpeachable repository of arcane information. And another in which I was a tabula rasa, almost no one at all. Just a facsimile of a person rather than anybody real and whole.

The dissonance of it was horrifying, a primal terror unlike anything I'd ever experienced before. The way, I imagined, some people might fear death, that ultimate disintegration of self if you truly believed nothing else came after.

Though to me, the idea of living with a mind that couldn't be trusted felt worse than even the possibility of a truly final oblivion.

I sank back onto my haunches, wrapping my arms around my chest. Goose bumps had erupted along the expanse of my skin, and I broke into a clammy sweat despite the buzzy warmth of the air, the humid heat that permeated the forest from the lake. "It's okay," I whispered to myself under my breath, rocking back and forth, feeling abysmally pathetic and weak even as Montalban nuzzled my cheek, desperate to provide some comfort. "You're alright. Try to relax and let it pass over you. Like a reed in the river, remember? Don't fight against the current, because the current always wins."

Sometimes, the simple relaxation mantra Ivy had improvised for me from her meditation practice worked, bleeding off some of the panic. Other times, it did absolute fuck all.

The worst part was that no one understood why this was *still* happening to me. As a Harlow recordkeeper, I should have been shielded from a conventional oblivion glamour in the first place. Given our role as the memory keepers of our community, Thistle Grove's formal occult historians, we were all bespelled to be immune to such attacks. But Nina's form of the spell had been super-powered, whipped to unfathomable heights by the kernel of divinity that had been lodged inside her, the deity's favor she'd been granted by Belisama.

Why that entitled Blackmoore bitch had been deemed deserving of a goddess's favor in the first place was still beyond me.

In any case, even after the mega-glamour dissolved—helped along by my cousin Emmy's and my uncle James's efforts—I wasn't rid of it entirely. Six months later, I still sometimes lost memories like this, little aftershocks of oblivion riving through me even after all this time. Other times, I reached for knowledge that I should have had—that I *knew* I'd once possessed—only to discover an utter, sucking absence in its place. As if some vestigial remnant of the spell lurked inside me like a malevolent parasite, a magical malaria that only occasionally reared up.

The lost memories did return sometimes, if I relaxed enough in the moment, or if I was able to revisit their original source— reread the page that held the charm, pore over the missing diagram.

But sometimes they simply didn't, as if my brain had been rewired and was now inured to retaining that piece of information. And it was all horribly unpredictable. Just when I'd begun to tentatively hope that I might be on the upswing, I'd tumble into yet another mental vortex, a churning quagmire where I'd once reliably found the diamond edges of my mind.

But the self-soothing methods Ivy had taught me were always worth at least a try. I repeated the sappy "reed in a river" mantra to myself several more times—trying my damnedest not to feel like someone who'd ever wear Spiritual Gangster apparel in earnest—all the while inhaling deliberately through my nose and exhaling out of my mouth. The familiar smell of Lady's Lake calmed me, too, the distinctive scent of the magic that rolled off the water and through the woods, coursing down the mountain-side to wash over the town. It was the strongest up here, an intoxi-cating smell like some layered incense. Earthy and musky and sweet, redolent of frankincense and myrrh laced with amber and oakmoss.

As a Harlow, my sense of the lake's magic was both more in-timate and more acute than that of members of the other families—and the flow of it up here, so close to its wellspring, reassured me. Left me safe in the knowledge that I was still Delilah of Thistle Grove, on her knees on Hallows Hill with her beloved familiar on her shoulder. A Harlow witch exactly where she belonged.

Abruptly, the harvesting charm slid back into my mind. A little frayed around the edges, some of the words blurring in and out of sight, as if my memory were a dulled lens that had lost some of its focus. But it *was* back, restored, intact enough that I would be able to use it to collect the viridian.

"Oh, *thank you*," I breathed on a tremulous sigh, my limbs turning jellied with relief, unsure whom I was even thanking. Ivy's mantra, the goddess Belisama, the magic itself? When it came down to it, it didn't really matter.

Sometimes, you had to take the smallest of victories and run with them.

Sometimes, they were all you had to cling to.

2

Mystery Objects

IT WAS PAST nine by the time Montalban and I got home, the harvested viridian pulsing in my backpack, safe inside the transparent little globe of magic I'd conjured for its keeping. I lived on Feverfew, only a few streets over from Yarrow Street and Tomes & Omens, the family occult and indie bookstore that was now largely my charge. Not even a five-minute walk away, but far enough and residential enough to cushion me from the relentless hubbub of rowdy tourists that traipsed through Thistle Grove almost year-round.

Witch-crazy visitors were Tomes & Omens' bread and butter, but that didn't mean I had to *like* the noisy bumblefucks, or the overly familiar way they pawed my books and artifacts. You'd think tourists itching for a slice of occult history would approach it with more respect, and yet they dropped fragile artifacts, spilled their obnoxious unicorn lattes into sticky puddles on my floors, and chased my poor raven around the store as if they had the slightest hope of clapping their grubby paws on her.

But that was people for you, and why I generally preferred to stick to books and familiars.

Dipping into my cargo shorts pockets in search of my house key, I paused in front of the renovated colonial that held my second-floor duplex unit. Protective candles flickered in my windows—I'd learned to always ward my home that way from my uncle James—while my woman-about-town landlady's below were dark as per usual; the chick's social life was tantamount to an extreme sport. The summer night felt like a bell jar lowered around me, silent and almost perfectly still. A warm hush that pressed sweetly against the skin, disturbed only by the faint, whispery rustle of the elms that lined the street. The air smelled of honeysuckle, which grew abundant around the base of Hallows Hill and drifted around the town in fragrant currents every year, as soon as spring began its softening yield to summer.

Perfumed peace all around me, just the way I liked it. If I closed my eyes, I could almost pretend to be the only human left alive in the entire neighborhood. The sole survivor of some subtle apocalypse.

Sometimes, the idea of that much solitude felt disturbingly appealing.

I located the correct pocket, still savoring my little triumph as I fished out my key and jogged up the stairs to the porticoed landing, hiking boots clomping against the concrete steps. I'd successfully snared a memory back from oblivion, something I'd managed only a few other times before. Maybe I *was* finally getting better; maybe the remnants of the glamour were loosening their lingering grip, claws retracting from my mind.

Shifting the weight of my backpack to my left shoulder, I lifted the key to slide it into the lock. And promptly forgot what I was doing, or what the ominously serrated piece of metal in my hand was even supposed to be *for*.

The panic that slammed into me was like barreling face-first into a wall. My heart battered against my ribs with what felt like bruising force, my hand shaking so hard I couldn't even keep the—the *thing*, the Mystery Fucking Object—lined up with the lock.

Had my life depended on it, a cold blade pressed to the soft flesh under my jaw, I couldn't have divined what the object in my hand was meant to do.

With a distraught caw, Montalban abandoned her perch on the landing balustrade and settled on my shoulder. But this time, even her loving presence, the warmth of her ruffled feathers against my cheek and the sharp, familiar dig of her talons into my shoulder, couldn't cut the rising terror.

The more I thought about it, the more sinister and wrong the thing felt, until some of that danger seemed to seep like welling blood into the texture of the night around me. Tainting it, turning it into the deceptively peaceful prelude of a slasher film. Why would something ever be *shaped* like this? That strange little circular head at the top, the menacingly toothy blade. Was it a very small weapon, maybe? An artifact intended to facilitate some malign spellwork? What was I even doing, holding something so clearly forged to nefarious ends without protective gloves between it and my skin?

I dropped my backpack with a thump, heedless of the englobed viridian inside, and turned to press my back against the door, sliding down the varnished wood until my butt met the floorboards.

I was drenched in a cold wash of sweat, and I could hear myself panting, harsh breaths that sounded like they were being dragged by a fishhook from my throat. Even Montalban's panicky croaking seemed to echo from a tunnel's distance away, though she was right next to my ear. I wanted to drop the Mystery Fucking Object more than I'd possibly ever wanted anything. But some deep-rooted stubbornness inside me resisted the impulse, the desire to take the easy way out.

A stupid, maybe-evil hunk of metal was *not* stronger than I was.

But I needed help; that much, I did know, even if the admission felt like chewing on poison ivy, like the sting of nettles burning down my throat. With my free hand, I fumbled in my pockets for my phone. Ivy was the first contact in my favorites, above Emmy and Uncle James, and she answered on the first ring, almost as if she'd been expecting my call.

Maybe she had. Thorns could be that way, as if they had a specialized sonar for long-distance emotional distress.

"Hey, Lilah," she said, her warm voice like a balm, an aural tincture with a honey base. Ivy had a beautiful singing voice; years ago, back when we'd still been together rather than best friends, she'd often sung me lullabies while I lay pillowed beneath her collarbone, the sweet vibration thrumming through my cheek. Some of that natural melody carried over into her speech. "What's going on, boo? Shouldn't you be in bed with your tea and Cheerios?"

I gritted my teeth, because yes, I damned well should have been. Most nights, I'd have long since been snuggled under my weighted blanket with a book, a mug of chamomile tea, and a snack cup of Cheerios and M&M's, Montalban roosting in the wrought iron birdcage that hung above my nightstand, making the dripping-rain sounds she made only when content. Once upon a time, the ritual had included a nightcap, a lowball of negroni instead of tea. But I'd found out the hard way that alcohol didn't play well with the aftermath of the oblivion glamour.

Yet another thing, a small pleasure, it had stolen from me.

"I went up to Hallows to harvest viridian teardrops," I said without preamble, my teeth chattering a little. My tank top was soaked through, stuck to me, and the balmy breeze cut sharp against the film of sweat clinging to my skin. "I just got back, and I'm trying to open my door but then I—I *forgot* again, Ivy. Now I'm, I'm holding this *thing*, and I don't know what it is but it seems fairly awful and I . . . Fuck, I'm scared of it."

A tiny, mewling sob escaped past my teeth before I could call it back. I clenched my jaw, furious with myself, struggling to latch on to some semblance of control.

"Okay, honey, I'm with you so far," Ivy said, sounding sublimely unruffled. "You got home, and it sounds like you were trying to unlock your door. What does it look like, Lilah, the thing you're afraid of? Can you describe it to me?"

I rattled off as objective a description of the Mystery Fucking Object as I could muster, without mentioning any of my suspicions about weaponry or baneful magics. I didn't want to bias her.

"Ah," Ivy sighed once I'd finished. Her pitch didn't change, but I could still somehow feel the wealth of aching sympathy rolling off her and through the line. "I got you. It's a key, honey. You're holding your house key—you know what that is. It fits into the lock, you turn it, and it undoes the mechanism keeping your door closed. Is that sounding more familiar now?"

A key. A fucking *key* had scared me out of my entire wits.

Because I'd remembered what it was, almost as soon as she'd

begun explaining it to me. Sometimes it worked that way, when the oblivion clouded my memory of mundane objects, infusing them with a sense of pervasive malevolence. It didn't happen often, but each time it did felt like the first. I needed a grounding reminder, a succinct explanation of what the object was.

But it had to come from someone else. I couldn't mantra myself out of this kind of spiral, not when it was an everyday item that I'd suddenly forgotten.

I despised this utter helplessness—this mortifying dependence on Ivy's help, the imposition and burden it turned me into, a flailing, needy creature instead of her friend—more than any other part of my miserable recovery. I hated it so much that the loathing felt close to rage, a bubbling cauldron of vitriol I couldn't tamp down, that threatened to boil over any minute and scorch everything around me into bitter dregs.

And beneath the fury was another, darker fear, a leviathan's shadow surging deep beneath the ocean's surface. What if, one day, the thing I forgot was my phone? How was I supposed to summon Ivy then? My best friend and my lifeline, the tether that kept me sane and reeled me back in to myself.

Flames and stars, what would happen to me then?

I started to cry, raw, croaking sobs that I could do nothing to suppress. "I'm sorry," I wept, swiping a hand over my horrible snotty face, succeeding only in smearing myself more. "Ivy, I'm so sorry to . . . to *be* like this. To do this to you."

"Lilah, honey, cut that shit out," she ordered, in the gentle and wholly uncompromising tone she probably also used with the more demanding clients she handled as the formal Honeycake Orchards event planner. The yoga she taught on the side was specifically an outlet for the frustration incited by the bridezillas, frazzled baby-shower hosts, and entitled-tech-bro retreats she managed at her day job. "Let me remind you that I love you, and that I volunteered for this. We agreed I'd be your person when you needed it. Tell me, did we not agree?"

"We did agree," I said damply, nodding as if she could see me. Montalban bobbed her head in unison, like a little shadow; she loved Ivy, and she knew that talking to her helped me when I was in this state. "We did. But you—you don't deserve this bullshit all the time. Having to fucking handle me like this, be on call any time of day or night. Like I can't take care of myself. Like I'm this utterly useless waste of space."

"Welp, that's it," she replied, and I could hear the soft rustling of thrown-back sheets—she, apparently, *had* been in bed. A shared love of early bedtimes had always been one of our things, back when we'd been together. "I'm coming over."

I lurched back against the door in horror, nearly dislodging Montalban from my shoulder to an indignant caw of protest. "No! Ivy, no, you have to be up so early for that wedding tomorrow. You don't have to do that, you really—"

"Again, and I say this with love," she said, and I could hear the warm fondness in her voice, "but *do* shut up, bitch. Of course I'm coming over, this is no longer remotely a discussion. There's no way I'm letting you be alone right now, not when this is the prevailing mood. And have you had dinner, or did you forget to eat while you were up on Hallows?"

"It's possible that I forgot," I admitted, chastened. "I had some trail mix, maybe? I was really focused on—"

"Harvesting the viridian, of course you were. Pearl Dragon

should still be open, I'll stop by and pick something up. I had a light dinner, anyway, I could use a dim sum snack. Want bubble tea, too?"

She'd probably had a healthy, substantial home-cooked dinner, but of course this was what she'd say. I closed my eyes and tipped my head back against the door, awash in equal parts guilt and gratitude, and suddenly aware of the seismic rumble in my stomach. The friendship that had grown out of my former romantic relationship with Ivy was one of the greater miracles of my life, one that I had no idea how I'd managed to pull off, given how clumsy and standoffish I often was with people.

Why she still chose to love me so hard was an enduring mystery.

"Thank you," I whispered into the phone. "Really, Ivy. I . . . I don't know what I'd do without you."

"Not much, I'd bet, because you'd have long since starved to death. Don't worry, though, fam. The dim sum's gonna be on you, to balance out the scales."

3

The Visitor

W HEN I LET myself into Tomes & Omens the next morning, after a night of highly restorative platonic spooning with Ivy, goddess-damned Nina Blackmoore was somehow already there. For a blessed moment I didn't even notice her, as the alert spell imbued into the brass bell above the doorjamb trilled a notification of my own arrival. *Now come Delilah Charlotte Harlow and the familiar Montalban!* it chimed inside my head in its dementedly cheerful, fluting tones. *Ahoy, Delilah Charlotte Harlow and Montalban, ahoy, ahoy!!*

"Yes, I *know* I'm here, you may proceed to chill out," I muttered to it under my breath, swinging the door shut behind me once Montalban had winged her way in toward her customary perch at the front of the store. I didn't mind the bell much during the day, once I was past my second coffee and used to tuning its chiming out as the foot traffic picked up. But first thing in the morning, it could be grating as hell. "It's still me. *Still* your boss."

The lingering echoes of *ahoy!!* trailed off in my mind almost wistfully, as if the alert were a sentient enough spell to be wounded by my brusque dismissal. The bell and I went through this maddening rigmarole every day, and every day I remembered that I needed to tinker with the embedded alert spell such that it wouldn't feel obligated to recognize me as a visitor to my own store. Then I routinely became distracted by whatever else my task list held, and the next morning, *Ahoy!!*, here we'd find ourselves again.

Then Nina slunk out from between the shelves in one of the outrageously expensive suits she always wore for her shifts at Tomes—as if she were clocking in to her in-house counsel position at Castle Camelot, rather than coming in for another grueling day of casting—one small hand lifted in timid greeting.

"Good mor—"

"Why are you here?" I said, cutting her off as I elbowed past her tiny frame into the maze of towering, creaky shelves that occupied the center of the store, their dusty tops disappearing into the gloom of the double-height ceiling. The storefront windows were bespelled to block the light spectra most harmful to old books, which meant the shop was always bathed in a shadowy murk. It was one of the first spells I'd restored, once I had enough wits about me to effectively cast again. Nothing was more damaging to ancient tomes than too much light, and if it made the store *spookier* for the tourists, so much the better.

As I stormed through the narrow aisles, the books rustled around me like roosting birds, shifting uneasily against one another as they picked up on my bristling annoyance. Over the years, the Tomes collection—and, to a degree, the brick-and-mortar structure of the store—had acquired a collective sense of self, keyed in to its Harlow keeper. Normally, early morning at the bookstore was my favorite part of the day; the precious time I had it all to myself, to breathe the musty magic of its air, sort through the ledgers, and shelve new acquisitions before the hordes descended. Yet Nina had made it a point of pride (an extremely annoying one) to beat me here on her days in, as if this display of earnest punctuality would somehow endear her to me.

It stunned me, sometimes, the degree to which someone supposedly bred to politesse and decorum could be so completely divorced from objective reality.

"It's Tuesday," I went on, dropping my backpack behind the imposing, claw-footed glass counter that held a display of athames, crystals, and lockets for impulse purchases at checkout. "You don't come in on Tuesdays."

As part of the punishment imposed on her this past Yule by my cousin, in Emmy's role as Victor of the Wreath, Nina had been charged with applying her heavyweight Blackmoore magic to helping me restore the wards she herself had wrecked. And in all fairness, she'd vigorously flung herself into the task, showing up twice a week without complaint, and even on weekends if I asked her to come in. She also treated me with absolute deference; not speaking unless spoken to, never complaining about the mindnumbingly repetitive spells I sometimes assigned her for my own petty pleasure, giving me space unless I specifically requested her presence. It was almost embarrassing, the way her whole face lit up on the rare occasions I deigned to engage her in casual conversation. Even those impeccable suits were a misplaced gesture of respect, an indication that she took this task no less seriously than the work she performed for her own hideous family.

One of the reasons I hated her so much was that despite her Blackmoore trappings, she so assiduously made herself difficult to hate. If anything, interacting with her was nothing close to the chore socializing amounted to with most people. Under different circumstances, she and I might even have liked each other—and somehow, this made her presence even worse, like a tender toothache I couldn't resist prodding with my tongue. A constant reminder of all she'd stolen from me, in her brazen moment of vast selfishness.

Had her help in rebuilding the wards not been as invaluable as it was, I'd have cut her loose months ago; Emmy would've understood, deferred to my wishes. But Tomes & Omens had to take precedence over my feelings. I was just a steward, whereas this place was Thistle Grove's take on the Library of Alexandria, our Harlow-tended treasure trove of town history, records, and magical arcana. I couldn't let my own sense of loss and loathing get in the way of rebuilding its protections—and in an undertaking that massive, Nina Blackmoore's assistance was a necessary evil.

"I, um, spoke to Gareth about spending more time here," she replied, tucking a stray blond wave behind her ear, mascaraed brown eyes flicking warily between me and Montalban, who'd fixed her with a short-tempered, beady gaze from where she perched atop a bookshelf. Sensing my keen dislike of Nina, there'd been a transition period during which my familiar purposely made herself a nuisance. Stealing Nina's pens, dipping her bill into Nina's open beverages and snatching up her snacks, strafing her with the occasional fly-by droppings.

Highly entertaining as this hazing-by-raven had been, it had also gotten in the way of our actual task, so I'd kindly asked my familiar to refrain from further well-intentioned harassment. She'd grudgingly complied . . . at least, most of the time.

"To see if we could move the restoration along faster," Nina went on, "so we can be done by Samhain, ideally. I know you're worried about that many tourists trampling through here come Halloween, with the wards still only partially in place. Gareth agreed it'd be worth hiring a junior attorney to help me at Camelot, so I could—so I could be here more. If, of course, that's alright with you?"

I paused behind the counter, taken aback by such a display of consideration on her part—and on her brother's, to boot. She'd been right to pick up on my concern, and by now it wasn't *that* surprising to discover she'd been paying such close attention to my worries. But Gareth Blackmoore was the kind of person who'd have been dubbed a "rake" in a different time; a shitty, over-indulged princeling of a scion who'd spent most of his twenties variously fucking and fucking over the portion of Thistle Grove's female population susceptible to his dubious charm. Including, among a legion of others, my own cousin.

In short, he'd been exactly the kind of unapologetically trash scumbag who made me even more stoked to be gay.

And yet, he'd agreed to this proposition. Maybe Emmy had been onto something when she removed his mother, Lyonesse, from her position as the Blackmoore family elder and instated Gareth in her place on a trial basis.

"It's fine," I said shortly. "Tuesdays, too, then."

Nina nodded furiously, honey-streaked waves bobbing, her lips twitching as she fought against a smile. Clearly thrilled I was allowing her to do this, giving her yet another chance to demonstrate the breadth of her remorse. If only she wasn't so pathetically *insistent* about prostrating herself in front of me. Sometimes I got the sense she'd have happily flung herself down in front of me on a sidewalk like some medieval swain, to make sure I trod on her waiting back instead of stepping in a puddle.

Too bad all that regret counted for next to nothing, when not even an eternity of performative remorse could fix my stupid, broken brain.

"We're casting Marauder's Misery today," I informed her, turning away. "I have a viridian teardrop to grind down for it. Go get me my mortar and pestle, would you."

When she didn't immediately leap into action, Montalban cawed imperiously at her, as if in mimicry of my command. *Get thee to it, then, bitch*, being the general mood.

"Of course, Ms. Harlow," she muttered, flinging my raven a dirty look before heading toward the back of the store where we kept the apothecary tools shelved. I'd never given her permission to call me by my first name, and since she'd never asked, this was where we'd landed. "Right away."

FIVE HOURS OF grinding, sifting, and amalgamating later, I'd perfected the sticky amber paste that Nina and I would smear over our dominant casting hands before launching into Marauder's Misery. I'd forgotten that the paste also called for damiana and marjoram oil, neither of which I'd had on hand, so I'd sent Nina out to the Avramovs' Arcane Emporium not once but twice. I hadn't done it on purpose, but I couldn't deny how much perverse

pleasure it had given me to yank Nina away from the ward she'd
been casting and then interrupt her precious salad lunch to have
her play errand girl for me. She'd done it all in good grace, but by
now I understood her well enough to know she had the kind of
inborn pride that rivaled mine. It *had* to rankle her on some level,
to be bossed around without so much as a throwaway thanks.

Ah, life's simple pleasures. Maybe I needed to start stocking
even fewer ingredients in my apothecary's cabinet.

I was just about ready to call Nina over so we could get the
spell started when the bell tinkled above the door, the alert chiming *Now comes Catriona Arachne Quinn! Ahoy, Catriona Arachne
Quinn, ahoy, ahoy!!*

I scowled to myself, annoyed by the interruption, and a little
surprised that a non-local would be wandering in here alone this
time of day. Most tourists would still be at lunch right now, and
they typically traveled in pairs or packs, not solo. Tuesdays also
tended to be quiet at the shop; we'd had an only moderately irritating group bustle in earlier, but off-season, visitors usually flocked
to Thistle Grove for long weekends rather than dropping in on
random weekdays. Still, there'd been enough of them to drive
Montalban up into the rafters, and I hadn't seen her since, which
meant she'd probably settled into some aerie for her afternoon nap.

And that name, Catriona Arachne. It was unusual even by my
standards, and I'd grown up alongside the Thorns' flora-inspired
first names, the Avramovs' Slavic nomenclature, and the Blackmoores' overblown penchant for Arthurian mythology.

Sliding the pungent paste under the counter, I arranged my
features into what passed for my customer-service face, preparing
to be pelted with town history questions and requests to retrieve

books and novelty items (that this browser was almost inevitably not going to buy) from the highest shelves. So when the minutes ticked by in complete silence—whoever this Catriona Arachne was, she had such a quiet step that even the creakiest of the store's floorboards weren't giving her away—I shrugged to myself and went back to my final review of Marauder's Misery in the Harlow copy of the Grimoire.

By the time she finally made it over to the counter, I'd gotten so immersed in making sure I had the lead caster's lines memorized—Marauder's Misery followed a complicated call-and-response pattern, and there wasn't as much repetition in the stanzas as you often found in long workings—that I'd all but forgotten she was even here.

"Excuse me."

I glanced up, brow furrowed with preemptive annoyance before I remembered that I was supposed to be projecting courtesy. "Can I help . . ."

The words ghosted away from me, and for once, their loss had nothing to do with the oblivion glamour.

The woman standing in front of the counter was easily one of the most striking people I'd ever seen—and I lived in a town teeming with Avramovs, who looked like they'd been genetically modified to beguile victims into untimely ends. She was even taller than me, an inch or two over six feet, with what appeared to be naturally white-blond hair buzzed close on one side and falling just shy of her cheekbone on the other. Her skin was dramatically tan against that shining pale hair, a deep and tawny amber—and even more startling, her eyebrows and lashes were inky black, framing the most arresting green eyes I'd ever seen. Long, narrow, and tilted up at the corners like a cat's, they were nearly the color of verdigris, both vivid and pale. Such an unusual color that it tipped more toward uncanny than attractive.

Just in case I didn't have enough reason to stare at her slack-jawed, she also had a tiny, intricate tattoo at the corner of her right eye that I couldn't quite make out. And beneath an aquiline nose featuring a dainty septum piercing and two hoops in the left nostril, and cheekbones so sharp they cut an even harder line than her jaw, was a pair of breathtakingly delicate lips painted a deep, matte cerise.

Even if she hadn't also been rocking the kind of hard shoulders and arms you usually saw on MMA fighters, I'd already have been a lost cause. Women like this were my ultimate undoing; vaguely rakish, stunning without being conventionally beautiful, a tantalizing touch androgynous. It was the reason I'd fallen so hard for Ivy years ago. She and this woman obviously looked nothing alike, but the striking aesthetic and the general aura of brash sexiness pretty much embodied my type.

Catriona Arachne Quinn smiled at me, slow and a little crooked, almost smirky. As if she was plenty used to eliciting this exact reaction from mortals unexpectedly graced by her attention.

"I didn't mean to interrupt your reading," she said, with a flash of white teeth behind those black-cherry lips, her gaze flickering down to the open Grimoire. Her voice sounded exactly like she looked. Low and distinctive and slightly husky, like incense smoke. There was the hint of an accent there, too, something that softened her consonants a little, but I couldn't place it. "Must be a pretty compelling story, that. You looked completely engrossed. Practically worlds away."

"Oh, no, no, it's no problem," I assured her, flipping the Grimoire closed. Technically I shouldn't have had it out in the open in the first place—we were supposed to keep this original copy of the spellbook safely in the attic, away from any prying eyes or sticky fingers—but it wasn't like any tourist would even know what they were looking at. "Just, um . . . work. Very, very dull. Were you, uh, looking to make a purchase?"

Still with that lazy half smirk, she slid a pack of tarot cards across the counter. It was a relatively shitty oracle deck, fairy themed and mass produced, nowhere close to the quality of the beautiful handmade decks we also kept in stock. I wrinkled my nose, unable to hide my surprise that someone like her would've chosen something so unabashedly cheap and boring.

She laughed at my disdain, a silvery chuckle, higher pitched and more melodious than I'd have expected from that smoky speaking voice. "Ah, so it's like that. I take it you don't approve of my selection?"

"Well, it's completely up to you." I reached over to pick up the tarot deck and scan it. "I was just thinking that we carry a number of more . . . unique decks than this one. Some of them hand-painted, even, designed right here in town."

"To each their own, as they say," she said, flicking one of those gorgeous cut shoulders in a shrug. "And, hey, could be I'm hopelessly partial to trashy fairies. Sexy Tinker Bell here might be right up my alley, for all you know. We all have our afflictions, don't we?"

I burst out laughing, unable to help myself. The pouty illustrated fairy on the cover of the deck, scantily clad and sprawled very suggestively on an oversized leaf, did sort of look like the porno version of Tinker Bell.

She grinned fully at my laughter, crossing her arms on top of the counter and leaning over them, in a lazy way that struck me as both extremely hot and casually territorial, as if she were some-how staking a claim on the store. And possibly me, by extension. It should have made me bristle—and certainly would have, had it been anyone else smearing their bare arms all over my clean glass—but instead it sent a full-bodied flush traveling up my skin.

"For what it's worth, I'm not," she went on in a confiding tone. "Into trashy fairies, that is. Witches are much more my speed these days. Heard I could find a whole mess of them in this little slip of a town and thought, hey, why not come see for myself?"

"Where are you coming in from?"

"Chicago." A corner of her mouth quirked. "Mostly."

"Well, you're definitely in the right place for witches," I in-formed her solemnly. "We *do* take some issue at being referred to as 'trashy,' however. The ones you'll find here come with a very storied history. Highly dignified, by all accounts."

"This is my first stop, but I can already tell," she said with equal mock seriousness, tilting her chin at my dove-gray-and-white Harlow robes. I always wore them when working in the store, not just to cater to the tourists, but also because it felt right, in a sincere and symbolic way. As though I were already inhabit-ing my role as future keeper. "Occult, but make it classy, no warts or pointy hats cheapening the vibe. I love your tattoos, too. And your nails."

I'd rolled up my robe's sleeves while I worked on the paste, exposing the full-color floral tattoos that sleeved my arms like botanical illustrations. Sprawling peonies and lilies and thistles, wreathed with renderings of my favorite magical flora: bristling broombrush and lacy pink aurora, spriteslip and tinderweed.

And my nails *were* more interesting than they had any right to be, considering how much I worked with my hands, but I loved keeping them long. This week they were coffin-shaped and painted fuchsia and black, a sinuous line of silver glitter drawn through them like a meandering river.

"Thank you," I said, flustered that she'd noticed my details just as closely as I'd noticed hers. Her own strong hands were still resting on the counter, like the counterpoint and foil to mine; the backs veined, nails short and square and unpainted. She had an unusual bracelet around one wrist, black leather and cord in a complex knotted design that also held glinting little slivers of onyx. There was something very eye-catching about the way it was made; now that I'd noticed it, my gaze kept drifting back down to its knots. "I do my own nails—art therapy, I guess you could call it. And I sketched the designs for the tattoos, too."

Before I could regret inundating her with personal information she probably had zero interest in knowing, her dark eyebrows lifted with delight.

"Artistic. I like that," she said, tipping her head in admiration, that asymmetrical slice of hair falling into her left eye. "I'm a little crafty myself, as it happens. Enjoy a bit of weaving, here and there."

Weaving struck me as the blandest conceivable hobby for a woman like her; not that there was anything wrong with it, I just couldn't imagine someone who looked like a kickboxing pinup en-joying something so sedentary. Though maybe it meant she'd made that edgy bracelet herself. It felt much more in line with the rest of her.

"Did you want anything else?" I asked her, clearing my throat as I folded the garbage deck into a complimentary velvet cloth for her, not that it deserved any such protection. The cloth was prob-ably of higher quality than the cards themselves. "Or maybe a bag? I'm afraid we don't have any weaving supplies on offer."

"Oh, I always travel prepared," she replied. There was something oddly coy about the way she said it, some private moment of amusement as she tucked the deck into a back pocket with a half smile. "Never know when one might need the materials for an emergency crafting session."

"Right," I said, a little uncertainly, thrown off by this tinge of strange innuendo, like she was keeping some secret with herself. "Well. Thank you for stopping by, and enjoy Thistle Grove. If you're looking for things to do, I highly recommend a visit to Honeycake Orchards. No trashy fairies there, either, but it's a gorgeous place."

"Noted," she said, tipping me a little two-finger salute as she pushed back from the counter. "I'm Catriona, by the way. Cat."

"Delilah," I replied automatically, though I normally never told Tomes visitors my first name. If anyone asked, "the Witch Harlow, Proprietress of this Establishment" had a suitably more ominous ring to it, like someone you didn't necessarily want to bother *too* much about what such-and-such trinket cost. (Even if I wasn't, formally, the proprietress just yet. Those smug, presumptuous trespassers didn't need to know *everything*.)

"Delilah," she repeated, a gleam lighting in her eyes. The soft emphasis she put on each syllable made me acutely aware of the tip of her tongue flicking behind her teeth as she pronounced each of the *l*'s. "Beautiful name, one you don't hear so often. It was a pleasure to meet you, Delilah—and thanks for the insider info. It's much appreciated."

"You're welcome," I called after her, but she'd already turned away.

And as she disappeared into the shelves, with a lithe, rolling gait that put me in mind of predators roaming the savanna in nature shows, I couldn't shake the feeling that I'd detected some sense of recognition in her. Like she'd already known my name before I told her what it was, just like I'd known hers.

It also didn't occur to me until after I'd heard the door swing shut behind her that she'd never actually paid for the fairy deck.

4

That's Enough

NINA EMERGED FROM the shelves a few minutes later, looking put-upon. "Who was that?" she asked, glancing uneasily back over her shoulder. "That woman who just left?"

"I don't know, a tourist," I said testily, not inclined to share that I'd been so distracted by said tourist that I'd functionally allowed her to shoplift merchandise right under my nose. Under normal circumstances, that wouldn't even have been possible, but one of the wards Nina and I still hadn't fully restored was the one thwarting petty theft. I'd ranked it as low priority, and now here we were. "Why?"

Nina pursed her lips, making a disgruntled moue. "I ran into her in the shelves, and she just felt off. The way she looked at me . . . I don't know. It was weird, somehow."

"'Weird, somehow,'" I echoed sarcastically, more to hide my own outrage than anything, my mind racing. Why would someone even have *wanted* to steal such a cheap deck? Maybe Cat had been semi-honest with me during the deft misdirection I'd mistaken for real flirting. Maybe she just liked trashy things in general, especially if they happened to be stolen.

Or it could have been a ruse, a way to keep me from noticing some more significant theft, I thought, with a zinging bolt of alarm. I'd have to run an itemizing spell later, make sure she hadn't strolled out with anything of more value. It was highly unlikely—the anti-theft wards covering the most important books and objects were already in place—but not impossible.

"The ultimate offense," I continued, distracting myself from troubling thoughts by baiting Nina. "Wait, could it be that . . . did she fail to curtsy to you in passing?!"

Nina shot me a flinty look, squaring her little shoulders. "I didn't say 'rude,' did I?" she retorted, in one of the spicy flashes of spirit she managed to suppress most of the time. "There was something a little askew about her, that's all. She just made me uncomfortable."

"Well, *that's* completely unacceptable. If she comes back, we can kill her," I suggested, only mostly joking. If that brazen thief ever dared come back here, she was certainly going to find out some things, hotness notwithstanding.

"Now come on, I want to start casting Marauder's Misery before it gets too late." I slid out from behind the counter with the bowl of viridian paste, holding it out to Nina so we could both slather our casting hands with it. "I'll take point—can you manage second?"

Marauder's Misery was one of the warding spells that ideally called for a circle; in a pinch, only two witches would constitute a circle, especially if one happened to be a Blackmoore. Nina's knowledge of warding spells had been impeccable so far, but this one was a doozy, even if she'd had all that time to review it while I concocted the paste.

"Certainly. But . . ." She flicked me a doubtful look, clearly too wary to articulate her concern as she followed me into the maze of bookshelves.

I could read her mind anyway; Marauder's Misery was a long, convoluted, and demanding casting, hours of exhausting spell-work. And Nina knew that I was still struggling. I'd have died before admitting it to her, of course, but I plied myself with a daily regimen of mundane remedies for ailing memory. Ginseng, ash-wagandha, ginger root, lion's mane mushrooms, sage, turmeric, gotu kola, and an entire laundry list of other, mostly abysmal-tasting herbs. Some I steeped into the rank tisanes I swilled all day, and others I took as supplements by the handful. (There'd been a brief period of dabbling in Adderall as well, but that had done nothing besides making me even more prone to biting Nina's head off at the slightest provocation.)

Even someone as unfamiliar with herbal remedies as your average Blackmoore would've guessed by now what I was after.

"What?" I barked at her, my already brittle patience splinter-ing as we reached the bookshelf juncture that marked the rough center of the store. Sensing spellcasting action afoot, Montalban swooped down from where she'd been roosting in the ceiling gloom and lit on my shoulder with a raspy caw. "Is there a problem?"

Nina shook her head, hair sheeting her face. "No, of course not. Whenever you're ready."

Still glaring at her, I reached out to grasp her hand. We were both right-handed casters, which meant we had to form a circle by facing each other, left hands clasped between us. Which, in turn, meant hours of standing face-to-face while she made insufferable doe eyes at me, exuding medical-grade penitence.

Flames and stars, I'd be lucky if I had any uncracked molars left by the time this restoration was complete.

I counted us down from three. Then we lifted our viridian-pasted hands in smooth tandem, index fingers pointed up, both drawing counterclockwise circles in the air as I started chanting the charm, Nina following my lead through the long, lyrical couplets. The air began to circulate as we cast, ruffling our hair and my raven's feathers, coursing in purposeful currents like an elaborate knot being crafted around us. In Marauder's Misery, the element of air became the protective medium, galvanized by the magical viridian pollen adhering to our hands. Once we'd finished weaving its defensive web, it would settle invisibly into place over the bookshelves, a transparent, interwoven shield. If any vandals ever broke in with the ill intent of damaging my books with anything sharp—which, according to the will I was infusing into this working, covered anything from nails to scissors to blades—the air hovering above the bookshelves would repel them. Upon sensing any malign intention, the kinetic energy stored in its knotwork would activate, blowing them away from the books while leaving the tomes themselves untouched.

It wouldn't be pretty, but it also wouldn't kill them . . . probably. Just teach them some pointed lessons, pun *very* much intended.

For hours, Nina and I worked in nearly flawless tandem, a lockstep so neat and precise it felt close to joy even as fatigue accumulated between us, building up like slow sediment. I'd become used to working with her, but it was more than just experience;

while my magic buzzed inside me with a low, satisfying hum, hers nearly roared in response, like crashing waves. There was so much of it for me to draw on as the lead caster that it felt like having been granted access to a bottomless well, but it was her control over it that was the truly enviable thing. Her raw magic felt not just endless but deft, and even I found it damn near impossible not to feel impressed by the masterful way she handled it. Manipulating its ebb and flow, feeding me exactly as much as I needed from her and never any more or less.

Sometimes, collaborating with Nina felt almost disturbingly beautiful; there was a synchronicity that seemed like something innate, though as Blackmoores and Harlows, we had no reason to feel such a connection. Some of it might simply have been Nina's own unbridled joy at being allowed to flex her magic. As part of the punishment Emmy had imposed on her, Nina was forbidden from casting under any circumstances besides the ward restoration, or defending herself or someone else from mortal peril. This was her only opportunity to lose herself in the kind of complex working she'd probably been used to casting every other day.

Then, sometime around the fourth hour, I forgot my lines.

One moment, I was singing them out in a confident, clear alto, without so much as a waver to my voice or will. The next, I stumbled, tripped up by the abrupt onset of nothing—a sudden and jarring absence where the next line should've been.

Montalban sensed the surge of my panic, rasping out a harsh warning croak.

Nina's eyes snapped open at the sound, then narrowed as she felt the ensuing disturbance in the working. Without skipping a beat or undoing any of the progress we'd made, she fluidly switched places with me, intoning the lead caster's next line. Giving me time to recover, or to fall back into the secondary, supporting role, so we could both carry on with the spell.

The realization that she'd learned both parts in advance—setting herself up as my understudy, as if she'd suspected or even assumed that I'd need help—sent a gout of pure fury gushing through my veins.

"Stop it," I hissed at her through clenched teeth. "I *have* this. I just—I need a second."

"Don't," she said, sharp, holding my eyes with a steely determination I hadn't seen in her before. "Please. Don't do this. Can't you feel that it's already deteriorating? We've worked so hard, we can't just let it drop now. If you still know the secondary casting, we could—"

"Of fucking course I know it. It's a *Harlow* spell."

She clenched her jaw, refraining from pointing out the obvious, which was that I'd clearly already forgotten the words to the primary casting of a Harlow spell. Aggravatingly enough, I *did* still know what came next for the secondary caster; I just couldn't latch on to what I'd been chanting before, as though that part of the spell had transformed into a slippery, soaped-up rope that had wriggled out of my grasp.

"Just . . . just give me a second." I rummaged furiously through my mind, scrabbling for the next line; Nina couldn't feed the words to me like a prompter with a script, it didn't work that way. If she continued speaking them aloud, she'd become the primary by default, the spell's central energy bending toward her will rather than mine. Which meant any resulting casting would have much more of her in it than me. This Marauder's Misery would wind up a Blackmoore spell instead of my own—and I couldn't stomach that idea, not for something so vast and pervasive, a charm that would become so integral to the fabric of *my* store.

I'd always feel Nina's mark on it, even after she was finally gone.

And I'd be damned if I let this happen to me again, this egregious helplessness. The need to rely on a Blackmoore, of all witches, for the casting of a spell my own ancestors had crafted. And not just any Blackmoore, but *this* one, the one responsible for my predicament.

"I just need to *think*," I said, listing my head slowly from side to side. "I . . ."

As I fought furiously to remember, all the pleasure I'd felt in the ease of our joint working rushed away from me—and with it gone, the lyrics themselves faded like ghosts melting back into the ether, evanescing from my mind. As our casting lapsed, so did the spell itself. The complex over-under weave of those aerial knots loosened, until they unraveled from the cohesive shape of Nina's and my joint will, becoming nothing more than loose-floating strings of mundane molecules.

With a wistful sound like a sigh, the spell simply deflated around us. Wisping away as if it had never even been at all.

The sheer frustration of its loss spiked through me like a weapon, something that might shred me to pieces, murder me from the inside. I wrenched loose of Nina's hand and stumbled in place, reeling with futile rage and devastation. Because what was I even good for anymore if I couldn't tend to my own books? Yes, I could've let her take the lead—but what about the next time, and the time after that? How was I supposed to be a Harlow steward, the next master recordkeeper, when I couldn't even reliably remember my own family's spells?

I let my head fall back and *howled*, shrieking like an animal with its paw snared in a trap. Montalban took to the air, wheeling in furious circles above my head, screeching out my pain in her own strident octaves.

"Delilah!" I could hear the fear and panic in Nina's voice—a part of me was dimly shocked to hear her call me by my name, like she'd never dared before—but only faintly, as if she stood somewhere very far away. "Delilah, stop, *please*! We can just, we can fix it! We can start over, we only need . . ."

"*Shut . . . UP!*"

My vision shimmering at the edges, I shoved Nina away from me, so hard she stumbled back against the shelves, her face stricken as she gaped at me, ashen and aghast. Then I whipped around and stalked toward the front of the store, to the cabinet where I kept my herbal remedies. Painstakingly assembled little jars and tubs and sachets, all full of useless fucking bullshit that was clearly helping me not a whit.

The assemblage of glass caught the light, twinkling at me like damning evidence; a collection of the myriad ways I'd failed to help myself.

With a guttural roar, I yanked the doors open so hard the hinges whined in protest as the doors cracked back against the cabinet's sides. Then I began ransacking its contents, plucking out item after item and pitching them all onto the floor, my rage so pulsing and acidic it felt like something toxic I had swallowed. A vial of bitter, blistering venom I'd somehow managed to choke down. Everything that shattered as it met the ground, its contents strewing across the floorboards, only fed that bubbling inner turmoil.

"Fuck you," I muttered to each item under my breath as I

pulled it out and dumped it. "You pointless trash. And you, and you. And *especially* you."

Some of the shelves I swept clean in a single satisfying motion, sending everything flying off; others I emptied piecemeal, making them last. Like I was bloodletting, or lancing a series of agonizing boils. By the time I reached the bottom shelf I was on my hands and knees like some hunched creature, tossing things over my shoulder with savage abandon. I could barely hear Nina anymore, though I knew she hadn't stopped calling my name in that helpless, appalled tone that only enraged me all the more.

"Oh would you *fuck off*, you miserable Blackmoore bitch!" I snarled at her over my shoulder. "Just leave me the hell alone!"

The only reason I was even wreaking this carnage was to keep myself from falling on her instead, clawing at her dainty little face instead of smashing glass against the floor. The least she could do for me was keep well away.

From behind me I could hear a tremendous rattle, as the bookshelves quaked against each other in an echo of my agony. The entire store seemed to moan like a living thing, as books, floorboards, and rafters shifted and groaned, Montalban's cries piercing through it all. Resonating with the whirlwind force of my emotion like some inanimate Greek chorus as I played out my own personal tragedy.

Then the cabinet loomed empty above me, bare and bleak as my own mind. Nothing left to break; nothing else to throw.

I sagged where I knelt, pitching forward onto shaky arms, panting from exertion. I was so exhausted I barely even struggled when Nina's own arms slid gently around me from behind.

"Shh, Delilah," she whispered against me, soft tendrils of her hair tickling my cheek. I hadn't even realized how loudly I was sobbing, in raw, grating caws that sounded more like my familiar than me. "I am so, so sorry. But listen to me, we're going to set this right. We will, together, I *swear* to you."

I squirmed against her, fighting with what little energy I had left to keep myself from accepting the comfort of her touch. It would have been so easy to give in; to let her hold me just this once, let her apologies wash over me. Allow myself to absorb them, take them in. But that solved nothing, accomplished nothing besides giving her closure and relief, an outlet for her remorse. One she could never earn, would never deserve.

Instead, it helped to recite the litany of things I hated about her. The perfectly tamed loose curls of her hair; those deathly dull oval nails, rarely polished anything more thrilling than eggshell; the way she watched me with such overflowing, painful, seemingly endless hope. As though she kept thinking she might catch a glimpse of my forgiveness on the horizon, like the distant silhouette of some exotic bird.

Tough fucking luck to Nina Blackmoore, because I would *never* forgive her for reducing me to this, not if I somehow managed to live a thousand years. I would rather have died mindless and raving than let her hear words of absolution fall from my mouth.

But she was right about one thing; I was going to set things to rights for myself. And I was going to do it on my own.

I sat up and wrenched myself roughly away from her, still gasping for breath as I swiped one hand across my tear-streaked face.

"Enough, Delilah," I whispered, shaky but adamant, as if Nina wasn't even there. "That is *enough*."

5

The Malefica

AFTER BANISHING NINA for the night, I stayed at Tomes alone, sweeping and scrubbing at the mess I'd made. Salvaging what herbs I could, though almost everything had gotten hopelessly commingled, and what could be separated out was largely contaminated, spangled with slivers of glass. I'd burned through a fortune's worth of herbs with my tantrum, which probably would've served me right in some sanctimonious way if I could bring myself to care, which I couldn't. Though knowing myself, the guilt for causing such a deplorable waste would kick in later, when I was least expecting it.

Instead, I let my mind roam while I cleaned, riffling through my mental catalog of healing spells.

Not the kind that we'd already tried, the aboveboard sort you might find in the Grimoire, spellsmithed into existence by some benevolent Thorn. I'd already been plied with every mental acuity spell Ivy knew, and even the Thorn elders, Aspen and Gabrielle, had held a circle this past Ostara, with the intention of focusing their family's energies and harnessing the balancing force of the spring equinox into healing me. None of it had taken.

But just because we'd tried everything in the Thistle Grove witch arsenal didn't mean we'd tried *everything*.

By the time I stowed my broom and mop, full night had fallen beyond the Tomes windows. It was late enough that Montalban had returned to my shoulder to half drowse against the curve of my neck, clearly wishing we were already home; like her witch, my familiar wasn't exactly a party raven. Normally, if I was planning on staying late, I'd light candles in the many hurricane holders scattered throughout the store—all of Tomes was so bespelled to withstand flame that it was probably the most fireproof venue in town—but I didn't want their telltale flicker visible through the storefront windows, giving my presence away.

I didn't want anyone knowing I was still here, much less what I was planning to do.

Instead, I spoke the soft charm for a witchlight, a flicker of sinuous radiance springing to life above my palm. Then I headed to the back of the store and up the spiral staircase that led to the attic, where we held the store's collection of baneful spellbooks under lock and key.

It was easy to forget sometimes, when you lived in an enchanted town alongside three other innately gifted families, that other magic even existed in the world at large. Magic that had nothing to do with Thistle Grove or Lady's Lake; grimoires beside our own Grimoire, the book of spells contributed by the four families and penned by Elias Harlow, my own ancestor. But Uncle James and I specialized in rare and antiquarian books, and many of these were magical treatises. Arcane compendiums of the kinds of spells most Thistle Grove witches never even thought to consider—because why should they, when they'd been born to their own reliably eldritch talent?

Why even wonder what other shades of magic might lie beyond the ones they knew?

For me, it was different. On top of being a Harlow, the weakest of the families, I spent my days surrounded by these books, even when I wasn't negotiating for their acquisition in online auctions and specialized forums. I existed hemmed in by magic alien to Thistle Grove; I lived to learn these books' secret hearts, protect them with my own if necessary. The rest of the families called Uncle James's role, and what I would one day be, the master recordkeeper . . . but really, we were simply keepers. Of history, knowledge, and memory, and of the kind of power the rest of the families largely didn't even know existed, because it held so little relevance to them.

Sometimes, part of my charge as the master keeper in training was to protect the world from books that should never be used. Which, of course, meant that I had to have read them first, to fully understand the danger posed by their contents.

And I'd remembered reading a certain book that offered healing spells—and specifically one for enhanced mental acuity—if you were willing to pay its price.

Upstairs, the Tomes attic smelled keenly of magic as it always did, as if someone had snuffed out a censer of mugwort, frankincense, and amber only moments before you walked in. In the silvered shafts of moonlight slanting through the dormer windows, sparkling dust motes drifted alongside the free-floating skeins of magic that emanated from the potent pages of the books we kept up here. The witchlight flickering above my palm, I strode over to one of the biggest bookcases, glass-doored and triple-locked. The glass itself was deceptive; though it seemed like any ordinary pane, it was shatterproof and resistant to colossal force, the equivalent of a see-through vault.

The Tomes' malefica shelf, where we kept the worst of our baneful books and grimoires.

Before I began, I opened one of the dormer windows, then ran a fingertip over Montalban's sleek head to wake her. She roused sleepily, peering up at me with one bright eye as she ruffled her wings. "Fly home, precious," I whispered to her, transferring her gently to the sill. "I need to be alone tonight."

She hesitated for a moment, head cocked, clearly questioning the soundness of my judgment. Her place was by my side, and I rarely sent her away for the night. She'd be just fine without me—would likely bed down in the oak outside my bedroom window—but she wasn't used to us being apart.

"It's okay," I encouraged her, twitching my chin toward the warm summer dark beckoning beyond the window. "Trust me, and wait for me at home. I'll see you tomorrow, promise."

She cawed once, as if to have her protest formally committed to the record, then took off into the night, her diminishing silhouette a black cutout against the star-scattered sky. Even though it had been the right call—what I was about to do was dangerous and frightening, no place for an innocent like a familiar—I felt a wrenching ache at her absence.

Window latched shut, I turned back to the malefica cabinet. Closing my eyes, I held out a palm, then chanted the words to a summoning spell.

One after another, three tiny keys materialized into existence;

so small and with such lacy, filigreed bows they could have been meant for diary locks. They hovered above my hand, glimmering with reflected witchlight, each turning one full rotation before dropping onto my palm. We couldn't risk these being stolen, so rather than wearing them on a necklace or chatelaine, we kept them tucked in an invisible pocket in the store itself; a little fold of space-time that had been conjured here right after the store was built.

To open the malefica shelf, the keys had to be used multiple times in a sequence known only to the keeper and the apprentice, while intoning an unlocking charm at a precise pitch. Fear roiled my belly at the idea of forgetting the words or the melody halfway through, but the charm persisted as I cast it, holding steady and precise in my memory.

Maybe, I thought with a wry twist, the spectacular failure with Marauder's Misery had fulfilled my oblivion quota for the foreseeable future, though I doubted it. A bitch should be so lucky.

Once I completed the sequence, the doors swung open of their own accord, with an eerily blissful exhale like a sigh. As though they'd been waiting for this release for longer than I could imagine. Then the whispers began, sending a wave of chills rippling down my spine. Low, sinister laughter sifted through the darkened attic, threaded with snatches of muffled conversation, punctuated by cackles, hisses, and the faint echo of what sounded like distant shrieks, as if the bookcase were a doorway into somewhere altogether else. Somewhere, at any rate, that no one sane would wish to venture.

These shelves were the equivalent of a haunted house, hosting a collection of bound specters. Books so overflowing with malevolence that their forced proximity caused a psychic distortion, a seeping aura of menace. I knew from Uncle James that they weren't *really* generating any sound—the horror-movie soundtrack was manufactured by my own mind as it interpreted the overwhelmingly ominous feel of them.

My mammalian brain understood—even if my allegedly higher self chose to ignore all the warning signs—that this was something I decidedly shouldn't be fucking with.

Teeth gritted against the urge to slam the doors shut and relock them as quickly as I could, I yanked over a library ladder and scurried up the steps. The books were always shelved in order whenever we added a new one to the collection, but on the whole, they gave very few fucks about either our organizational system or the notion of staying put. I had no idea where I'd find the one I was looking for, so I'd simply have to search methodically, even if every moment spent close to this collection of aggregated evil made my skin want to slither off my bones.

I skimmed my fingers along the weathered spines, holding up my witchlight to illuminate their lettering. Four shelves down, I paused, breath catching as my finger landed on a gold-edged, oxblood leather spine.

Opes Sanguinis. Wealth of Blood.

I slid the book out from between its fellows—very carefully, not wanting to provoke the ones that weren't about to taste sweet freedom—and clambered down the ladder on unsteady legs. With the *Opes* tucked under an arm, I relocked the cabinet and re-tucked the three keys into their invisible nook. I had no idea how long it would take me to work the spell I had in mind, and I couldn't risk keeping that shelf unlocked. To my knowledge, the books couldn't literally creep or crawl away. But if they were capable of reorganizing

when eyes weren't on them, it wasn't a gamble I particularly wanted
to make.

The malefica safely in their glass prison again, I set the *Opes*
on the hulking pedestal desk backed into one of the attic corners,
flicking on the banker's lamps on either side. I cracked the cover,
meaning to look for the table of contents; despite the Latin title, most of the spells in this grimoire were in either Old English
or Chaucerian Middle English, two of the magically useful lan-
guages I'd had to learn as part of my keeper's education.

But as soon as my fingers brushed the maroon leather, the
book twitched under my touch; almost a small shudder, like muscles flicking beneath an animal's taut hide. Worse yet, it felt . . .
slimy, a kind of revolting slickness nothing like the visibly pebbled
texture of the age-worn leather. Then it split itself open with a
resounding *thump*, pages falling away in a cascade until it landed
on the exact spell I'd been searching for.

The one that very unnervingly translated to "The Light That
Calls for Blood."

I let out a panicky, high-pitched giggle, thoroughly rattled.
"Well, *that* was fucked," I muttered to myself under my breath, my
hand hovering warily over the pages. Even though the store might
respond to Harlow presence, the books themselves never behaved
this way once I engaged with them. They were only books, paper
and glue and bindings that felt exactly how they looked.

But this one had somehow intuited which spell I wanted, even
though I hadn't even said it aloud. It was as if the spellbook knew
that this time was somehow different. That this time it would be
used, and not merely read.

The deep sense of misgiving brewing in my stomach only

gained strength. I already knew that this was miles from the best idea I'd ever had, but what if it was so much worse than that? Harlows weren't just keepers, after all, but gatekeepers, too; keeping dangerous books locked away was part of our imperative. Which meant not only preventing others from misusing them, but clearly also *not* using them ourselves.

But how would I ever ascend to master keeper and fulfill my obligation as a Harlow, saddled with a memory that crumbled like shale, that failed me when I needed it most? Being the keeper was all I could remember wanting since I'd been a baby witch, spending every spare moment at Tomes with Emmy and hating my cousin—sometimes more than a little—for so blithely being the chosen one, the one who'd step into my uncle's shoes. That the role was now passing to me instead was total serendipity, a miracle in itself. A wondrous series of choices and happenstance that had played so beautifully in my favor, it felt like some hard-won fate.

Nothing had ever made me happier than knowing that this was who I would become; nothing else had ever felt so absolutely right. And if I wanted to keep this new destiny, this was a risk I had to take.

I MIGHT HAVE lived in Thistle Grove my whole life, but I'd never ventured into the Witch Woods at night before.

Like most of the witch community—besides the necromancer Avramovs, who considered its gloomy, sinister sprawl an extension of their demesne—I knew better than to wander here past sundown. The twisted tangle of forest that grew along the edge of town and abutted The Bitters, the Avramovs' rambling Victorian manse, had been haunted at least since the founding of the town. The trees here grew thick and gnarled and crooked, like woods transplanted from a Brothers Grimm tale. The kind of place that made you feel like slitted yellow eyes were boring into your back, icy exhales whispering down your neck, phantoms sliding like smoke along the edges of your sight.

Only, in the Witch Woods, it wasn't your imagination fooling you into paranoia, nor some trick of the light—what little light there even was, since the shrouding canopy overhead grew so dense it thwarted Thistle Grove's crystalline night skies. The veil that separated the realms of the living and the dead was notoriously thin and filmy here. Shades—ghosts of the restless dead—took that as an invitation to filter through, take up residence inside the trees themselves. Their own prolonged torment, the lingering echoes of whatever unresolved emotion kept them tethered to this plane, was what warped the trees into such unnerving, often grotesque shapes.

Most of the shades were content enough to inhabit their possessed trees without bothering passersby. But the ones that weren't tended to be the sort you very much didn't want to run across at night.

I did come here during the days sometimes, when it was easier to take sensible precautions against the more aggressive shades. Like the Hallows Hill woods, magically potent flora grew here as well, the kind useful for your edgier, less family-friendly wards. Unlike the Avramovs or teen normies out on a drunken dare, I'd never found a compelling enough reason to set foot here after dark.

Tonight, I'd had no choice but to come. Back at Tomes, I'd cast a dowsing spell on myself—one that turned me into a human compass needle drawn not to water, but toward the ley line nexus that the Light That Calls for Blood had instructed me to find.

I knew from past reading on the subject that ley lines were all over, an invisible web that enmeshed the globe—made up of natural conduits of magical energy, which could be tapped into by those who knew how to go about such rituals. But when it came to Thistle Grove, their appeal paled in comparison to the massive, much more readily accessible magical reservoir of Lady's Lake. Even I'd never found ley lines particularly interesting to study, hadn't even bothered to explore how they might affect our town.

But when I'd realized that the dowsing spell was drawing me on a direct path toward the Witch Woods—its pull so intense and implacable it felt as though a metal cord had been threaded through my sternum and attached to something motorized—the pieces had slowly fallen together. If a powerful ley line nexus existed within town lines, it would likely be either on Hallows Hill or in the Witch Woods. My bet would've been near the lake, but the haunted forest made sense, too. It would explain something I'd always wondered about, which was *why* the veil was so ragged here in the first place. Even if invisible, ley lines were compellingly attractive, the magical equivalent of life; of course restless spirits would be drawn to such a vibrant nexus, congregating there. Over the years, such a steady influx of shades would have gradually thinned the veil, worn it away.

Back at Tomes, I'd daubed my eyes with a night vision balm I'd made myself—a tincture of deadly nightshade, spikestar flower extract, and dew I'd collected from the thistles that ringed Lady's Lake. When the dowsing spell finally drew me to a breathless halt, I could clearly see that it had stopped me at a seemingly random juncture. About halfway between a towering, twisted oak and a slender sycamore whose branches grew in creepily sinuous curves, like arms beseeching the sky. There was nothing special about this spot, certainly nothing to indicate I was standing on some wellspring of metaphysical power. But the dowsing spell pulsed inside me like a supernova; a burning, throbbing glow of certainty that made me suck in my breath in a sharp gasp before it vanished in a rush.

Oh yes, this was definitely the place.

Biting the inside of my cheek, I knelt, setting my backpack down beside me. Against the ominous silence of the woods, I could suddenly hear the *Opes Sanguinis* whispering to itself, as if it could sense the proximity of the ley line nexus, too. I'd memorized the incantation, but I'd had to bring the awful book with me as a backup, just in case I slammed up against the oblivion glamour and needed it for reference. I could almost make out the faint hissing of its words; something like, *eat the light*, or possibly, *feed the light*. Lines I recognized from the spell itself.

Just what you wanted to hear in the small hours of the night, in the middle of an egregiously haunted forest where nobody knew you even were.

A wave of prickling trepidation swept over me; what the actual fuck did I think I was doing here, and all by myself to boot? This was baneful magic, the oldest and craftiest sort of malefica, and I hadn't so much as left Ivy or Uncle James a note. Yes, I didn't want either of them to know what I was up to before the deed was done . . . but what if something went terribly wrong, and no one knew where to look for whatever was left of me?

Then I would deal with it, I told myself, setting my jaw. The way I always dealt with my problems—self-assuredly and on my own. And even if something *did* go sideways, could it be that much worse than my moth-eaten mind, as tattered and threadbare in its own way as the veil itself was here?

This was the last remaining path. The only trail left that might actually lead me back to my old, lost self.

Mustering my courage, I reached into the backpack for the one tool the spell had called for, a ritual knife I'd sharpened and sterilized back at Tomes; just because I was fucking around with blood magic didn't mean I was also stupid enough to risk literal sepsis, thank you very much. Then I cleared my mind and brought myself into the meditative state that best facilitated spellwork, focusing only on the slow coursing of my breath and the fleshy beating of my heart. Once I found that internal center and held it steady, I summoned a mental image of the page that held the Light That Calls for Blood, written in a slanting, spidery scrawl.

When the words began pouring from my mouth, they barely sounded like me at all.

I'd pitched my voice quiet and low, but it dipped further with each incantation, echoing in my ears as if I were deep in some stalactite-dripping cave rather than the woods. The words themselves felt sharp and somehow angular, as if I were speaking through a mouthful of nails. When I uttered them, they emerged as an eerie susurrus, like the sinister, furious scratching of quill tip against parchment. Much more profoundly strange than Old English when used in normal conversation, the way I'd practiced it with Uncle James.

Even weirder, the spell had a *taste*—an acrid tang like blood and rusted metal, coating my tongue and dripping down my throat. I'd never done a casting that came with its very own flavor, and it ignited another flare of panic—*Delilah, what the* fuck *are you doing? This is one thousand percent unhinged of you*—that I ruthlessly quelled as I continued chanting the words. Once I'd run through the seventeen spoken iterations the spell called for, I gritted my teeth and sliced a neat line across my palm, then held my dripping hand just above the forest floor.

Because that was part of the price that all *Opes Sanguinis* spells called for, lifeblood as fuel and as sacrifice. At least this one required only my own.

As soon as the first drop touched the mulchy soil, the ground began to glow.

I caught my breath as the glow swelled like a seam of magma opening far beneath the forest floor, bursting through all the strata below but not quite breaching the surface. The light was a rich ruby red, pulsing in an irregular pattern like Morse code. For a moment, I just gaped at it, mesmerized.

Then the pain began, like I'd known it would.

At first it was only a throb, timed to the flickering of the light and confined to my hand; so manageable that I relaxed a little, reassured that this spell was something I could handle. Though the slice on my palm was fairly shallow—I'd been careful not to do myself any unnecessary damage—my blood dripped much faster than it should have, as if responding to the beckoning, seductive rhythm of that light. I could hear it spatter as it hit the soil, magnified to the sound of falling rain, like I was bleeding streams rather than just droplets. And suddenly I did feel light-headed, both dizzy and faint, like I might be losing much more blood than I'd actually shed.

With each drop, the pain in my palm intensified—then the light flared so bright it flung my flesh into transparency, revealing the intricate framework of the bones beneath. Dainty metacarpals and slender phalanges suspended in luminous pink, like some macabre art exhibit.

Then pure, white-hot pain swept up my arm and engulfed my entire being . . . and flames and stars, it hurt *so much*.

What came next wasn't a world of pain, but a whole universe of it. Churning scarlet galaxies blooming behind my eyelids like terrible flowers, unfurling and unfolding as I flung back my head and shrieked until my throat felt stripped. Unalloyed agony fissured through my skin; a riving, raw sensation as if my flesh and organs had turned to glass, begun shattering. And somehow, even as I shrieked, the words of the spell kept speaking themselves through me. Ancient and implacable, heedless of my distress. Seemingly uncaring if I, their vessel, even lived through this.

And still that awful crooning whisper coursed all around me, like streams of scouring sand. Sifting into my ears until reality itself seemed to shiver and still.

The briefest flicker of a face sprang into my mind, too fleeting to identify. Then the red behind my eyelids grew brighter yet, blotting out everything else. Until I felt, with a scorching leap of terror, that I might go blind even with my eyes squeezed shut.

Because there was nothing left but red.

Bloody oceans and rivers and scarlet lakes, bearing me away like a savage tide.

6

The Aftermath

I CAME TO with the vague, disconcerting sensation of cold cob-
webs trailing over my face.

Groaning, I shifted my head from left to right; something poky
was digging into the base of my skull. Even with my eyes still
shut, I could tell it had lightened to day—which meant I'd been
lying here for hours, long enough for dawn to break. As sensation
slowly trickled back in, full-body soreness rolled over me, a pervasive ache unlike anything I'd ever experienced. I felt like I'd
been steamrolled and then worked over with a mallet, no part of
me left unscathed.

And there was also that faint breath of chill drifting against
my cheek, even though the rest of me felt sticky with dried sweat.
With another groan, I risked opening my eyes—and found myself
face-to-face with an unmoored shade, the roiling vortices of its
empty sockets not an inch away from me.

With a clipped shriek, I yanked myself upright and scrabbled back on all fours. As the shade wisped away, nearly as spooked as I was, I realized it wasn't the only one.

A bobbing host of them had ventured out of their tree house homes to encircle me, hovering in place. The tenebrous gray of their billowing silhouettes just opaque enough to give them shape, like untethered shadows—hence, *shade*. Even with a flash flood of adrenaline crashing through my veins, I recognized that this pack of shades didn't seem overtly aggressive. If anything, they appeared . . . curious, intrigued by me. Like young wild animals that hadn't learned enough to know that a human trespasser should make them afraid.

Emboldened by my stillness, the one that had been investigating my face rushed back at me, moving with uncanny stop-motion speed, like it had drifted right out of the nearest horror film.

Oh, absolutely fuck *that*, and especially now.

Bracing myself on one shaky arm, I flung out my other hand and barked out a banishing spell; a quick and dirty one, simple enough that it didn't require anything near an Avramov's proficiency, or even all that much will to back it up. Still, I rammed enough "get the shit away from me" energy into the casting that the shade blew itself apart in midair, its wispy shreds spiraling away from one another like droplets of ink dispersed in water.

It would almost certainly re-coalesce—this wasn't the kind of spell capable of permanently banishing a spirit from the mortal plane—but not until long after I'd gotten the hell away from here.

Before they could get any vengeful ideas, I turned to the rest of the clustered shades and dispatched them one by one with a neat series of banishing spells. A few persisted, stubbornly holding their own, enough that I had to call on more obscure workings. But in less than five minutes, I was alone again, filaments of pale early-morning sunlight filtering through the tiny chinks in the thick foliage overhead.

I slumped forward, catching my breath, as two simultaneous realizations spilled over me.

One, I hadn't faltered on a single word in any of the spells I'd used. And even though every inch of me still felt battered, my mind was stunningly clear; airy and somehow fresh, the way a house felt after a good spring cleaning, once you'd flung open all the windows and chased the must and shadows out. As if I'd gotten used to living with a murky brain, hadn't even fully realized how sludgy my thought processes had become until the muck was expelled.

And two, the floral tattoos that sleeved my arms had lost their previous riot of color and were now a uniform ruby red.

I shifted onto my heels and lifted both arms, turning them over and over to inspect the ink more closely. I'd spent many painful hours getting those tattoos, and sketched the original designs myself; I could immediately see that aside from the bloody new color, the flowers themselves remained unchanged. But tiny markings now trailed complex paths between them—what looked like spiky runes, an alphabet entirely different from the Old English the spell had been written in.

It was as though the Light That Calls for Blood had turned me into a human scroll, emblazoned itself into the still-living vellum of my skin.

I sank back onto my haunches, mind racing with the implications. On the one hand, my brain felt crystalline, scrubbed clean with cool water—clearly the spell's handiwork. On the other, there was no way that tattoos turning bloodred augured anything remotely positive.

Once I managed to lurch to my feet, a shimmering veil danced at the edges of my vision, as all the wooziness that the adrenaline had chased away came flooding back full force. Whatever the spell might have accomplished in terms of mental healing, it had also left me weak and wobbly; so drained it would take all the scant energy I had left just to drag myself back out of the Witch Woods.

Then I was going to badly need Ivy's help.

OVER AN HOUR later, I staggered onto the shoulder of the road that wound along the Witch Woods and flopped myself into the passenger seat of Ivy's blue Sentra with all the grace of a trash bag being tipped into a dumpster. The fact that I'd even had enough verve to slog back here and then drop a pin for Ivy felt like a tremendous personal achievement, something that should've won me a prize. Getting my affairs in order was starting to feel like an increasingly not-terrible idea.

"Lilah," Ivy breathed in shock, running her practiced healer's hands down my face and over my shoulders, alarmed eyes swiftly assessing me. "Holy shit, boo, you look like a goddamn *ghost*. Are you okay? What in the entire fuck happened to you? Why are you even all the way out here in spook city?"

"Went camping," I cracked with a rusty giggle, so exhausted I was beginning to feel a little punch-drunk. "Got a lil lost."

"Very funny. Try again."

"I'll 'splain later," I mumbled, tipping my swimming head back against the headrest. "And no, I am not okay. Something . . . I think something might be pretty wrong with me, in fact."

"Yeah, no shit," she replied grimly, leaning across the center console to wrap both hands around my face and tilt it toward her. She smelled enticingly of pastry, caramelized sugar and melted butter; she must have come directly from sorting out a catering order at the Honeycake Orchards bakery. "Let me just take a closer look."

I closed my own eyes with a sigh, the emerald and amethyst swirls of her healing magic unscrolling behind my lids as Ivy performed the Thorn equivalent of medical imaging, sending her healer's awareness spiraling through my body, all the way down to my cells. Unlike a clinical exam, this magical scan felt languorous and warm, like a honeyed bath that lapped at you from the inside. By the time she was done, I felt even woozier, but pleasantly so.

"Well, no wonder you look half-dead," Ivy declared, sounding appalled as she drew back. "Delilah Charlotte Harlow, almost a *fifth* of your blood is not where it should be. And given that I'm not sensing any wounds or internal bleeding, I'm over here wondering just how the hell you managed to do this to yourself."

"Woooo, a fifth!" I marveled giddily. "That a lot? *Sounds* like a lot."

"It is. Under most circumstances, you'd need an emergency transfusion. How you managed to walk your exsanguinated ass out of those woods on your own steam is its own fucking mystery. You should be in hypovolemic shock right now!"

"Natural stamina?" I suggested, my head lolling. "Robust hiker, sturdy calves, et cetera."

She rolled her eyes, running an exasperated hand over her

buzzed head. "Lucky for you, you've got me to tide you over. Do I have your consent to help you produce a bunch of new blood for yourself?"

While Thorn healing magic couldn't cure any of the big baddies when it came to disease, it could still speed up healing significantly; close wounds, mend torn ligaments, help broken bones knit back together much more quickly and cleanly than the normal course of things. And accelerate blood production, apparently. The more talented the Thorn, the more intensive the healing they could do—and though Ivy was a third cousin to the main line, proximity to the central familial branch that traced back to Alastair Thorn rarely factored into ability.

"By all means," I pronounced, waving one hand grandly in the air. "Please and thank you."

"Don't thank me yet," she cautioned. "You're in a bad way. Could be we'll still have to get you to the hospital."

"Not after you're done with me," I said as she pressed her palms back to my cheeks, that blissful heat spreading through me again in warm runnels. Even through the light-headedness, the smell of baked goods on her hands coaxed a rumble from my stomach; from what I dimly remembered, I hadn't eaten since maybe noon the day before. "And then maybe you could feed me, too?"

"When am I ever *not* feeding you?" she said with a wry little laugh, closing her eyes. "It's one of life's constants. Death, taxes, and 'Delilah forgot to eat.'"

I wrinkled my nose. "Was that a compliment? Doesn't seem like it."

"More an inescapable reality. Now, try to hold as still as you can, even if it stings a bit."

)) ● (((

BY THE TIME Ivy was done—after the excruciating agony of the baneful spell, even the smarting ache of legions of new blood cells bursting into existence in my marrow had barely fazed me—I'd felt more than well enough to head back to Honeycake Orchards with her for breakfast, and what was clearly going to be a non-optional debrief.

Once we'd arrived, Ivy had swooped into the bakery attached to the farmhouse restaurant to snag us a picnic basket of assorted goodies; she'd already gotten one of her underlings to cover for her before coming to rescue me. (Wednesdays were the one day a week that Uncle James still liked to helm Tomes & Omens solo—part of the reason I'd chosen to forge ahead with the spell the previous night—so I hadn't had to worry about calling in fake sick.) She'd also let me into an unoccupied room at the Honey-cake B and B for a badly needed shower, along with a borrowed change of clothes. Mine were a grimy rainbow of sweat, blood, and assorted Witch Woods ick that no amount of bleach was going to lift.

Now we sat together in one of the secluded niches of the "haunted" hedge maze, where Thorn-animated flowers swayed and sang for the tourists who traipsed through the orchards each year for apple, pumpkin, and cherry picking, along with a variety of witchier-themed activities. But they never saw special enclo-sures like this, reserved only for friends and family. A checkered picnic blanket lay spread under us, the green walls of the hedges rising like fortress gates to our backs, casting just enough shade to offer respite from the bright flood of late-morning sunshine.

Pink eglantine roses with sunny egg-yolk centers wound their way through the leaves, humming in three-part harmony and shedding their distinctive apple fragrance all over us.

Ivy referred to this little niche as the Sweetbrier Enclave. Like the others, it would open only to a whispered password from a Thorn.

"You *sure* you're up to this?" Ivy asked, studying my face as we both tore into melty ham-and-gruyere croissants. "Clearly I'm more than owed an interrogation. But I could wait a day or two, give you a chance to at least catch your breath."

"I told you," I mumbled through a hearty bite, tilting my face toward the sunshine. The warm breeze combed pleasantly through my still-shower-wet hair, lifting it off my neck. "I'm better than good. Whatever you tinkered with in the pipes really did the trick."

And it was true; I felt almost bonelessly relaxed, better than I had in months. As if I'd finally released a breath held for so long that I'd gotten used to keeping it trapped under my diaphragm, locked down deep in my chest. And the sunshine, this picnic, Ivy's company . . . it all felt like part of the recovery the spell had triggered. A rediscovered ability to actually *enjoy* nice things, without the pall of possible oblivion hanging over me.

But Ivy shook her head, worrying at her silver lower-lip hoop with her thumb. Her skin was such a deep, dark brown it gleamed lustrous under sunlight, but even with that healthy sheen she looked unusually drawn, her brow still furrowed with concern for me.

"Listen, all I did was boost you back to normal plasma, blood cell, and platelet levels," she said with a slow shake of the head. "I didn't want to mess with your system too much. Whatever you're feeling, it's not because of anything I can take full credit for. So level with me, Lilah—why exactly *are* you looking so bright-eyed and bushy-tailed, when you were giving potent *Walking Dead* vibes not an hour ago?"

I stalled with another bite, while a rose extended its pretty head to settle on my shoulder, stroking its petals against my neck. The flowers had been poking at me relentlessly since we'd sat down; straining to wrap themselves around my wrist, resting on the top of my head, even nuzzling ticklishly into my ear.

"And why do the eglantines keep doing all that?" she demanded, narrowing those big dark eyes at me. "It's like they're suddenly obsessed with you. They don't even get that worked up over *me*. Something's different about you, Lilah. You feel all . . . jangly. Buzzy, somehow, not quite like yourself. What happened to you, out there in the woods?"

"I cast a healing spell on myself," I said, still hedging a little—though it was making me nervy, too, the way the eglantines had taken such a keen interest in me after having virtually ignored me for years. "And I needed to be in a certain spot for it to work. A spot that happened to be in the Witch Woods."

"What do you mean, a healing spell? We've done dozens of those already. My whole family's spent months casting every working that might make some difference for you."

"It's not a Grimoire spell," I clarified, knowing she'd pick up on the capital *G*. "It's from one of the other books. The ones we keep at Tomes."

"What the hell kind of a book," she said slowly, that already intent dark gaze intensifying more, "would ask you to wander into a haunted-ass forest in the middle of the night, then somehow siphon off that much of your blood? Not to mention turn your tattoos that . . . that *color*, and throw in all those creepy little marks?"

I glanced guiltily down at my arms, the newly scarlet hue of the flowers. "So you noticed that part."

She cast me a flat look, folding her arms tightly across her chest, the stacks of her vintage Bakelite bracelets clinking against one another.

"How many years have I known you now, Lilah, and you think I'm not familiar with what color your ink's supposed to be? What is it that you're not telling me here?" When I didn't respond, she huffed out an aggrieved sigh, flicking her gaze away from me before dragging it back to mine. "This is bullshit, you know, what you're doing right now. We don't pull this withholding, secretive shit with each other. It's not part of our deal."

I worked my jaw from side to side, considering. I owed Ivy the unvarnished truth; she'd been my bedrock and touchstone for months while I struggled, without an ounce of resentment on her part. And it wasn't as though she'd had an easy time herself this past half a year. She'd gone through a whirlwind romance and then a difficult breakup with one of the Avramovs, along with an ongoing rift with her little sister over a disagreement that had begun as a misunderstanding and evolved into something much deeper—which would've been hard on anyone, but especially a member of the highly sensitive Thorn family. Even with all that going on, she was rarely willing to share her burdens with me, even when I badgered her about them. The spotlight of support tended to be almost exclusively on me.

It was one of the many reasons I felt profoundly guilty for imposing on her with my own infirmity, even if she always insisted that she'd signed up for it.

And besides all that, she was right. Three years ago, when we'd decided to stay friends even if we weren't going to keep on being romantic partners, being real with each other had been part of the conversation. A commitment we'd made to be the sort of chosen family that didn't traffic in lies or passive aggression.

"It was from one of the malefica books," I admitted with a gusting sigh, flicking a slantwise glance at my backpack. If I focused, I could still hear the *Opes* inside it, hissing sullenly to itself. It didn't appreciate being stuffed in there, jostled ignominiously against my other belongings, and it was making its displeasure known. "The ones we keep in the locked shelf upstairs. You know the one. I've shown it to you."

Ivy's jaw dropped, and for a moment she just gaped at me, speechless. Then, she shook her head, slow and incredulous.

"Delilah. You're telling me you cast baneful magic on purpose, and on *yourself*? Why would you take an insane risk like that? Isn't the whole point of that bookcase—of you and James keeping it locked down—that those books are fundamentally evil? So unpredictable and dangerous that the spells in them shouldn't ever be cast?"

"If that were true, then we wouldn't keep them in the first place. We'd destroy them." I bit down on the inside of my lip, trying to keep my nerve, even though Ivy's fear and disapproval were contagious. Stirring my own dormant unease at having cast a spell this frightening—not to mention, compounding the greasy guilt that sat in my stomach like a lump of lard. I'd betrayed my uncle's trust, and my family's by extension. What I'd done, even if justified, was no small breach.

"Oh sure, tell me another one," Ivy snapped, crossing her arms over her chest. "You Harlows are glorified librarians—there *are* no books you'd willingly destroy, no matter the contents. Book burning isn't in your makeup. And that impulse to preserve is fine—noble, even. Hell, it's necessary, given the world at large. But you've always told me you read those books cover to cover only so you'd know exactly what's in them. What you're charged with never letting out."

"You're making it sound like I had half a fucking choice here!" I shot back, sudden fury boiling up in me. Ivy flinched a little, and I instantly regretted the harshness of my tone. We didn't mince words with each other and never had, but we also took care to never raise our voices, either.

I gazed down at my hands twisted in my lap, avoiding her face, trying to even out my ragged breathing before I spoke again.

"I'm sorry. I didn't mean to yell. And yes, maybe it wasn't the most prudent call," I admitted. "But I had to do something, Ivy. I *had* to. I can't—I couldn't live like that anymore. The supplements aren't working for me, none of the spells you've tried have made any difference. The meditations do help a little, sometimes, but even then it's only temporary. And yesterday . . ."

I described what had happened the day before; the way I'd forgotten Marauder's Misery halfway through, the utter meltdown my failure had catalyzed. Ivy watched me silently as I spoke, her limpid eyes torn between fear and sympathy.

"That must've been terrible for you," she finally murmured, reaching out to fold my fingers in hers, giving them a squeeze. "And in front of Nina, no less. You must've *hated* that."

"I wanted to kill her," I admitted. "I mean, not really, but you understand. For letting her, of all people, see me that way. And then she tried to *hug* me. Can you imagine?"

Ivy let out a low whistle. "Damn, did she really? That chick might actually be worse at reading the room than you are. Which is, in its own way, quite impressive."

"Harsh," I noted, "but accurate. For what it's worth, I don't think her social skills are the problem. She just . . . tries too hard when it comes to me. Pushes too much. And it only ever makes things worse."

We sat in silence for a moment, the eglantines crooning at us, soft birdsong trilling from the nests tucked within the nooks and crannies of the hedge.

"But why a malefica spell?" Ivy asked finally. "There's gotta be thousands of books in that store of yours. Why start with baneful magic?"

"We don't tend to acquire many spellbooks that focus on healing," I explained. "According to Uncle James, it's a waste of time and money when we already have access to your family's spells. The healing-based grimoires that've come into our possession over the years pale in comparison to what you can do—and I know, because he and I have tried most of those outsider spells on me, too. The benign ones, that is."

"So what was the one you used last night?"

I grimaced, anticipating her reaction. "The Light That Calls for Blood. It's from a, uh, book called the *Opes Sanguinis*. The 'Wealth of Blood.'"

"Oh, fabulous all around." Ivy swiped a hand down her face, moaning quietly into her palm. "Fantastic. Wait, no, *phenomenal*. Now tell me everything, please. Since you didn't even give me the option of backing you up on this fool's errand, I at least deserve a full rundown."

I described the events of the previous night as closely as I could, trying to ignore the canvas of emotions playing over her face as I detailed each step. Ivy was always transparent that way, incapable of hiding her visceral reactions.

"What else do you know about the spell?" she asked once I'd wrapped up, ticking questions off her fingers. "Spellsmith, origin, historical context?"

"Almost nothing." I spread my hands. "The *Opes Sanguinis* doesn't come with any foreword or preamble, no spellsmiths, editors, or aggregators are credited, and there's no explanation for why the title is in Latin while the spells themselves are in Old or Middle English. There's nothing in our storewide index about it, either, except for date of acquisition—which was about three generations of Harlows back."

"Then you need to talk to your uncle about this," Ivy pressed. "He's been master recordkeeper for decades . . . even if there's nothing in writing about the *Opes*, he might still know *something* about it. That spell is inside you now, Lilah. At the very least, you have to understand how it works. What you did to yourself when you cast it."

"I can't drag him into this, Ivy," I argued, shaking my head. "He'd be *furious* with me. I broke our most important rule, doing what I did last night. Depending on how he chooses to look at it, I also broke his trust. Possibly the sacred trust, even, when it comes to Harlow keepers."

There wasn't technically a prohibition on Harlow keepers helping themselves to the spells in the malefica books, but that was only because one so obviously didn't need to be made explicit. Casting baneful magic from an external grimoire we were charged with protecting went against everything we stood for. If he ever found out I'd done this, there was a better-than-good chance that Uncle James would never forgive me—and that he'd reconsider having appointed me as the next keeper.

"Lilah . . ."

"And look at me!" I cut her off, gesturing broadly at myself, all but thumping my chest to demonstrate my newfound haleness. "I'm fine—*better* than fine, so much better than I've been since all this began. Whatever this spell's origin—whatever else it might do—does that really matter right now? What matters is that it helped when nothing else did. I can think again, properly. I feel like *myself*, like the way I used to be. Ivy, please. Can I just be allowed to enjoy that for a while?"

Ivy subsided, closing her eyes and releasing a whooshing exhale.

"Okay," she said a moment later, weariness settling into every line of her striking face. "Alright. Let's do it your way, at least for the moment. Because you're right—I can't begrudge you a little peace, not after everything you've been through. You might've gone about it possibly the worst way imaginable, no question, but I can understand why you did it."

"Thank you," I whispered. "Really. That means so much."

"But if *anything* starts going wrong," she cautioned, her face taking on an even graver mien. "Lilah, I mean it. If you start feeling *any* type of way, you need to take this to James."

"If something happens, of course I'll come clean with him," I assured her, a swell of vast relief and gratitude expanding inside my chest at her support. It meant so much more than she knew to have her on my side like this, so staunch and unflinching, when I had so few real friends to count on. "You have my word, okay?"

But even as I said it, I knew that nothing was going to happen. Nothing would steal this hard-won peace and clarity from me.

Because I wasn't going to let it.

7

The Beguilement

AS SOON AS I got home from Honeycake, I flung open my window to let Montalban in from where she'd been roosting in the oak that shaded my bedroom, exactly where I'd known she'd be. She was overjoyed to see me, nuzzling her head against my cheek and showering me with the gentle pecks from her curved bill that passed for kisses. But then she paused, as if sensing some subterranean disturbance; walking her way down to my shoulder, cawing insistently until I turned my head to face her.

"What is it, sweetness?" I asked, nonplussed as she peered into my eyes, scrutinizing me. Unnaturally still, like a carved jet figurine of herself. "What are you . . ."

Then, I saw it; a ruby gleam sparkling to life in each of her glossy dark irises, like a bloody pinprick floating in ink. As if her own gaze reflected something crimson that glowed deep in my own eyes, a light that only she could see.

She cocked her head back and forth, considering me, for so long that a clot of fear curdled in my gut; nothing had ever thrown my familiar like this, not since we'd been bonded. But then she gave a dismissive little head bob and nestled back against me. Whatever she'd detected, it clearly wasn't enough to dilute her affection or our bond.

So I'd been right to tell Ivy not to fret over me, I thought to myself, the scrim of fear breaking apart, loosening and melting into relief. We might all need some adjusting to this new normal, but we would be fine.

I would, at long last, be fine.

THE NEXT TWO days, I swept around Tomes with my old assertiveness, my every movement efficient, competent, and deft, my mind clear as a bell. Thursday morning, I got up at the crack of dawn to hike back up to Hallows Hill, and this time I found and harvested a whole spate of viridian teardrops in under an hour. Since Thursday was another of Nina's days at the store, that afternoon we recast Marauder's Misery, in record time and with no hiccups at all.

And when Morty Gutierrez—Nina's partner, and owner of the quirky Shamrock Cauldron bar—dropped in to bring her lunch, I even felt magnanimous enough to accept their turkey-apple-and-brie sandwich offering. (Through careful observation of my ordering habits, Nina had deduced that this was my favorite item on the Shamrock's menu, but most of the time I demonstratively declined anything Morty brought me when he came to visit her. Free food from the Shamrock didn't *exactly* count as a Blackmoore bribe, but it felt close enough that I liked turning it down on principle.)

That Friday, I spent a serene day almost entirely by myself, largely unbothered by tourists and able to restore four separate wards on my own. Casting without any fear or doubt hanging over me felt like flexing a newly healed muscle; a little tentative, but deliciously satisfying all the same.

By the time I got home, I was feeling cocky enough to chance something I hadn't dared in months—a negroni nightcap, once the headliner of my bedtime routine. When the first couple of sips left me neither spinny nor nauseous, I drained the cocktail and made myself another in a little impromptu celebration. Tucked up under my weighted blanket and surrounded by the prints of botanical illustrations I'd plastered all over my bedroom walls in lieu of wallpaper, I felt a kind of pure contentment I'd been afraid I'd lost forever. Because this was all I really needed out of life; a book in my lap, a lowball in my hand, my muscles still aching pleasantly from yesterday's hike. And the warm knowledge that I'd wake tomorrow fully equipped to live the dream that was running Tomes.

I was so relaxed I drifted off between one page and the next, having barely managed to flick off my bedside lamp before succumbing to sleep, Montalban already drowsing in her open cage. So when I woke to a room shrouded in a darkness, the shadowy silhouette of a figure floating just beyond the window across from my bed, I barely registered any alarm at all.

Just a dream, I thought hazily to myself, as the silhouette clicked long nails in a beckoning rhythm against the glass.

Only a dream, as I flung off my blankets and set both feet on the floor, the parquet much colder under my soles than it should have been, as though something were sucking the ambient heat from the room. The window itself was rimed with ferns of frost, but only in the places where the shadow's hands grazed the glass. I had to come all the way close, nose nearly pressing against the panes, before I could make her out.

Because it was a her. And flames and stars, she was beautiful.

The shadow hovering in front of my window was no shadow at all, but a nearly naked woman with midnight hair that streamed in glossy, sculpted currents to her waist. Folds of some gauzy, weightless fabric, like the night air given texture, draped across her full breasts and twined just below her waist. She all but glowed against the dark, with the kind of pure and poreless milky skin that had clearly never withstood sunlight. Her face was heart-shaped and impossibly lovely; a chiseled nose with nostrils as precise as blown glass, a soft sweep of cheekbone under gleaming alabaster skin, and curved lips the color and lushness of summer strawberries. Her eyebrows were feathered black arches so symmetrical and dense they might have been sketched by someone who had personally witnessed the eyebrow version of the Platonic ideal.

Everything about her was an invitation, from the nip of her waist to the wide flourish of her hips.

And her eyes . . . her eyes were blackest black, pools of spilled ink with no whites around them, fringed by thick, silky lashes like trimmed mink. When I met her hypnotic gaze, I could see that the pupils themselves were elongated, like topaz teardrops suspended in that unrelenting onyx darkness.

There you are, my freckled beauty, my fawn-faced lady, she whispered, though even as I saw those perfect lips shaping the words, I heard the crystalline chime of her voice only in my head. *Finally awake, after I called and called to you.*

The surge of lust that bolted through me made me literally

weak in the knees, turned them to water. I licked my lips, pressing both palms against the window, so overcome with the yearning to touch her that I'd have promised her anything, everything she wanted, in exchange for her skin under my hands. The fact that she was *floating* in front of my window, her shadow long and eerily thinned out on the empty street below, barely seemed to register as problematic within the context of this strange dream.

Oh, the way you shine, she crooned at me, her eyes widening with delight, long, curved black nails (*like talons*, some distant part of my mind clamored in alarm) still clicking against the glass in that coy, rhythmic little rap. *So warm, so red. Like hearthfire itself, or a beating heart. Will you let me in, my fawn-faced beauty? Will you invite me to share your warm, warm bed?*

I nodded so vigorously I nearly sprained my neck, that dreamy feeling still enveloping me, granting me permission to do whatever I pleased. Fumbling hurriedly with the latch, I flung the window open, the gust of summer air that rushed in almost huffing my protective candle out. But it stayed lit—if anything, the orange flame blazed even brighter, to an aggressive height far out of proportion to the slim taper's length.

Almost as if it thought it was protecting me from something that meant me harm.

How silly of it, I thought giddily to myself, almost giggling out loud. What a *stupid* candle. How could I think anything but the best things, the *nicest* things, about this gorgeous, irresistible, exquisite creature that had chosen to bestow a visit on the likes of me? I was so, so lucky she was even here!

As if in echo of my thoughts, she flicked a contemptuous glance down at the candle's flame, tucking her fine-boned feet away from it.

I can't come to you, my pretty freckled fawn, not while that *vile thing is still lit.* Each word felt like a caress, like it had been designed to insinuate itself into the folds of my brain and stroke me from within. *If you'd like me to come visit, you must first extinguish it for me.*

Another faint alarm sounded from the deeper recesses of my mind, even as I bent over the candle, lips pursed in readiness. *She needs an invitation, and she can't bypass a ward, and you* know *what she is, Delilah, you know this isn't safe!*

But that dream haze of pure lust persisted, throbbing between my legs, fogging up all reason. I wanted her inside, with me; I wanted all that creamy skin spread out under my hands, her sharp-tipped fingers tangled in my hair. Her red mouth clasped over my own, as she swallowed my gasps like she was drinking them.

I blew out the candle, murmuring the charm that laid its ward to rest. It flared for one last, desperate moment, wanly resisting my command, and then guttered.

With a triumphant croon, she surged through my window in a billowing rush of silky hair, landing so lightly I didn't even hear those pretty feet meet the floor. Her toenails were black, too, I dimly noted, glossy and shining like polished jet; the same color as her eyes and hair, shockingly dark against the sweet-cream pallor of her skin.

Then she stepped fluidly toward me, winding her arms around my waist, those long nails tracing over the thin T-shirt I'd worn to bed, scarlet lips hovering not an inch away from mine. I gasped instinctively as the heady wash of her perfume engulfed me whole, a hypnotic scent unlike anything I'd ever smelled, jasmine and sharp moss drenched in the slow drip of honey. And underneath it, something mulchy and somehow damp, like the soil in the Witch Woods' most impenetrable depths.

I cupped my hands around her face, shocked at how smooth she was, her cheeks like satin as I swept my thumbs over them. When she leaned in to kiss me through a smile, my breath hitched at the lushness and heat of her lips. Whatever analytical part of my brain was still awake had expected her to be chilly, from the way her touch had sucked warmth out of my window and the air inside my room.

But she was the opposite of cold, her tongue sweet and silky and scalding against mine.

So hot I could feel my own essential heat respond to her, yielding to her command. Like a gush of warmth searing up my throat, rushing to meet hers. As if she were drinking me somehow, just the way I'd wanted her to.

Impossibly, the notion of her drawing some vital sustenance from this kiss felt more seductive than anything I'd ever felt before, so overwhelmingly sexy it made me want to swoon. Whatever she wanted, I would give to her. Anything she needed from me, it would be my pleasure to sacrifice.

"What's your name?" I whispered against her lips, panting into her mouth. "What should I call you?"

*Oh, why would that **ever** matter?* she replied archly, nipping at my lower lip. *Now isn't the moment for such tawdry trifles. Now is the time only for desire.*

My legs went so weak they nearly gave out from under me. I could feel one of her arms tighten around my waist, fearsomely strong, like her frame was made of rebar instead of bones; supporting me, folding me easily against the lush contours of her form. With all my toned muscle, I probably weighed much more than she did, but she handled me as if I were made of feathers, or dandelion fluff. Her other hand slipped under my shirt, trailing up and down my spine, stroking me with a light, insistent touch that sent trembling waves of desire coursing down my legs and coiling at my core.

She pulled away from me, breaking that sucking kiss for long enough to whisk my shirt over my head, then bury her face in the tumble of my hair and the sensitive crook of my neck. When her slick open mouth pressed against my skin, I moaned aloud, hips rolling against hers.

You taste so good, my freckled beauty, she murmured against my neck, low laughter in her voice. Her exhale brought a delicious stippling of goose bumps unfurling down my side, my mind roiling into a decadent whorl of chaos, a tumult that made it impossible to form a thought beyond sheer want. *Like some sweet cut fruit dusted with flecks of salt. And all that heat in you, the light in you, like a well of melting sugar boiling over in the sun. Will you let me taste you even more?*

"Yes," I whispered urgently, in a low, needful rasp I barely recognized as my own. "Please. Any . . . anything you want."

With another silky laugh, she walked me backward until my calves pressed against the mattress edge, pushing gently on my shoulders to sit me down. Then she slid into the space between my legs and knelt, reaching up to cup both my bare breasts in scorching hands. I let my head fall back as she pressed and rolled them beneath her palms, then pushed them together and drew my nipples into the forge of her mouth—sucking them into hardened, throbbing peaks until I thought I'd really melt, turn into the pool of sun-warmed sugar she said I tasted like. Spurred on by my moans, she trailed licking kisses down my sternum and my navel, then dipped lower still, using her teeth to tease up the edges of the boy shorts that I slept in. Sinking sharp, luscious bites into the insides of my thighs.

I wanted her to peel those shorts off me with such mindless ferocity that I felt like I'd die if I didn't feel her mouth on me at once. Like I'd crumple beneath the crushing force of my own lust.

Just as her fingers slid under my elastic waistband, nails grazing against my skin, an image crashed into my mind—a bold, intent, almost hawkish face, white-blond hair obscuring one verdigris eye. The other narrowed in fury and revulsion, an intricate tattoo nestled in its corner. The same face I'd seen when I cast the Light That Calls for Blood, only clearer, much more focused now. And this time the vision lingered instead of winking out, for long enough that I managed to recognize her.

Catriona Arachne Quinn, who'd stolen a fairy oracle deck from me three days ago and was now cat-burglaring her way into my mind.

Wake up, Delilah! she hissed at me. I felt an almost physical mental lurch, as if she'd snatched me by the shoulders and given me a robust shake. *Stop her! She's a succubus, and she's fucking eating you right now. If you don't stop her, you are going to die tonight.*

Am not, I argued, like a petulant child. *And I want her.*

As if she could tell something untoward was happening, the beauty—the . . . succubus?—stilled between my legs. Then she gave a delicate shudder, like a cat twitching off an unwanted touch. Montalban began to stir in her cage, too, issuing a disgruntled squawk; maybe she'd also felt the psychic shock waves of Cat's intrusion in my mind.

What is that, my fawn-faced lady? the succubus whispered with a new touch of wariness, black-and-topaz eyes snapping up to mine. That underlying odor of mulch and darkness deepened, taking on a sharp note that was close to rank. For the first time, I sensed a low current of menace emanating from her; a spine-tingling sense that maybe she was the kind of houseguest I should have thought twice about before inviting in. *Or should I say, who?*

Delilah, she's going to kill you, Catriona repeated, her voice knelling like a church bell in my mind. *I know it feels goddamn wonderful right now, but trust me—the foreplay's not going to last, and I promise you're not gonna like the main event. That's what succubi do, it's their only nature. And I know she's strong, but so are you. Resist the pull—banish her now.*

When I hesitated another moment, I felt an even more foreign sense of frustration in my mind, something like an impatient sigh. Then a shocking, icy flood of sensation crashed over me, like the psychic equivalent of a freezing shower. It sluiced the lust right off me, grounded me in place.

Reminded me of myself, and the profound wrongness of what was happening right now.

"Succubus," I whispered aloud, a torrent of panic gushing through me even as Catriona's presence in my mind blinked out. I knew their lore from the books; demonic temptresses, supernatural beings that fed on the life essence of their victims while seducing them. Like more traditional vampires, if vampires were more inclined to fuck you to death than drain your blood.

But for all my knowledge of their lore, I'd never thought I'd meet one in the flesh, glowing like a fallen star on my bedroom floor. Before tonight, I hadn't even been totally sure they existed; as far as I knew, not a single one had ever made her way to Thistle Grove.

So you do know my name, she whispered from between my

legs, tucking a sheaf of glossy hair behind one small shell ear. And this time her red smile split wide, showing pearly, even teeth with delicately pointed canines. Not sharp enough to bite, not like I imagined a vampire's would be; but sharp enough to at least hint at what she really was. What kind of family she belonged to. *Or one of them, at least—and the least important one, at that. Still, how impertinent of you, to feign ignorance. And here I thought you wanted to be mine!*

"I do not, and I want you to go!" I snapped back, scrambling away from her, even more frightened by the unmistakable new edge of warning in her tone. Now fully awake, Montalban had begun causing a ruckus in her cage, flapping her wings and rattling at the bars. But I sent her a stern mental command to stay put; the last thing I needed was for the succubus to somehow target my familiar and entice her, too, if that was even possible.

As soon as I'd put some distance between us, my teeth began to chatter. The comforter under my knees was crisp and freezing cold, as if she'd already consumed most of the room's warmth. "Be—begone!" I added, as if my voice weren't shaking.

When we were having such lovely fun, you and I? she purred inside my mind, crawling onto my bed on her hands and knees, her flanks and shoulders rolling with the lithe grace of an apex predator. That sweet overlay of perfume, moss and flowers and sticky honey, rose to the fore again, and I could feel renewed waves of beguilement battering at me like breakers, threatening to recapture me in their undertow. *Oh, no, I think I won't go just yet . . .*

Gritting my teeth against the onslaught, I frantically riffled through my mental grimoire of banishing spells. The ones I'd used on the Witch Woods shades wouldn't even begin to faze her; she was a chthonic creature of another order of magnitude. But the spells I remembered that specifically targeted succubi always required the entity's true name to bind and banish them.

What utter bullshit, I thought to myself as she settled back to hover over me. How exactly were you supposed to discover the name of a creature about to consume your essence? Take a fucking quiz? Phone a friend?

Just as her parted lips drifted back down to mine—flames and stars, she smelled *so* good, and tendrils of her hair drooped like the softest fern fronds over my cheeks—a spell blazed into my mind. It was ancient, inscribed in one of the crumbling grimoires that Uncle James and I hadn't dared crack open more than once, afraid that even with preservation spells in place they might disintegrate under the oil of our touch. It wasn't a succubus-specific banishment, but one intended as a catchall, a last resort for situations like this.

When you were inches away from fang and claw, staring your demonic end dead in the face.

Normally, I wouldn't even have considered it; it was another baneful spell, this one wholly fueled by the caster's pain. But all's fair in love and war and death by sex, I thought wildly to myself as I stared into the succubus's eyes, glistening like chitin shells right above mine.

Then I bit down on the inside of my lip as hard as I could, at the same time as I scratched deep, vicious grooves into my palms. As the pain blazed up, I spat a word—multisyllabic and harsh, in a language long since dead and buried—directly into the succubus's face. Infusing it with as much get-thee-gone will as I could muster.

Sensing the current of magic, Montalban gave a sharp caw and homed in on the spell; funneling it through herself, making it that much keener when it struck the succubus.

With a clipped, insectile screech, the demon *lifted* off me— dragged away by something that I couldn't see. That invisible force yanked her away like a rag doll, then simply sucked her out the open window, as if my room had turned into a breached space-ship hull leaking into outer space.

8

The Huntress

I DRAGGED MYSELF into Tomes the next morning after a miserable, sleepless night.

I'd spent the darkest hours purifying my apartment with a censer of rosemary, mugwort, and sweetgrass, then cast every ward I could think of to secure my home against intrusions. It was now likely much safer there than at Tomes, so I instructed Montalban to stay put rather than come with me to the store—in the guise of asking her to guard our home, after she threw a screechy tantrum over being parted from me again.

But even as wrung out as I was, I couldn't cast off the churning fear, the new questions that whirled through my mind like dust devils. Why had the succubus singled me out as her target? I'd never even heard of a paranormal manifestation in our town that wasn't the direct result of a spell cast by a Thistle Grove witch. (That *was* a remote possibility, but I doubted that even the most daredevil Avramovs would summon a succubus. And from what I knew, they were perfectly capable of hosting life-draining orgies without any paranormal assistance.)

As much as I hated to admit it, the much likelier explanation hinged on the fact that I'd recently cast a baneful blood spell and accessed a ley line nexus. Maybe something about that combination was oddly irresistible to succubi? Or maybe it had been an isolated incident, the timing just a bizarre coincidence.

But I couldn't quite bring myself to believe something so improbable, when a connection between the events was so much more likely. And how in the flames and stars had Catriona Arachne Quinn wormed her way into my head? Yes, the Avramovs could cast oblivion glamours and the Thorns were empaths, but none of our witches could read thoughts, or directly invade someone else's mind.

So, instead of huddling under a fort of blankets and denial in my magically barricaded home, as would have been my strong preference, I did what I always did. I turned to my books.

By early afternoon, I'd managed to unearth nothing, even after having speed-read my way through Thistle Grove records of every Harlow keeper going five generations back. It wasn't that my ancestors didn't believe in what they referred to as "cryptids"; there were numerous accounts of the keepers and other Thistle Grove witches having encountered them on their travels outside of town. Some of the books in our collection had apparently even been acquired from creatures of a paranormal bent.

But the more I thought about it, the more their complete absence here struck me as strange. Thistle Grove was home to a tremendous magical repository in the form of Lady's Lake, and its entire reputation and tourism industry revolved around its occult history—wouldn't supernatural creatures be drawn here in hordes?

And yet, they weren't . . . unless you counted the shades that haunted the Witch Woods, which I didn't. Restless spirits were everywhere, and in a town overrun by a clan of unearthly gorgeous necromancers descended from Baba Yaga, an absence of apparitions and possessions would've been much stranger. But in more than three hundred years, no one had reported a single encounter with any cryptid other than a shade. (Besides a very dubious mention of a satyr in the Hallows Hill woods during the Beltane of 1943, which was wryly dismissed by the recording Harlow keeper as a case of wishful thinking and too much spring wine.)

But the succubus had been very real—and she'd homed in on me, specifically.

By the time I slumped over the counter with a tension headache brewing behind my eyes, not even four cups of industrial-strength coffee could dispel my growing dread. It seemed almost certain that my spell had triggered something unforeseen, something that had resulted in a personalized invitation to that succubus. And if that was the case, how could I be sure it wouldn't happen again?

I was dismally contemplating a fifth cup of coffee, just to see if more caffeine might forcibly lift my spirits, when the alert bell chimed. *Now comes Catriona Arachne Quinn, ahoy, ahoy!!*

My entire body sprang into full alert, and without thinking, I cued up a list of defensive spells and began drawing on the magic it would take to cast them. Yes, she'd helped me last night—without her intervention, chances were very good that I'd have wound up a succubus feast—but she was clearly no ordinary tourist, either. For all I knew, she'd saved me just to corner the market on killing me herself.

By the time she appeared from between the bookshelves—hands raised and palms out, a corner of her mouth quirked with amusement—my own hands were all but crackling with restrained magical energy.

"I come in peace," she called out theatrically, sauntering over to the counter. Again in a simple, stretchy tank, this time black, formfitting charcoal pants lined with a multitude of subtle pockets, and heavily scuffed combat boots despite the summer heat. She jerked her chin at my hands, lifting a dark eyebrow. "So no need for any sparkies, unless it puts your mind at ease."

"What are you talking about?" I said, inanely, given that we were clearly far past the stage of playing dumb. She shouldn't even have been able to sense my burgeoning spells; a normie certainly wouldn't have. Both the locals and tourists seemed completely unaware of the lake's magic, the fragrant roil of it throughout town, the way the air itself seemed to fizz and shimmer with raw potential.

But Catriona Quinn was obviously miles removed from being a normie.

She rolled her eyes, tossing her head to clear that blond swatch of hair away. "Listen, I know you're a witch, and I don't mean you any harm," she said bluntly. "Which isn't to say I *haven't* killed witches before. But only what you might consider the wicked ones."

I stared at her, slack-jawed. "Who the fuck *are* you?"

"I the fuck am Cat," she replied coyly, tilting her head to the side, platinum hair swishing right back over her eye. "I thought we already covered this bit."

"That much, I do know. Catriona Arachne Quinn." A flush of

satisfaction surged through me at the look of surprise and calcu-
lation that flitted across her face, before she schooled it back into
the smooth neutral of that self-assured amusement. She hadn't
expected me to know her full name; now she was reconsidering
what else I might know. "So, let me rephrase. *What* are you? Not
a normie, that's for sure."

"Oof, is *that* what you call them around here?" She pulled a
face, sucking air in through her teeth. "A bit on the nose, don't you
think? Verging on offensive."

"Oh, you mean 'offensive' like barging into someone else's head
uninvited?"

"What was that?" She cupped a hand around her ear, cocking
her head. "You know, I've never heard 'many thanks for saving my
life from a sex pest demon, please accept my eternal gratitude'
sound like that before. Must be a regional dialect thing."

Despite myself, I sputtered a chuckle. "Okay, yes, so I'm in your
debt for that. But this isn't going to be like the other day, where
you talk me in such circles that I let you stroll out of *my* shop with
something stolen." I paused for a moment, outrage resurrected.
"Whatever you are, you have abysmal shoplifting taste."

She grinned at that, white teeth flashing against cerise lips.
"Touché. Sorry about the deck—that was a necessary evil. I needed
to establish a telepathic link with you, and stealing something
symbolic is one of the easiest ways to create one. In my defense, I
deliberately chose something I assumed didn't matter very much
to you. If anything, you should be twice grateful that I took that
awful schlock off your hands on top of saving your life."

When I didn't say anything, struggling to process the notion
of a telepathic link—one I hadn't consented to, to boot—she added
a dry "You're welcome."

"How is a fairy oracle deck symbolic of *anything*?" I demanded, my head beginning to spin like a shoddy carnival ride. Yet again, in my rush to delve into the research, I hadn't eaten anything today except for half a stale bagel and a handful of lentil chips. In combination with shock and too much coffee, the results were suboptimal. "And why won't you just tell me what you fucking are, instead of talking around it?"

"Occupational hazard," she said with a crisp shrug, those impressive shoulder muscles bunching under her tawny skin. "Or maybe you could call it an identity disorder. I have . . . a hard time staying linear, occasionally. Why don't you come eat with me; I'll explain what I can. You need to eat anyway. I can smell your blood sugar plummeting from here."

"You can *smell* my blood sugar? And you—you want to have dinner with me?" I asked, flummoxed, finally lowering my hands. Thrown as I was by this bizarre conversation, I'd at least decided she didn't constitute any imminent threat.

"More of a late lunch, given the hour. And unlike last night, I wasn't even planning on having the meal be you! See?" She spread her hands, tipping me a wink and a broad, winning smile. "I'm already a way better date."

TWENTY MINUTES LATER, we were at Cryptid Pizza, because my life had become surpassingly strange and meta even by Thistle Grove's standards. Pop culture depictions of werewolves, vampires, Bigfoot, Swamp Thing, and the Creature from the Black Lagoon hung on the walls in neon frames. One of the walls had a claw-mark decal, making it look as though something with huge talons had rent it; another featured a rotating black-and-white spiral that formed a swirling, hypnotic tunnel if you stared at it too long. The chandelier was shaped like a UFO, complete with twinkling lights and occasional *X-Files* sound effects.

Cat seemed thoroughly delighted by the twee quirkiness of it all, chuckling to herself as she dispatched her slices in efficient, fastidious bites while I gobbled mine down. She'd been right about my sorry state; the caffeine had masked my hunger, but with creamy goat cheese, caramelized onion, and glistening coins of pepperoni actually in front of me, it had taken everything I had not to drag the entire pie over to my side of the table and snap at Cat's hand every time she reached for a slice.

"This is a *ridiculous* place," she said, gleefully taking in the decor. "What a fucking brilliant way to hide real magic in plain sight. Kudos to your local fiendish masterminds."

"Speaking of hiding in plain sight, or, for instance, posing as a clueless tourist with a fairy fetish," I said pointedly, washing down the last of my second slice with a swallow of soda, "here we are, breaking bread—or rather, bread and cheese and processed meats. Just like you wanted. So. What are you."

"You're remarkable, do you know that?" she said, verdigris eyes locking on mine, and the avid intensity in her gaze stirred something low in my stomach. I could make out her tiny tattoo now; a delicate, stylized spider perched on an equally small and intricate web, just to the left of her eye. "So relentlessly forthright. No wiggle room with you whatsoever. What's that about?"

I shrugged a shoulder. "I am, apparently, 'just *rude*,' as my little sister will happily tell you." Genevieve and I had had our share of disagreements over the years; we had very different ideas on how to approach social mores and niceties. Gen built her life around elevating them into an art form, while I preferred to circumvent them altogether, thereby avoiding the waste of time they inevitably entailed.

"A lack of patience for sugar-coated bullshit isn't rudeness," she replied, eyes shifting between mine, and I got the sense she meant it. "It's an enviable quality. Believe me, I would know. Where I come from, frankness can be very hard to come by."

"And where might that be? The place you come from."

"Chicago, mostly. That part was true." She leveled a solemn gaze at me, with none of the archness I was becoming accustomed to from her. "I lived in a sort of enclave—a community of creatures and other not-quite-mundanes. Like a co-op of weirdos, if you will. Fae, shifters, witches . . ." She skimmed her gaze over the monsters hanging on the walls, lips quirking. "Can't say I've ever run across the Creature from the Black Lagoon, but many of the others were present and accounted for."

So there were cryptid enclaves in major cities; that wasn't something I'd ever read in one of our books. I remembered Emmy complaining that she'd felt no magic at all during her nearly nine years in Chicago, but a community like that would likely be heavily glamoured, well shielded from the uninvited and uninitiated. As a witch whose magic was waning with distance from Thistle Grove, there was no reason she would've stumbled across them, especially if they didn't want to be found.

"It makes sense that paranormal creatures would congregate," I mused, as much to myself as her. "Safety in numbers, common interests. Protection from discovery by . . . mundanes."

"Exactly. We call it the Shadow Court." She smirked a little at that, a corner of her mouth curling. "Big drama and intrigue, I know, but it's headed by a very old fae—they go in hard for that sort of thing. Many of its members are fae as well, belonging to one of a number of factions; we call them clans. Other, less-human-passing creatures don't tend to stay long enough to put down those kinds of roots. Usually they're just passing through."

"Fae," I echoed, running a mental tally on what I knew about them. There were many different variants in the lore, but the creatures that normies often called "fairies" all tended to be morally ambiguous in one way or another. Sly, conniving, tricksters at heart; silver-tongued, often dangerously charismatic and beautiful. Experts at blurring lines and enticing humans into playing bit parts in their elaborate narratives. The literature all indicated a tendency toward megalomaniacal dispositions that favored self-interested scheming, the kind that in humans usually led to venture capitalism and politics. "So, is that what you are? You still haven't said."

"I'm only half fae, like many of us are. Full-blooded fae are low on moral strictures in general, and then humans often find them pretty sexy, too, so . . ." She spread her hands like, *That big fae energy, what are you gonna do?* It certainly explained her striking face and coloring, the magnetism of her presence. "It all adds up to quite a few halflings running around and causing all manner of spicy mayhem. I'm a little unusual, in that I'm fae on my mother's side—she's cat sith, if you happen to know anything about them. They're quite rare, compared to some of the others."

I did, in fact. I'd run across several references to them in my reading on Celtic mythology. The sources couldn't seem to agree if they were a type of fae shifter native to our plane, like a sort of fairy werecat, or actual felines that had slunk their way in from an external fae realm. They were often accused of stealing souls, but also occasionally imparted blessings on those who earned their favor, too. Beyond that, the details were nebulous.

"So, can you . . . turn into a cat?" I asked, feeling more than a little idiotic. "Also, 'Catriona,' really? A half cat sith named *Cat*?"

"I cannot turn into a kitty cat, no. But I do have certain physical advantages. Heightened senses, a few other handy upgrades here and there." She chuckled, rolling her eyes in wry agreement. "And trust me, I'm well aware of how ridiculous the name is. Most cat sith hail from Scotland, so 'Catriona' made sense, and I imagine my mother thought she was being *very* clever with the obvious nickname."

She caught the face I made in response to that, and laughed, canting her head. "I know, I know. But I think part of it was in earnest, too; my father raised me on his own for nearly half my life. I didn't find out about the Shadow Court—or about my mother, what she was—until I was sixteen. It was her way of keeping her mark on me. Branding me as hers, until she could have me back."

"Until she could have you back?" I prodded, as gently as I could, though *branding* your own child in any way while planning on abandoning her struck me as baseline abominable. "Why leave you and your father behind in the first place?"

"She and my dad had a bit of a whirlwind thing, so he was never part of the long game for her. And she didn't think the Shadow Court was a very good place to raise a child. The clans I mentioned don't always get along, by which I mean there's a steady stream of complicated fuckery and power struggles that don't always end well. I love it now, but it's a complex place. It was her way of shielding me, until I was old enough that she thought I'd be able to find my footing there."

I was watching her so closely that I caught another of those brief expressions rippling across her face, like a reflection wavering in water. There was something more beneath the surface here that she didn't intend to tell me. But I could see from the way her features meticulously smoothed out that there'd be no use in pushing.

"Which clan are you?" I asked instead. "I assume you have an affiliation."

"Arachne." She tapped the tiny spider by her eye. "Same as my mother. We're more involved with brute force than politics, which means we keep what passes for peace in the Court, and the city at large. What you might call pest control."

"So, you're a monster hunter," I clarified, even as I wondered why a faction that made that kind of outright aggression its business would choose a sly, reclusive creature like a spider as its sigil. Shouldn't she have been a wolverine or something? Or leopard, grizzly, cobra? Even a mongoose would have made more sense.

"More or less. Very few creatures are full evil, but some are. Others just can't restrain a violent or carnivorous nature, and the Shadow Court can't tolerate any threat to mundanes large enough that it runs the risk of exposing all of us. Not to mention, sometimes we're the targets of the violence; some of the predators aren't exactly discerning when it comes to what they consider prey."

"So why consider me prey, specifically?" I asked, my mind snagging on a shard of what she'd said. "I've been wondering what drew the succubus to me."

"I don't know, but she was making a beeline for you." She toyed with the straw in her soda, twisting it deftly between her fingers, almost as if she were dancing a coin along her knuckles. "I'd been tracking her in Chicago for a while. She'd killed a couple of high-profile mundanes, the kind that result in real questions getting asked, and it was past time to put her down. Then she switched up her pattern entirely, hightailed it your way like you'd sent her an engraved invitation. I managed to beat her here."

"But how could you know it'd be me she was after?" I asked, a thorny prickle of suspicion bristling in my chest. "You showed up days before she attacked me. I may have . . . some idea of what I might have done to catch her attention. But even that, I didn't do until after *you* were already here."

"Oh, you're a quick one!" she drawled, eyes widening in admiration, and despite my discomfort, my uncertainty with her, the pit of my belly warmed at the compliment. "This is where those cat sith tweaks I mentioned come in. We have some telepathic and prognosticating abilities. Which means that occasionally, if I try very hard, I'm able to catch a murky glimpse into the future. Helps with hunting and tracking, which is part of why I'm in Arachne in the first place. When I realized the succubus had changed direction entirely, heading away from the city, I focused those abilities on her."

"And what did you see, exactly?"

"Looking forward tends to be nebulous stuff—probabilities rather than certainties. But I caught enough clues to piece together which town to aim for." She flicked up a shoulder. "The name of your store, for one, and you working in it. And you on your knees, bleeding in that fucked-up forest on the edge of town. I saw that you were casting something; something very big and, from the looks of it, exceptionally nasty. Many demonkind have powerful future sight; I'd wager that's how she knew to head your way, too, even before you cast the spell."

"I felt you in my head that time, too," I said, the pieces still not quite falling together. Something about this story didn't track, but I couldn't put my finger on what. "Just for a second. But how is that possible? If seeing that spell was part of what led you here at all, that would have been *before* you established the psychic link with me at the store."

"I know, it's confusing as hell." She pulled a sympathetic grimace. "Future sight can get squirrelly that way. I actually witnessed that moment over a week ago, before I ever came here, much less had a link in place with you. You only felt me at all because I experienced an emotional response strong enough to briefly filter through to you. Once I arrived and found you, I knew I'd need a *real* connection. To be able to try to protect you whenever she eventually made her move."

I scrutinized her, chewing on the inside of my cheek. "So why didn't you just tell me she'd be coming for me, that day at Tomes? Let me make my own preparations?"

"Oh, my mistake." She tilted her head to the side, all mock earnestness. "'Excuse me, a supernatural creature you may not even know exists is very likely on her way to eat you. Well, it's about a seventy-odd chance, no guarantees. But just trust me, okay, I know these things.'" She raised both eyebrows at me. "*Deeply* convincing, yeah? What reason could you possibly have had to believe me?"

"Fair enough. Well . . . thank you, I guess," I said, a little grudgingly. Something about this explanation still wasn't sitting right with me, but I couldn't discern what or why, and her intervention *had* saved my life. That much was incontrovertible fact. "Is the link still active? Because while I might be grateful for your help, I do not want or need you lurking in my mind like a stowaway."

She gave her head a brisk shake, making a face. "It doesn't work like that. Think of it as more of a panic button. It activated only because I sensed the disturbance once she began the beguile-ment. I can't just access your thoughts on a whim. For something that deep, you'd have to give me permission."

"Well, you don't have it. In fact, I want you to . . ." I waved my hand vaguely, unsure what to call it. "Sever it. Switch it off. How-ever that works."

With an elaborate sigh, she slid her hand into a concealed pants pocket and fished out the oracle deck, sliding it back to me. "There. Nothing of yours is mine anymore. Token back in your possession, link broken. We cool now?"

"For the moment." I drew the deck toward me, tucked it into my own back pocket. "Do you think she'll be back for another go? The spell I used on her was strong, but it wasn't a permanent ban-ishment."

That crescent-moon smile surfaced again, this time even sharper, a knife's-edge glint. "Oh, no, you won't have to worry about her again. Part of my job, remember? I caught her later that night, once you cast her out. She's . . . let's say, permanently de-clawed."

I shuddered a little at the idea of what kind of bloodshed had transpired, if succubi had anything like human blood. Even the murder of a creature that had been trying to kill me in the first place wasn't something my conscience particularly wanted to grapple with.

"The thing is," Cat said, draping her forearms over the table and leaning across them, "just because she won't be back doesn't mean something else won't take her place. Another of her kind, or maybe a different nasty altogether."

I wrapped my arms around myself, dread sweeping through me. She wasn't wrong; there was no reason to think I'd become some kind of specialized flare, a beacon exclusively for succubi. Who knew what else might be coming for me even as we spoke.

"You need to figure out just what it is you did to attract her attention, and then undo it," Cat went on, eyes taking on a steely glint. "In the meantime, I'd suggest casting defensive wards around yourself everywhere you go. The strongest you can manage."

I nodded, chewing on the inside of my cheek. "I've already warded my home."

"Good. You should do the same to the bookstore—tonight, in fact. And if I may be so forward," she went on, still with that unnervingly solemn mien, "I'd also suggest inviting me to stick around while you figure out why this is happening to you. Because I'm getting the feeling that pest control isn't one of your strengths."

9

Look Away

BY THE TIME we'd walked back to Tomes—Cat had insisted on accompanying me, to watch my back while I cast defensive wards before locking up for the night—I was still grappling with the idea of inviting her to stay while I sorted out whatever was happening to me. On the one hand, she'd already demonstrated her willingness to protect me, and she clearly had an aggressive skill set far beyond anything at my disposal. And it wasn't as though I had anyone else to ask.

The Blackmoores might have been strong enough to act as my bodyguards against whatever might come after me; Nina was so desperate for my favor that she'd probably even have agreed to keep my secret, if I asked her for assistance. But since I'd rather have been torn to sexy soul shreds by an entire succubi horde— *What would the appropriate collective noun be? A harem? A boudoir?*—than solicit Blackmoore help, that wasn't a viable option. I'd also briefly toyed with the idea of approaching an Avramov for protection, but they were so tight-knit and clannish that any one of them would walk my request up the chain to Elena Avramov, their matriarch. Given that Emmy was our current Victor of the Wreath as well as scion Natalia Avramov's partner, and Uncle James was Elena's fellow elder, there was no way my predicament wouldn't get back to them.

And I wasn't willing to own up to what I'd done yet, not without giving myself a chance to set things right on my own. Ideally without having to relinquish all the beautiful benefits of my restored mind.

On the other hand, Cat was a complete stranger. I knew nothing about her outlandish origins and motivations besides what she had chosen to tell me, no independent verification possible. How could I trust a half-fae outsider with my safety, the secrets of my town—especially a tricky cat sith, about whom even the lore largely couldn't decide?

I needed more information, at the very least.

"Do you know anything about spellbooks?" I asked Cat as I let us into Tomes, feeling a little calmer as soon as the store's dusty, incensey scent of paper and magic billowed up around us. *Ahoy, Delilah Charlotte Harlow, ahoy, ahoy!!* the bell fluted in my mind, a slightly frantic note to its chime. *Ahoy, Catriona Arachne Quinn, ahoy, ahoy!! Ahoy—*

"Oh, cut it out already," I snapped, closing my fist in the sharp quelling motion that momentarily dampened the spell. My nerves were too shot for any further heraldic announcements delivered in that shrilly chipper tone, and it wasn't like I didn't know Cat and I were here.

"Excuse me?" Cat said, bristling. "*You* asked me a question. And I hadn't even said anything yet."

"Not you, sorry." I pointed up at the bell, rolling my eyes. Insistent fragments of *ahoy, ahoy!!* continued to echo in my head, but I twisted my fist closed even more emphatically until they vanished altogether. "Alert spell. It can be a little grating sometimes. I keep meaning to tinker with it, make it less abrasive, but somehow it always falls to the bottom of the priority list."

"You don't want your alert spells all mellow anyway," she pointed out, with irritating logic. "They're supposed to alarm you, not bliss you out."

"Well, that's the thing. It's an alert, not an alarm," I said, admittedly splitting hairs, turning back to the door to cast an all-purpose protective ward against anything that might try to barge in here after us. "So I don't see why it needs to be quite so—"

Cat froze in place, flinging one hand up in the air to quiet me. The change in her posture was so startling that it made the bottom of my stomach drop out; a predator's unnerving stillness, eyes narrowing to slits, her head twitching this way and that as if seeking some elusive sound.

Then her nostrils flared rapidly, once, twice, and three times as she sniffed the air, an expression of sheer revulsion twisting the bold lines of her face.

"There's a fucking dhampir in here," she hissed, angling herself in front of me and falling into a warrior's loose-limbed ready stance. "Stay behind me, and keep your eyes peeled. Sometimes those sneaky fuckers like to—"

Before she could finish, something dropped from the ceiling to land about ten feet in front of her, emitting an unearthly hissing screech.

The sound was so wrong, so unmistakably inhuman and malevolent, that my blood turned to frosty slush in my veins, running cold in a way I'd previously assumed was strictly a figure of speech. The thing swayed back and forth in front of Cat, shifting its weight from side to side, its overly long, scythe-clawed arms dangling by spindly bare thighs. It was stark naked, its mottled, sagging skin a grayish white leached of any living pigment, its huge yellow eyes slanted and pupilless. It had no nose, just vertical slits for nostrils, and an enormous, gaping, lipless mouth lined with multiple rows of jagged gray teeth. Sharply pointed ears swiveled on either side of its tapered head, and a pair of vein-riddled, near-translucent wings twitched at its back.

It looked like a bat crossed with a hairless cat, with a pinch of goblin thrown in for ugly-fucker measure.

Given the option, I'd have hands down chosen to go another round with a succubus instead. This had to be the most hideous monstrosity I'd ever clapped eyes on, and I'd seen some unabashedly gory woodcuts and anatomical sketches in my time.

"What the fuck, what the fuck, what the fuck," I heard someone droning under their breath, until I realized that someone was, unfortunately, me.

"Be *quiet*," Cat snapped at me over her shoulder, and with a shock, I saw that her eyes had changed—that distinctive green now glowed with amber striations, and the pupils had narrowed and slitted, exactly like a cat's. "They're dumb as rocks and can barely see, but they can sure as shit hear a pin drop. Stay behind—"

Then the dhampir rushed at Cat, and everything smeared into a blur.

Somehow, a pair of knives had appeared in Cat's hands—each with a central handle, wickedly curved blades shining on either end. I could see her lunge toward the thing, slashing at it with both knives, with an agile grace that was somehow both fluid and precise. But both of them moved with such preternatural speed, my eyes soon lost the ability to track their clash. I caught only a series of crystallized snapshots, isolated glimpses of motion:

A long, ragged gash from one of Cat's blades appearing across the creature's chest, accompanied by another of those eldritch screeches; a ferocious backhanded swipe that sent Cat's head rocking back before she recovered herself; a swift booted kick delivered to the monster's spindly calf with a gut-wrenching crunch, drawing out an even deeper howl from the dhampir; a threshing whorl of claws slicing across Cat's midriff and making me gasp, even as she spun away.

But by then, my mind had come to quasi-terms with the horror of it all and begun functioning again, and I realized there was something we could be using to our advantage: Tomes' own built-in defenses, the very ones Nina and I had been restoring.

"Get close to the bookshelves!" I bellowed at Cat, from my safe vantage point several paces back. "Make it lash out at you, and then duck!"

"Kind of busy over here, Delilah," she snarled through her teeth, fending off the whirring blur of its claws as it advanced on her. "Maybe I just do it my way. You know, the way that historically fucking works?"

"Trust me," I pressed. "Just *try* it!"

She flashed an impatient, mistrustful glance at me over her shoulder, hesitating for a split second, then gave a brusque nod.

In two steps, she deftly maneuvered them both so that her back was pressed against one of the shelves; seemingly cornered, unable to retreat. The dhampir rasped what must have passed for a triumphant cackle with its kind; a guttural *har-har-har* that would have been almost comical, if it hadn't issued from that tooth-riddled maw. It clearly hadn't dawned on it that Cat had purposely rendered herself vulnerable. Still cackling, it swiped at her—only to catch nothing but air in its curved claws, as Cat fell to one knee and then rolled away in a neat somersault, springing back to her feet behind it.

But the dhampir's claws *had* caught something; they'd sheared close enough to the vulnerable, exposed spines of the books that lined that shelf. Triggering the Marauder's Misery that Nina and I had worked so hard to cast.

The kinetic energy captured in the invisible web that encased the bookshelves detonated with a *whoomp* of displaced air that made my ears pop. A miniature tornado whipped up from out of nowhere, wrapping itself around the dhampir like invisible chains. The spell was intended to deliver a punishment commensurate with whatever sharp and pointy threat had been posed to the books—and in this case, it had clearly categorized the dhampir as a top-tier, red-alert, no-holds-barred marauder.

While Cat and I watched—me slack-jawed at getting to see the activated spell in full effect, her grinning with unbridled delight—Marauder's Misery spun the shrieking creature all the way back up to the ceiling, gave it a thorough pounding against the rafters, then slammed it back down to the floor so hard that it bounced before collapsing on the floorboards, spindly limbs in a starfish splay.

"Possibly you were right," I conceded, after a long moment of considering the dhampir's prone form, the bellows wheezing of its labored breath, the yellowed fangs bristling out of its slack mouth.

If it hadn't been for Cat, I'd now have been twice dead. "Could be a good idea for you to stay a spell."

"Glad we're agreed," Cat panted, flashing me another fierce grin even as she pressed a hand to her midriff. "Shit, that was *fantastic*. You witches really do put on the best special effects. Stellar teamwork, forgive me for doubting you. But now, if I were you, I'd look away."

"Why?" I managed, slumping over with hands pressed to my thighs, still struggling to catch my breath as waves of adrenaline battered against my insides. Two near brushes with death in twenty-four hours felt . . . excessive.

"Because I'm going to finish off that shitty, half-rotted beastling," she replied, brandishing one of her blades as she stalked toward the dazed dhampir, still struggling to lift its head off the floor. "And I have a feeling that isn't something you need to see."

"LOOKS LIKE YOU owe that alert spell of yours an apology," Cat quipped, smiling down at me in the warm light of my bedside lamp.

She sat on the edge of my bed with me kneeling beside her, dabbing antiseptic onto the livid scratches the dhampir had scored into her abdomen. Before we'd left Tomes, I'd cast flame-based protective wards on both doors and all the windows; any cryptid that tried to sneak its way in while I was gone would be in for a zesty surprise. And when I rewound the alert bell's last handful of announcements, *"Ahoy, dhampir!!"* had indeed been among them, which I'd have heard if I hadn't shut it off in my moment of pique. In lieu of apology, I'd removed my ability to override it, and instilled a distance warning into the spell—this way, it could chime an alert in my mind even if I wasn't inside the store.

"Mistakes were made," I admitted. "I won't be ignoring it again."

"You could say sorry? An apology never hurts, even with a magical alarm system. Maybe especially with a magical alarm system."

"I'll consider it."

I pulled my hand away when she caught her breath, hissing a little through her teeth.

Montalban rustled her wings in warning at the sound; she still wasn't sure what to make of Cat. When we'd first arrived, she'd been playfully provocative, almost flirtatious; flitting into Cat's face, grazing her shoulder, fluttering in little circles around her. I wasn't sure if it was the cat thing, the fae thing, or the simple fact that I found Cat so striking myself. Sometimes my familiar could be that way; not just her own personality, but also a landscape in miniature of my own emotional terrain.

"Montalban?" Cat had said when I introduced them, her mouth curling with amusement as she held still, letting the raven inspect her from every angle. "After Madeline Montalban, I'm assuming."

"That's the one," I replied, surprised she'd caught the reference. "I have a weakness for British ceremonial occultists. The more extravagant, the better, generally."

"Who could blame you? That crew knew how to live." She glanced over at my familiar, still preening in Cat's general direction. "Ever call her Monty?"

I stared at her, appalled. "Of course not."

"Right, right. Tawdry of me to even suggest."

Now my familiar perched atop her cage, talons wrapped around the filigreed curlicues of the wrought iron, peering down at us in open fascination as I doctored Cat.

"I just want to make sure I didn't leave any trace of dhampir gunk in you," I said, gingerly returning to her wound. "I doubt you want to find out what happens when whatever lives under those claws gets a chance to multiply."

"I'm fine, do your thing," she assured me, leaning back to afford me better access. "Not at all keen on becoming a paranormal petri dish."

She'd shucked her shredded tank and now wore only a black sports bra, affording me a profoundly distracting view of her taut stomach, sheathed in silky skin that gleamed over the kind of carved abs I hadn't thought existed in real life. And from this close, she smelled intoxicating; a sweet, richly floral fragrance like dewy wildflowers that seemed to rise from her bare skin like a natural perfume. Maybe some fae pheromone, meant to entice susceptible mortals.

The fact that it was making me a little dizzy even as I tended to her injuries probably meant it worked exactly as intended.

"And trust me, I've felt much worse," she added, letting her head fall back. "I'm usually the one messily patching myself up, so this is a welcome change."

"Least I could do, this being the second time you've saved my life." I pulled a face, my stomach roiling at the memory of mopping up the heap of greasy ash left behind after Cat dispatched the dhampir. She'd been right to ask me to turn away; I had no desire to know what she'd done to reduce it to that gruesome clump. "Though I will say this time was considerably more disgusting and dramatic. That thing was foul."

"Suckers of any kind always are, even the ones with prettier faces. How did that rotter even get into your store?" Cat mused, a fine wrinkle appearing between those shockingly dark brows. "I can understand why it decided to lurk once it picked up your scent, rather than ambush you at the pizza place; they don't venture out before dusk, and even after that they can't stand bright artificial light. But a place like your bookstore . . . you must have it warded against malign paranormal intrusion."

"Actually, no," I replied, a little abstractedly. Satisfied that I'd staved off the likelihood of infection, I switched to a dense healing balm, slathering it across her torn skin. My home first aid kit contained not just the standard drugstore necessities, but also a variety of herbal pastes, salves, and tinctures that worked much better than anything store-bought or prescribed. "There's never been any reason for wards like that. We don't get any cryptids in Thistle Grove."

To be fair, it was possible that one of the wards Nina had blown away last winter had been designed to protect against exactly this eventuality—but if that was the case, it wasn't one Uncle James and I had even discussed restoring, when there were so many more pressing protective spells to attend to first.

"Which is bizarre," Cat replied, echoing my own earlier train of thought. "This place *reeks* of magic, as soon as you set foot past town lines. It should attract all kinds of beasties as a matter of course—most creatures love proximity to natural wellsprings of magic. Almost catch a contact high off it."

"So it's like . . . rolling in catnip to them, would you say?"

She rolled her eyes, smirking. "Just terrible, but I did set myself up for that one, so you're forgiven. That's the thing, though—even I couldn't feel anything unusual about this place until I'd actually arrived. It's as if there's a dome around it, keeping any magic from trickling out."

I hesitated, wondering how much I should tell her about Thistle Grove's witch community. Divulging our secrets to an outsider went against my grain, against every instinct I had about keeping our magic private and protected, something that had been instilled in all of us since we were little.

But if she was really going to be my bodyguard—ugh, could that sound more ridiculous?—until I got to the bottom of this, then presumably I had to be willing to at least share relevant information with her.

"There is a town-wide oblivion glamour in place—you know what those are?" When she nodded, I went on. "It's there because I'm not the only witch in residence here. There are hundreds of us, descended from the four witches who originally founded the town."

Her eyebrows flicked up. "No shit. I read as much in the tourist center brochures, but thought for sure the witch founders yarn was just a cutesy bit for the tourists."

"I mean, we present it as 'legend has it,' but yes, it's fact. We're a little like your enclave in that sense, and the oblivion glamour is one of the ways we protect ourselves from exposure. It prevents local and tourist normies from remembering any genuine spells they happen to see being cast, while letting us all lean into the whole witch-tourism thing."

"A fake-real Halloween town," she marveled. "Or would that be the other way around? In any case, that's genius, and probably nicely lucrative. So, you're thinking that glamour extends to cryptids? But in a broader sense?"

"I'm not sure." I paused, thinking it over. "It could be there's an entirely separate one, designed specifically to keep them out. But if there were, I'm the one who'd know about it—my family specializes in keeping this town's secrets, guarding its history. Something of that magnitude . . . it should be in the records. But it isn't."

"Even secret keepers aren't always privy to all the secrets," she murmured. Her eyes had fallen to half-mast, as if she found my touch much more enjoyable now that I'd finished with the astringents. "Especially the more valuable ones. If there's anything I've learned during my time at the Court, it's that."

It was certainly possible. As it was, we'd only recently discovered that it was a totem of the goddess Belisama, sunk deep in the lake, that fueled the town's magic like a massive generator. Seemingly no one knew how or why she'd wound up down there in the first place, and I'd always thought it strained credulity to assume that no one had *ever* known anything about her origins. Thistle Grove witches lived secure in the conviction that we were the biggest secret around, but maybe there was much more to our town than even we understood. Layers of illusion, a treasure trove of things that still lay hidden and unknown.

Given my current predicament, the prospect of further question marks shouldn't have thrilled me, but it did. The idea of uncovering something fresh, unearthing something wholly new—it appealed to the explorer in me, the archeologist adventurer. Now that I was charged with Tomes & Omens, Uncle James was the one who got to spend as much of his time as he wanted on the road, which meant any electrifying finds and acquisitions were more likely to be his than mine.

But this time, I might be the one on the brink of some grand discovery.

"Well, we aren't going to get to the bottom of it tonight," I concluded, gently smoothing an adhesive bandage over the scratches, now shiny with salve. "And you're all set. I'm not sure how half fae do with healing, but this should give you a nice boost—it's based on a spikestar extract emulsion. One of the magically active plants that grows by the lake."

"You're very skilled at this," she remarked, a slow smile curling those fine-cut lips as she sat up, carefully twisting her torso back and forth to test her range of motion. "Barely felt a thing. Is healing one of your affinities?"

"Oh, no, that would be the Thorns," I said, hastily gathering up the contents of my first aid kit and scrambling to my feet, suddenly much too aware of my closeness to her. "They're green magic practitioners, natural healers. I'm just an herbalist. I specialize in magical flora. The kind that, as far as we know, grows only around here."

"I do see you like flowers," she noted, green-and-amber gaze skimming over the botanical illustrations plastered on the wall across from my bed. I'd noticed that her eye color hadn't returned to normal yet, the pupils still a little feline. Maybe it took a while for her equivalent of adrenaline to subside as well. Now that I wasn't distracted by tending to her, I could also feel the high-octane buzz still juddering through me, a belated tremor thrumming in my hands. "Though the ink was a dead giveaway from the jump."

As she rose from the bed in a lithe, sleek movement, her gaze strayed down to my arms. Trailing slowly over the flowers winding around them, narrowing at their scarlet color and the lines of tiny, angular runes now marching between the stems and blooms like an army of sinister ants.

"But that color . . . that's new. And some very juiced-up power sigils, to boot." She reached out to graze a fingertip over the inside of my forearm, tracing the designs. Bringing a flood of heat rushing to the surface of my skin, narrowing to the fine point of her touch. "My, my, that must have been *some* baneful spell you cast in that forest of ghosts and ghouls. I'm no witch, but even I know you don't cast a blood working like that on a whim."

She brought that uncanny green-and-gold gaze up, locking it with mine. The intensity between us felt magnetic, like something pulsing and alive, especially with how much of her skin I could now see, that dew-and-wildflower scent surrounding her like a fine mist. A much softer smell than you might imagine, for someone as fierce as her.

"So tell me, Delilah," she said softly, mink-lashed gaze shifting between my eyes, "what brought someone who clearly doesn't suffer fools to that kind of reckless brink?"

"It's certainly a story and a half," I replied, clearing my throat and drawing my arm away from her, turning toward the living room. Anything to bleed off some of that burgeoning tension between us. "You know what . . . I could really use a drink, and I bet you could probably do with one, too. Why don't I pour us both a nightcap?"

"Oh, hell yes," she said ardently. "I can't think of anything I'd like more. And could I trouble you for a shirt? Mine doesn't exactly qualify as clothing anymore, but if you're in the market for an extra-nasty new rag, we can consider it a trade."

10

Burnt Sugar

B Y THE TIME I'd mixed negronis for both of us, it was past ten. Besides Ivy and Montalban, I hadn't had much in the way of company in years, and sitting with Cat, curled up on opposite ends of my plush couch, felt more intimate than it should have. I'd cracked the window to let in a sweet waft of breeze, the summer darkness outside like a gauzy curtain separating us from the rest of the world.

And there was a surreal element to it as well; sharing bittersweet cocktails with someone not entirely human, the first real cryptid (who wasn't trying to kill me) that I'd ever met.

"Penny for your thoughts," Cat said, taking a sip, those mesmeric eyes glimmering over the tumbler's edge. I didn't go in much for material extravagance, but I liked having beautiful glassware, and the cut-glass facets heightened the vivid sparkle of her irises, their reflected light dancing over her spider tattoo. Her eyes really did seem to almost glow, like a cat's at night. "Though I'd bet yours are worth quite a bit more than that."

"I was just thinking how strange it is, to meet someone like you. I've been around witches all my life, but half fae? Very new to me." I took a sip of my own, scrutinizing her. "And to be honest, I'm not sure why you're still here. Why you'd want to be. Your allegiance is to your Shadow Court, right, so why stay with me? Why continue to protect me, instead of heading back to the city?"

She shrugged a shoulder. "Because it's what I do. Monster hunter, remember? I keep people—and non-people—safe from the things that go bump in the night. And it's starting to seem like you're becoming quite the epicenter of monster activity. Seems to me like here is exactly where I need to be."

"Hmm." I took another long swallow, trying to organize the tumble of my thoughts.

"You don't believe me," she observed, cutting me a keen look. "Why?"

"I've read enough about fae to know that ulterior motives—mind games and machinations, that type of thing—are your calling card. And I don't truck much with deception or obfuscation, as you've noticed. So I suppose I'm wondering what's really in this for you."

"That's fair enough," she replied, tipping her glass to me. "For the moment, would you be satisfied with simple curiosity? I've never seen activity like this before, multiple predators flocking to one person. Given my line of work, it's in my best interest to understand aberrations like this. I'm also curious about your strange little town—and I'm *very* curious about this spell you cast. The one you think caused all this."

"I'm going to refrain from a curiosity-killed-the-cat joke, but please know how deeply the restraint pains me."

She snickered into her glass. "Duly noted. And appreciated."

When I continued to hesitate, she leaned forward, the simple white V-neck I'd lent her tightening around her shoulders. Along with the inches she had on me, she was also much more muscular, leggy and broad-shouldered and lean-hipped in a way that was even more distracting half a negroni in.

"Look, you're in some fairly deep shit here; I'm sure you realize as much. So you're going to have to trust someone," she said quietly. "And seeing as you're clearly unwilling to go to friends or family with this—for reasons that you'll note I haven't asked about, out of courtesy—it might as well be me. Not to mention I've already put my life on the line for you once. If that's not proof enough of good intentions, what is?"

I mulled her words for another moment, considering my options. She was right; I did have to trust someone, as much as the idea of relying so heavily on anyone other than myself and my familiar pained me even more now that I'd clawed back my mind and former independence. The old Delilah hadn't needed to depend on *anyone*, and the notion of reverting to my helpless, post-oblivion self rankled deeply. And Cat was a near-total stranger, and a supernatural one to boot. She'd appeared in my life only a handful of days ago and immediately proceeded to steal something that belonged to me, to establish a psychic link without my knowledge or permission.

As magnetic as I found her, how could I trust that her motives were what she claimed them to be?

But I wasn't willing to go to Uncle James or Emmy with my predicament, and drawing Ivy any further into this thorny tangle would only put her in danger, place her squarely in the path of whatever sharp-toothed shadow thing might make for me next. So what choice did I have but Cat?

"Asking for help isn't a weakness, Delilah," she urged softly, still fixing me with that piercing gaze. "But being too proud to accept it *is*. Believe me, I know."

I gave a single nod, running my free hand through the loose fall of my dark hair, toying with the ends where they curled by my waist. I caught the way she followed the motion, the subtle shift in her posture, an almost imperceptible lean toward me. I'd wondered if the attraction I felt had been entirely manufactured, a ploy to steal that deck from me, but I was increasingly feeling the genuine weight of her attention.

Whatever misgivings I had about her, the spark flaring between us felt very real, and decidedly mutual. Nothing like the (admittedly delicious) artifice of the succubus's compulsion. There was nothing dreamy or hazy about Cat's presence here, the warm, hyper-vivid reality of her sitting across from me, so close I would barely have to reach to touch her.

"Six months ago," I started, licking my lips, a nervous lump expanding in my throat. I couldn't believe I was about to admit this to her, and yet, here we were. "Something . . . happened here. A member of one of the other families, the Blackmoores, experienced a massive spike in power. She tried to steal something of importance to her from my shop—and to cover her tracks, she cast an oblivion glamour on me. A much, much more powerful one than it should have been."

I was omitting some crucial details here, but even if I had decided to trust her, it was to the degree strictly necessary. If I didn't absolutely need to share things with her, like the existence of

Belisama's statue in the lake, then I'd keep them to myself, at least for now.

"It wreaked havoc on me," I continued, my chest tightening. "I lost almost a week of memories completely, and even after it was reversed, it left . . . aftereffects. It destabilized my mind, left me prone to memory loss and disorientation. Basically stripped away many of the things that make me *me*—and that make me capable of doing my job, the thing I love most in the world."

"Fuck, that sounds terrible," she murmured, and the empathy in her voice twisted in my stomach like a clenching fist. "To be vulnerable like that. I can't imagine what I'd do if I couldn't trust my body anymore. Much less my mind."

"It was terrible, yes," I said, clearing my swollen throat. "I . . . had to depend on people in a way I'd never needed to before. I hated it. And nothing helped undo the residual damage. The family of healers I told you about, the Thorns, tried everything. Everything safe and aboveboard, anyway."

"So that spell you cast," she said, putting the pieces together. "It was for healing?"

"Yes, for enhanced mental clarity and cognition. But a baneful working, from a blood-magic grimoire. One of the ones my uncle and I are charged with keeping locked away." I shook my head, torn between fury at my circumstances and frustration at my own choices. "I shouldn't have done it, I know. It was stupid, dangerous. Reckless. That's not me. I think everything through, analyze every scenario half to death—and this time, I couldn't bring myself to even consider any adverse outcomes."

"Desperate people do desperate things, Delilah." She reached out and set a sympathetic hand on my knee, the lightest graze, though it sent a warm wash of sensation spiraling up and down my entire leg. "Yeah, you've wound up with a profoundly fucked situation. But you'll only make matters worse by beating yourself up about it."

I nodded, biting my lip, distracted by the runnels of heat still wending through my leg, that wildflower scent of hers making my head swim. It wasn't like I was any stranger to arousal—though it had been a while, unless you counted the succubus, which I definitively did not—but the draw to her was much stronger than what I normally felt. An almost irresistible compulsion to get closer. Maybe the succubus had left behind some lingering vibes; or maybe it was that Cat was so compelling, her raw charisma more magnetic than anyone I'd ever met before.

"What spellbook was it? Fae can work magic, too, though differently than witches do. But we also use grimoires sometimes, and the Shadow Court has an extensive library. Most of us study magical praxis as part of our education. Could be I've at least heard of it."

"It's the *Opes Sanguinis*," I said, struggling to form coherent thoughts, the heat of her hand slowly edging out everything else. "Do you know anything about it?"

"I haven't heard of that one." Her voice had dipped lower, gaining a husky edge, and the way she was watching me, heavy-lidded and intense, made me want to squirm. "But it might be helpful to take a look at the spell together. It could give me some sense of why it has the beasties so taken with you."

I hadn't moved my leg away, and she'd taken that as permission to begin stroking my knee in slow, concentric circles, sending tingles spiraling through me like ripples in a pond.

"Maybe." I swallowed hard, letting out a quaking little sigh. "I was thinking, uh, we could go to the Witch Woods first. The spell required an offering of blood to a ley line nexus. Whatever side effects it brought about, they started there."

"Oh, that's interesting," she breathed, sliding closer to me, until our knees almost touched. "I do know quite a bit about ley lines. Yes, let's start there. About tonight, though . . ."

"What, uh, what about it?" I half whispered, my breath snaring in my throat.

"I was wondering if I could stay here, instead of heading back to my motel." She quirked her head coyly, lifted those black eyebrows. "It could be safer for you, having me close. I know you've warded everything, but even the best wards aren't ironclad. If anything else took a shot at you, I'd be right here to take it on."

"Right. That makes—it makes sense. I don't have a spare room, but this couch isn't entirely terrible to sleep on."

"Good. Now that we have that settled . . ." She slid her hand farther up my leg, resting it on my thigh, her eyes a green blaze in the dim lamplight. "Do you want me to stay . . . or do you want me to *really* stay?"

"*Really* stay," I said, without even having to think about it. The idea of not kissing her was becoming physically painful, the very notion of it like an impossibility.

"Oh, I was so hoping that's what you meant," she said with a flash of that bright, ferocious smile. Then she leaned in and wrapped a hand around my nape, pulling me in for a kiss.

It was deep and silky-hot, as if we'd leapt right into the middle of an achingly delicious make-out session rather than the beginning of one; her tongue sweeping slick against mine, her lips deft and soft and insistent. She tasted like negroni and burnt sugar, and combined with that dizzying wildflower smell, it brought a furious pulse of desire throbbing to life between my legs. When she tangled a hand in my hair, pulling it tight enough to hurt a little, I moaned aloud into the kiss.

"So you like things a little sharp," she whispered against my mouth, sinking her teeth into my lower lip until I gasped. "I had a feeling you might."

She was right; for all that I came across as relentless and assertive in every other aspect of my life—or brashly aggressive, depending on whom you asked—I loved to be the one to yield in bed, to feel someone else's edge pressed hard against me.

"How did you know?" I whispered back.

"Maybe I smelled it on you." She kissed me again, hard and deep, a melting roil of tongues and lips that left me panting for breath. "Or maybe I just knew."

She tugged on the hair wound around her hand until I let my head fall back, her lips on my earlobe, then the delicate spot right under my ear. She kissed her way down my throat, hot and open-mouthed, the stroke of her tongue against my skin sending lightning bolts of lust streaking down my sides and simmering between my legs. I loved having my neck kissed like this, with such devouring abandon; when she scraped her teeth over the juncture between my neck and shoulder, biting down until I writhed against her, I yelped out a needful little moan that drew out a low and husky chuckle from her.

"The way you respond," she murmured, exhaling against my skin. She ran a hand down my throat and traced my collarbone, then let it drift down to cup the weight of my breast through my thin T-shirt. "It's so fucking sexy."

"Can't help it." My hands had been roaming her back, exploring the hard contours of her muscle, but now I slid them around to the front, up the sides of her rib cage and over the constraints of that tight sports bra. "How could anyone not respond to you?"

"It's rare," she admitted, coaxing a laugh out of me. "But I'm not *everyone's* flavor."

"You're definitely mine," I said breathlessly, leaning in for another kiss.

She moaned against me, releasing my hair, both hands moving to my waist to grip me tight and draw me closer. She was so strong it felt like she could lift me with barely any effort, hoist me onto her lap like a bundle of feathers, an idea that made me lose what little I still had of my breath.

But the motion tugged on her bandaged midriff, and she drew in a sharp, pained breath. The sound of it struck me like something physical, slicing through that lust-fogged haze and abruptly reminding me of the reality of our circumstances. This was a wounded stranger sitting on my couch. Someone who had fought on my behalf hours ago, and someone who'd let me tend to her injuries. But still a person—creature—I'd only just met.

And I wasn't exactly one to throw caution to the passionate winds and leap into every one-night stand that came my way.

"I'm so sorry," I mumbled, skittering away from her, feeling like I'd been doused with a bucket of icy water. Even with the heady cocktail of post-adrenaline endorphins and negroni buzz coursing through my veins, how had I allowed myself to be so captivated by her? "That wasn't—that shouldn't have happened. We don't even know each other. And you're hurt. And you're my guest."

"Well, agree to disagree on whether such details should get in the way of us enjoying each other," she replied blithely. "But you're right. That kind of activity would have been less than optimal, considering."

"Exactly. Yes." I stood, my head still spinning a little, the throb of wanting her still pulsing between my legs. "Why don't I go get you some sheets and pillows, make you a little more comfortable out here? I think it'd probably be best for both of us if we just went to bed."

She made a mischievous little moue at me, like, *That's what I was* trying *to do*.

"Separately, I mean," I clarified, backing away from her as if she were physically dangerous, an open flame. "We'll . . . we can talk more in the morning."

"Sure, Delilah." She settled back into the couch like a nesting cat, arranging her body into a languid sprawl. "And this will do just fine, don't worry about sheets. I've slept on much worse."

11

The Missing

"A VISITING SCHOLAR?" I could almost smell the skepticism dripping from Nina's tone, like some pungent sap. She'd been following Cat's meandering progress around Tomes with such a suspicious glare it would have been almost comical, had it not been unnecessarily complicating my life. "But she was here the other day, and I thought you said she was just a tourist."

I blew a stray curl out of my face and peered testily up at her from the mixture I was grinding with my mortar and pestle.

"She's also an old friend, and maybe I didn't feel the need to share my personal business with you," I retorted. "Are you, unbeknownst to me, composing some vital record of who I choose to keep company with? Or did I miss something, and *I* report to *you* now?"

"No," she muttered, letting her eyes drop, her hands twisting together in front of her waist like a fidgeting schoolgirl's. "Of course not. She's just . . . new to the equation, that's all. And she's barely spoken a word to me this morning. I thought, if I at least knew who she was to you and what she was doing here, I could be the one to try to break the ice."

Given Nina's quasi-pathological obsession with observing social mores and also appeasing me, this was likely partly true. But I sensed something else at play here; the vibe she'd picked up off Cat that first time had rubbed her wrong, and it was clearly a gut feeling she still hadn't shed. And it hadn't helped that, as she said, Cat hadn't bothered to acknowledge her beyond a breezy initial greeting, as if Nina's presence barely registered. My new bodyguard was here today only because restoring the wards was still my responsibility, along with running Tomes; I couldn't just abandon it in favor of getting to the bottom of what had happened to me. Not to mention, my uncharacteristic absence would raise eyebrows, even if I attempted to pass it off as illness. I practically lived here; the only sick days I'd taken since I began working with Uncle James almost two years ago had been in the immediate aftermath of the oblivion glamour, the terrifying week in which my mind had felt like a crumbling edifice ready to collapse at a passing breeze. If the curse of the glamour had come with any silver lining, it was that I remembered only bits and pieces of the painstaking dismantlement Emmy and Uncle James had performed while they stitched me back together as best they could. The process had not been painless.

With that kind of precedent, if I suddenly began blowing work off, it would be immediately obvious to anyone who knew me that something was awry.

So we'd agreed that I'd continue with my business as usual, with Cat spending the day at the store in her guise as a visiting academic with an interest in antiquarian books, in case any peck-ish cryptid came shambling inside in search of me. That persona gave her an excuse to prowl around the bookstore, browsing what-ever caught her interest while keeping an active watch on the per-imeter. According to her, predatory cryptids tended to be more active at nighttime—but in her experience, they were also unpre-dictable enough that she'd been reluctant to keep a distance from me even in daylight hours.

This concern for my well-being warmed me, despite myself. I was still reeling from our encounter last night, that blisteringly passionate clash, so out of character for me. I dated when I could scrape together the time, and I'd been with Ivy for several years before we parted ways. But I didn't do . . . *that.* Swoon directly into strange women's arms like some kind of bodice-ripper heroine with more supercharged libido than sense. And the rippling heat was still there this morning whenever Cat and I caught each oth-er's eyes, anytime a whiff of that lush wildflower scent drifted its way to me.

I'd never had a fantasy about sexy encounters between book-shelves in my entire life, but I was more than making up for that now. And the fact that she'd clearly taken against Nina on sight only endeared her to me more.

"She's just a reticent person. A little socially awkward, espe-cially with people she doesn't know," I said to Nina, internally awash in hilarity at the idea of Cat as anything but completely self-assured and poised. "I'm sure she'll come around eventually, so just . . . let her be. You and I have plenty of work to focus on today."

Nina flicked another ambivalent look back at Cat, who'd reap-peared from between the shelves with a stack of books in her arms. Cat returned the stare with a slantwise glance of such nonchalant equanimity that I nearly laughed out loud. Nina could have been a lamp or a signpost for all the attention or respect Cat chose to pay her, and seeing a member of the monumentally self-important Blackmoore family so casually dismissed—by someone other than myself—gave my serotonin levels a very pleasant spike.

"You're the boss," Nina said evenly, though I could still see the unease stirring in her dark brown eyes. "Ready whenever you are."

BY MIDAFTERNOON, NINA and I had finished casting all three of the wards on my agenda, hours ahead of time. "You seem better," Nina had said to me before she left, back to her usual treading-on-eggshells tone, but tinged with a newly hopeful note. "And I just—I'm really glad to see it."

"Getting there," I'd replied briskly, unwilling to give any more quarter. "Found a new supplement. See you Thursday."

I'd closed up early once she cleared out, keen to reach the Witch Woods while it was still light outside, when the more dangerous shades were less likely to manifest. Before Cat and I left, I made a point of standing directly beneath the little brass alert bell, clearing my throat as I peered up at it. It twinkled down at me, something distinctly defiant about the way its metal caught the light.

"Um," I wavered, feeling like an entire idiot. Beside me, I could feel Cat radiating suppressed amusement, but she gave me an encouraging nod when I cut her an irritated look. "Bell. I, uh, beg your pardon. I shouldn't have switched you off the way I did, the other day. It was uncalled for, and rude of me."

Ahoy, the bell agreed in my head, in tone somewhere between miffed and charitable, like it was still semi-pissed but willing to be the better person.

"Right. And I know you were just trying to help, and that it's your responsibility to watch over Tomes as much as it is mine. So, by all means, proceed—Tomes is yours to hold fast in my absence. And now I'll be able to hear you even from outside of the store. We're . . . partners, now."

Ahoy, ahoy!! the bell chimed, much more warmly this time; I could feel its pleasure, and even something like gratitude for my acknowledgment of its service. For the first time, it struck me as disrespectful that the spell that governed it was so rudimentary, when it had clearly developed at least the inklings of a personality, and one that seemed genuinely attached to both Tomes and its occupants. Maybe I'd give it a wider vocabulary one of these days, more words and phrases to work with.

"See? That wasn't so hard," Cat teased as we stepped out.

"You were right," I admitted. "It liked the apology. I still don't want to hear any more about it."

"Yes, ma'am," she replied, snapping a crisp salute. "Subject closed."

After I'd finished recasting protective wards and sent Montalban winging home—even if we'd all be warded to the hilt, I wasn't about to expose my sweetheart to whatever might be lurking in the Witch Woods—Cat drove us to the woods' outer periphery in her rental. Beyond that, we struck out on foot, attempting to retrace my steps from the night I'd cast the Light That Calls for Blood.

"You know, Chicago has a lot of paranormal hot spots, too," Cat remarked, glancing around us with a hunter's sharply assessing gaze. Weak daylight sieved like sparkling dust through the cracks in the overlapping mesh of boughs overhead, the trees around us bent and gnarled, their bark contorted into unsettling shapes. The air was dank with wet leaves and decaying mulch, heightened by the summer heat. There was a watchful quality to the silence, with none of the usual background noise you found in wild places; even birds and insects proceeded with caution here. Even if I knew she was much safer at home, I found myself wishing for Montalban's reassuring presence on my shoulder, her familiar shadow falling over me as she tracked me by sky.

"So it's not like I'm any stranger to zones of vastly heightened creepiness," she continued. "But I have to admit, this forest is giving me pause. It's like an infestation on the macro scale, bigger than anything I've ever felt. I can't believe you came traipsing in here solo in the dead of night, just to cast a spell. Ballsy move."

"Needs must," I said with a shrug. "Like you said, I was desperate. And at least this time, we're going in prepared."

"If we were any more prepared, we'd be rattling." She held up an arm, giving it a shake. "I feel like a walking castanet."

I'd loaded us both up with protective talismans and amulets from the Tomes trove of magical objects, and it seemed to be working. I could feel the hairs on my neck prickling, as the presences in the trees took note of our passage, but nothing had ventured out so far; I was keeping fingers crossed that we'd reach the nexus unbothered.

"My theory is that the ley line nexus here is so strong that it caused this large-scale possession in the first place—that it's been attracting shades for centuries. Do you think that tracks?"

"It very well could be the case," she replied, her gaze skimming the forest floor. "We're walking along a line right now; I can feel its current below. It's potent, that's for sure. And if it crosses another of similar strength, that could be explosive, metaphysically speaking."

"You can actually feel the ley line? Fascinating. If I hadn't had a dowsing spell guiding me, I'd never even have known I was following one." I glanced over at her in the gloom, the sharp, aquiline cameo of her profile, those delicate lips. "Have you always been able to sense things like that? Ley lines, magic? If you grew up surrounded by normies, I have to imagine that would have been disorienting."

"Oh, I acquired quite the impressive rash of diagnoses," she replied dryly. "ADHD, oppositional defiance, borderline personality disorder, schizoid tendencies. Human doctors didn't know what to make of me. My father was very kind about it; he always just said I was special, *sensitive*. But, yes. Growing up feeling like you're on the brink of losing your mind was maybe not the smoothest coming-of-age experience."

"And you really had no idea at all, about what you were?" Having grown up in the magical haven that was Thistle Grove, I couldn't imagine such alienation, the desperate, crushing isolation she must have experienced even with a human father who did his best to understand the de facto changeling he'd wound up parenting alone. Like someone adrift in a foreign land with no one to cling to, no one to share and validate her unique reality.

Even as introverted (and antisocial) as I was, I'd only ever been alone because I chose to be. I wasn't particularly close with my immediate family, except for Uncle James and more recently Emmy—but we all belonged to the Harlow family and to our larger witch community, even if we weren't constantly in each other's faces and business like the Thorns and Avramovs tended to be.

Not having been given the choice of belonging seemed

barbaric, monstrous. An exceptionally cruel thing to do to your own child, no matter your intentions.

"None," she replied, a little grim. "As far as my dad was concerned, he'd fallen madly in love with the most beautiful, charming woman he'd ever met, then got his heart shattered when she walked out on him and their three-day-old infant. They were only together for a little over a year, but he never got over her. Which, understandable. How was any human woman ever going to compare to Liusaidh of Arachne? Even if he did somehow genuinely buy that her name was Lucy Barnes, and that she was a classics professor at U of Chicago."

"Hard to imagine a 'Lucy' who looks anything like you."

She snorted a little, lips quirking. "Exactly. And trust me—I'm the palest possible shadow of my mother. But my dad . . . He does data analysis for insurance companies, of all things, if that paints any sort of picture for you. Even for a mundane, he has a very mundane mind. Limited imagination, extremely grounded."

I pulled a face. "Ouch."

"I do mean that mostly as a compliment. He's exactly the kind of stable, decent person you're probably imagining. Clean-cut Michigander, penchant for smoked meats and cold *brewskies* and Friday night lights. Went to college on a basketball scholarship, studied econ . . . almost married his high school sweetheart before he met my mother. You know. That guy."

I wondered why a creature as presumably exotic and intriguing as a full-blooded cat sith would ever choose someone so pedestrian-sounding for a dalliance, especially one that led to a child. If her mother was anything like Cat, she could have had her pick of mortal lovers—and her father sounded like the human personification of a yawn.

"You're thinking, why go for someone so milquetoast?" Cat noted, with wry amusement. My chin snapped up, a bolt of shock needling through me at the way she'd seemingly read my thoughts. "Don't worry, I'm not in your head; it's just the obvious question. The answer is, I have no idea, and she's never seen fit to explain it to me. It might have been an opposites attract sort of thing—fae aren't known for their levelheadedness and decency. From what I know, her life had been very exciting up until then, a constant parade of interesting times. Maybe she was craving some stability."

"I could understand that. From what you've said, it sounds like the Shadow Court isn't exactly a paragon of civility."

She barked out a rough laugh at that. "No, indeed. 'Den of vipers' would be more appropriate. Not everyone's always scheming and jostling for power, of course; many of its more peripheral members are just living their lives. But it's not the kindest place, and members of Arachne don't enjoy a particularly calm existence there."

"And what, when you turned sixteen, she just scooped you out of your life?"

"More or less. My father and I were living in a northern suburb of Chicago, I was going to private school; on the crew team, even, if you can imagine that. Then she just appeared in my room one night, scared the shit out of me. Told me who she was, gave me a wholly terrifying demonstration of what my body could do, the psychic abilities I'd been suppressing. Informed me in no uncertain terms that the Glencoe chapter of my life was over."

"I can almost understand why she'd do it that way, I suppose," I said. "Better to make a clean break, maybe. But to leave you behind to grow up with mundanes and then just claim you years later, uproot you from everything you knew?" I shook my head. I was far from the gentlest of people, or the most considerate, but I still couldn't wrap my brain around such disregard for someone else's feelings. "It sounds brutal. Awful for you."

She cast me an unreadable glance, eyes narrowed. "It was, at first. And Liusaidh's a difficult person, even at her best. Spectacularly talented at what she does, and extraordinary in many ways. But it would never have occurred to her to factor in such a minor detail as my feelings. Getting used to her after growing up with someone like my father, while learning to navigate the Shadow Court . . . Let's say it was a rough transition."

"Maybe you do take after her, then," I said, teasing just a little. "The way you treated Nina today, like she was barely a step above an inanimate object. I'm given to understand that this is nonstandard behavior for most humans."

"Well, I'm not human, am I? And I was polite enough to her," she said with a shrug. "Why strain myself beyond that? She's irrelevant to me—and besides, you clearly can't stand her."

"True. She's the one who cast the oblivion glamour I told you about, the one that wrecked my brain. Working at Tomes with me to restore the wards she also blasted to hell is part of her rehabilitation." I snorted, shaking my head. "Though most days, it feels more like some punishment I don't deserve."

"I thought it might be something like that." She smiled at me, slow as spreading honey, her eyes glinting brilliant green against the dim. "All the more reason to keep putting her in her place, then."

I fought back a smile of my own, inordinately pleased that she'd taken my side so instinctively, especially against Nina. Then something occurred to me, a piece of her story she'd left out.

"What about your father?" I asked. "What did he do, after you disappeared like that? There must have been an Amber Alert, a search for you. He doesn't sound like the kind of person who'd have given up easily on a missing daughter."

She looked away from me, setting her jaw.

"No," she said, subdued. It stirred something in me, to catch this small glimpse of suppressed vulnerability, the deeply human part of her. "He isn't. I told you fae can do magic as well, right? Well, we're no strangers to oblivion glamours, either, or to tinkering with other people's memories. Liusaidh planted false memories in his mind—of him and me fighting, me telling him she'd reached out to me, that I'd chosen to live with her in Chicago. That I—that I'd always hated living with him, was bored out of my mind, couldn't stand it anymore."

"Cat. That is . . ." My stomach twisted at the idea, balling itself up like a rag. "That's horrible."

She shrugged, jaw still stiff. "It was the best damage control she could come up with. And she was right to take me; I couldn't have survived there. My fae blood would only have gotten stronger, my 'medical' problems worse. He wouldn't have been able to handle me for much longer, and halflings can be very dangerous when left untrained. It was in everyone's best interest."

Then she stopped dead, her entire body tightening like a coiled spring as she twitched her head to the left. "There's another ley line just over there, running crosswise to this one," she said, pointing. "And a *third* one at a diagonal, which is very unusual. I've never seen a three-way nexus before, but I can feel the pull . . . Which means it should lie directly ahead of us."

I glanced around, taking in our surroundings; I recognized

some of the trees, along with a distinctive pile of rocks, furred with moss and lichen, tumbled between the gnarled root balls of two towering oaks. "That seems right. I was fairly out of it when I got here in the dark, but I do remember a very rude awakening the next morning pretty close to here."

"Another fifteen feet or so, and we should be right on top of it."

We traipsed ahead, picking our way over the rotted branches and plant debris that littered the forest floor. My heart rate kicked up as we neared the nexus, though I wasn't even sure what I thought we might find there. What kind of magical evidence was I expecting, anyway? What could there be to indicate why a spell intended for mental clarity had transformed me into a monster magnet?

"Whoa." Cat stopped dead, a look of pure bewilderment sweeping over her face as she dropped into an easy squat. "This . . . can't be. This is wrong."

I frowned, squatting beside her. The ground looked completely normal—or what passed for normal in the Witch Woods, at any rate. "What? What are you sensing?"

"That's just it." She shook her head, flummoxed. "I'm not sensing anything. The nexus is supposed to be here—it *has* to be here. The line we followed here ran roughly west to east, the one that's just over there runs north to south, and the third one cuts at a diagonal to them both. This, right here, is the spot where they should all intersect."

I nodded, casting another gaze at the trees around us. "This is definitely where I made my blood offering. Though I'm not seeing any . . . remnants of it here."

"There wouldn't have been anything left behind. Blood magic

absorbs the offering completely, in exchange for whatever else is granted." She set both palms on the ground. "Let me look a little farther. Maybe it dives far below the surface, somehow? Or something's shielding it?"

Her pupils narrowed and elongated, the green of her irises streaking with that feline amber as her gaze turned inward. I stayed silent, not wanting to interfere, though I was desperately curious about what she might be sensing.

"This is wild," she murmured after a few moments, refocusing on me, palms still pressed to the ground. "I know what a nexus is supposed to feel like. There are two of them in Chicagoland, and they're turbulent, scintillating. Like maelstroms of magic. But the one here . . . it's simply gone. It's as though someone excavated it, or extinguished it somehow. All three of the lines simply *stop*, like they've been sheared off. There's nothing between them. Just magically inert, mundane space. A hole, basically."

"How could something extinguish a ley line nexus?" I asked, equally perplexed, a lurch of fear juddering through me. "There was nothing in the spell to indicate that anything like that would happen."

"Because it's not possible," Cat said firmly, with a brisk shake of her head. "Ley lines and their nexuses are inexhaustible, infinite resources of magic. You can't just *suck* one dry, like a well. Clearly the spell you cast harnessed the nexus's power and put it to use in restoring your mind, but something like that shouldn't have interfered with the existence of the nexus itself."

"I don't understand," I murmured. "What did I *do*? It isn't like I suddenly have superpowers. I might be clearheaded again, back to my old self, but my magic isn't any stronger or different than before. It can't have been that immense of a spell. Something that sounds like it might be unprecedented."

"I don't know how this happened," Cat said, meeting my eyes with a gaze so grave it rimed the pit of my stomach, encased it in frost. "But a disturbance like this? In my experience, that never bodes well for anyone."

12

The Nightmare

WE WALKED BACK together, both adrift in separate pools of silence. My mind wheeled like a bird flung off course by a storm, trying to alight on anything concrete. Whatever I'd expected to find in the Witch Woods in the way of evidence, an entire missing nexus hadn't been on the list. We were both so lost in our private musings that it took a moment for either of us to realize that something out of the ordinary was happening.

Cat caught it first, reaching out to grab my arm. "Delilah," she said, low, her grip on me tightening. "Look."

Following the jerk of her chin, I realized that an entire row of trees in front of us was sieving ribbons of gray. Sooty streams of ectoplasm sluiced out of them, merging in the middle to form a roiling, inky mass that hovered six feet above the ground.

"Is that normal?" she asked me under her breath, in the same dangerous, blade's-edge tone. "Something that always happens here this time of day?"

"Definitely not," I replied, voice rasping through a throat suddenly clogged with fear. Flames and stars, where was an Avramov when you needed one? Uncanny shit like this was their specialty. "It's like the trees are . . . *bleeding* ectoplasm. Normally, when shades vacate their trees, they immediately re-coalesce into spirit form. I've never seen pure ectoplasm flow out of wood and then just hover this way. Unformed."

"Then some other entity must be using them," she said grimly, releasing my arm to whisk both of her double blades out from the hidden pockets in which she kept them sheathed. "Like raw material, to allow itself to manifest."

Slowly, the nebulous mass began taking shape into dark, swagged, trailing folds, like translucent robes that barely brushed the ground and draped over the suggestion of skeletal limbs, gaunt and reaching hands that stretched hungrily toward us. And above the "robes" floated a bony face with flecks of arctic blue glowing in its sockets like luminous ice, its skull shrouded by an ectoplasmic cowl. Its maw hinged slowly open until it gaped to an unnatural, macabre degree, revealing huge, curved ectoplasmic fangs, the lupine kind you saw only on predators.

And then it began to howl, an eerie vacillation between high-pitched keens and deep, velvety growls, in a purely hellish timbre that broke my entire body into gooseflesh.

"Oh, *motherfucker*," Cat muttered through her teeth, lifting her blades. Her eyes had gone green and gold again, her entire posture vibrating with tension. "Yeah, this is terrible."

"Cat, what is that?" I asked, my voice fluttering high with panic as we both backed away from the floating apparition, my heart slamming against my ribs. I prided myself on being level-headed and pragmatic, but *this*—this was somehow ineffably worse than both the dhampir and succubus had been. At least those had both been flesh-and-blood monsters, as opposed to an eldritch nightmare. This looked like it shouldn't even fucking *exist*, like something torn from a horror story that teen witches told each other around crackling bonfires on Samhain, when shadows seemed to leap the highest. "I don't—I've never seen anything like that."

"It's a wraith," she replied, her voice raspier, dipping closer to a growl. I hadn't noticed it last time, but her nails had changed, lengthening into glossy claws where she gripped her hilts. "Another sucker. But this one doesn't drink blood, or feed on your life essence. These nasty bastards dine exclusively on souls. I've never seen one before, either. They're pretty damn rare."

"But we're warded against shades! It shouldn't even have been able to manifest."

She flicked her gaze up at what was visible of the sky through the entwined branches, then shook her head. "It's close enough to dusk, and this thing isn't a shade. Wraiths are demonic entities, in the same family as succubi. It doesn't manifest in the physical plane unless it wants to feed, and then it builds itself a material form from ectoplasm. It's much, much stronger and more cohesive than a shade—and I'm guessing it isn't here for me."

As if in answer, the wraith's form finished gaining substance—then it streaked toward us in a blur of black and gray, still keening that awful howl. Snarling, Cat leapt in front of me, bringing both blades together in a sweeping slash. The thing evaded her easily, sliding away, but she'd managed to at least nick it; I could see the shaved-off wisps off ectoplasm catch fire in midair before burning away.

So her knives weren't just ordinary blades, which stood to

reason for someone who fought monsters. To affect something made of spirit matter, they had to be bespelled, capable of inflicting damage on creatures not of this plane.

The wraith rushed her again, coming at her in a series of flitting, erratic movements that made my head spin—the way a moth might move, if moths were viciously single-minded and flew nearly too fast for the eye to track. Cat fought back furiously, dodging and leaping, steadily slicing away at its edges like a flenser, evading those wicked fangs and claws. When it swooped in low to the ground like a bat skimming for bugs, aiming to cut her off at the knees, she somehow catapulted herself over its head, tumbling through the air in a series of lithe turns and flips before landing weightlessly behind it.

Which left nothing between the wraith and me.

A low, harmonic chuckle issued from it, a triptych of harsh notes laid over one another. Its icy eyes narrowed in something like anticipation, and it began floating inexorably toward me.

I backed away, tripping over a fallen branch and losing my footing, landing so hard on my ass my tailbone twanged. The wraith flew at me even as I scrabbled backward like a crab . . . until my back pressed hard against a tree trunk.

No escape, nowhere to go.

The wraith began to settle over me, spectral jaw unhinging even farther until I stared into the abyss of its gaping maw, its dank breath bringing with it a gust of such awful, bone-chilling cold I could feel the warmth leach right out of my face.

You're going to die, Delilah, you awful idiot, I thought to myself, drowning in terror, choking on it. *This is how it ends. You thought living with a broken brain was worse than being dead, and now you're about to find out if you were right.*

"Hey! Knockoff Skeletor! Did I say we were through?"

One of Cat's knives came spinning through the air like a throwing star. It whipped through what passed for the wraith's chest before burying itself in the tree trunk right above my head, so close to my scalp I could feel where it'd pinned some of my curls to the bark. Its passage blew open a flaming hole in the wraith through which I could see to the other side, its ragged edges hissing with crackling little flames.

Roaring with pain and rage, the wraith whipped away from me and darted back at Cat. She rushed to meet its advance head-on, her blades melding into a whirling blur of attacks and parries until I could barely discern where its clawed strikes ended and her onslaught began. Even terrified as I was, some distant piece of my brain noted what a pleasure it was to watch her move—the utter confidence and economy of every movement, a lissome grace without an ounce of energy wasted. Each sweep of an arm or placement of a foot was gorgeous and lethal and ruthlessly precise, like some deadly performance art.

You could see the true nature of her when she was in motion. No normie or mundane could dream of commanding space with such authority.

Then the wraith abruptly pulled back, billowed like smoke under her blades, and materialized close enough to gouge its ghostly claws into her chest.

Cat stumbled and fell to a knee, her shriek of pain piercingly higher pitched than a human scream, her knife tumbling from her hand as she clapped a palm to her chest. I could see from the way blood welled bright between her fingers that the gashes were bad—much worse than what the dhampir had inflicted on her. The wraith issued something like a satisfied sigh, in that same harmonic timbre; it thought it had her dead to rights, defenseless where she half knelt on the ground. Her gaze still fiercely pinned to it, but her face gone ashen from pain, her upper body swaying from the effort of keeping herself upright.

Unless I did something—anything—it was going to kill her.

"Hey! Hey, over here!" I bellowed at it as I struggled back up to my feet, frantically flicking through the repository of spells stored in my head, waiting for one to spark. "I'm the soul you want, remember? The one you came to steal?"

The wraith hung in place for another moment, as if debating. Then it rotated to face me, its spectral features contorting into a grotesque approximation of an eager, toothy grin. As it streaked toward me, I raised both hands and let a shimmering rush of magic sluice into them, speaking a charm I'd used a thousand times before under my breath.

The incendiary charm even Harlows could do, useful mostly for lighting candlewicks and setting fires in hearths.

As the first spark caught hold, the wraith barely paid it any mind—but I'd felt its frozen breath and seen the way its ectoplasm went up in flames when severed by Cat's blade, in a way that made me think fire might be this creature's natural enemy. If I was wrong, then we were both likely worse than dead. I had nothing else in my arsenal; Harlows weren't warriors, and even with the significant power boost Emmy's tenure as the Victor of the Wreath had lent our family, I didn't have the sort of raw power you needed to fling battle magic around.

But as the spark grew into a proper licking flame, eating into all the roiling gray around it, the barest moment of shock flitted across the wraith's face, its icy eyes widening. Then, like dry tinder, it simply went up in flames, in a massive, all-consuming column of fire. Leaving behind nothing but smoky, wispy remnants of dissipating ectoplasm.

As soon as it was gone, I rushed over to Cat, falling to both knees beside her.

"My hero," she croaked at me with a shaky grin, her lips trembling. Beads of sweat had popped up along her hairline, and her eyes had taken on a frightening glaze, the blurry distance I associated with shock. "How'd you . . . how'd you even know to use flame?"

"I rolled the dice. How bad is it?" I demanded, my heart pounding like a mallet, not wanting to disturb her stanching hold on the wound to examine it myself. I could see that her hand glistened with bright blood, along with slick little runnels of a deeply disturbing black.

"Pretty bad," she admitted, with a rasping cough. "That ugly fucker cut me deep. And I can feel something . . . something like a venom, spreading through my system. I think it might've left some of its ectoplasm behind."

"Fuck," I mumbled to myself, thinking furiously. Even if I had my first aid supplies, that kind of damage was far from something I could fix—and it wasn't like I could take her to the nearest hospital, not if she was harboring some sort of metaphysical infection.

As much as I hated to do it, there was only one place—or one person, rather—I could think of to take her to instead.

"You're really making a habit out of this," Ivy remarked, flicking me a charged look over her shoulder as she knelt by an unconscious Cat sprawled out on my couch. "Should start charging you concierge doctor prices."

After patching her up with the most rudimentary of healing charms, the magical equivalent of a flimsy Band-Aid, I'd managed to half drag Cat back to her rental car at the border of the woods and get us both back to my place. By the time Ivy had shown up, Cat's eyes had fluttered shut and I hadn't been able to rouse her at all. That frightening ashen pallor had only worsened, and now there were creeping little tendrils like black veins extending from the bandaged edges of her wound.

I was no Thorn, and my medical knowledge didn't extend far beyond tinctures and poultices, but even I knew that had to be very fucking bad.

"Think of this one as a service to the community."

"What the hell is that supposed to mean?" Ivy muttered, her hands pressed to either side of the bandaged wound on Cat's chest as she ran a magical scan of the internal damage. She'd managed to stanch the worst of the blood flow, but even so, the bandage had been seeping alarmingly since she began. "Who even is this person? She doesn't look local. I'd have remembered a face like this."

"She's a visiting monster hunter. Protector against things that go bump in the night."

"A monster hunter," Ivy echoed, her voice heavy with skepticism. "One who isn't all the way human herself? There's . . . I don't know what, exactly, I've never felt this kind of energy before. But I sure as shit know what it's not, and it isn't your garden-variety human essence. Lilah, where'd you find her? And what *happened* here?"

"She's half fae, from a creature enclave in Chicago," I replied, calculating how much I needed to tell her, and feeling like the most treacherous jackass even as I did it; there was no one closer to me than Ivy, and she should have deserved nothing but the truth. And I'd already dragged her too far into my mess as it was. "She followed a rogue succubus here, from the city. A succubus that attacked me."

"A succubus here, in Thistle Grove?" Ivy asked, her voice skewing even more suspicious, even as she kept her head bowed in concentration. "We don't get that type of nasty around here, as far as I know. And what would one want with *you*, Lilah, huh? Could it, I don't know, have some connection with a baneful spell you recently cast?"

"That's what Cat's helping me find out," I admitted. "We were exploring the Witch Woods, looking for answers, and we got ambushed by something else. A wraith. Like a demonic vampire, only more interested in souls than blood."

"Well, I've never even heard of any heinous shit like that, but it did some terrible damage," Ivy murmured, momentarily distracted by whatever she was sensing through her scan. "I can take care of the gouges easy, but there's a taint embedded in her. Ectoplasmic, something I can't do anything about; you know green magic doesn't play well with that. To clear something like this, I'll need backup."

"What do you mean, 'backup'?"

"I mean an Avramov." She heaved a sigh, leaning back onto her haunches and opening her eyes. "I can't heal the damaged tissues because it'll seal the infection in, and that's the last thing we want. It'll permeate her system with deathly matter, kill her as certainly as sepsis would. So we'll have to wait until Dasha gets here."

"You're going to call *her*?" I asked, appalled. From her perch on top of my living room bookshelf, Montalban rasped out an equally aghast croak of agreement; besides me, Ivy was her favorite person, and she knew that any mention of Daria Avramov boded only ill. Last I'd heard of Dasha, she and Ivy had gone through a tumultuous breakup that had taken Ivy months to bounce back from. Whatever had happened between them, it had been so painful for my best friend that even I hadn't been privy to the details.

"You got any other Avramovs on speed dial?" she shot back. "That's what I thought. And yeah, you'll owe me like ten thousand for making me call in a favor with her, of all people. I haven't talked to her in at least half a year, and I'd been hoping to keep it that way forever, ideally."

"But you think she'll take the call?"

"Oh, she'll take it," Ivy said, so chilly it made my own stomach tighten—Ivy *never* sounded like that, so distant and frigid—and I wasn't even about to be on the receiving end of this call. "Just give me a minute, and stay with your new buddy here. Hold her hand, talk to her. Whatever she is, she's in a bad way. She needs someone to hold on to."

After Ivy stepped into my bedroom for privacy, I scooted closer to the couch, perching on its edge to sit next to Cat's side. Bedside manner wasn't exactly one of my strengths, but I'd seen the appropriate medical TV dramas and had enjoyed the benefit of Ivy's more tender ministrations over the years, all of which had left me with some vague notion of what you were expected to do. With a sigh, I took Cat's icy, clammy hand and wrapped it in mine, trying to warm it in my lap. Taking cue from me, Montalban fluttered down from the shelf and landed on the couch's arm above Cat's head, bending down to delicately peck at strands of Cat's pale hair in her approximation of lending support.

"Hey," I said quietly, feeling silly to be addressing someone who was dead to the world. "I, uh, I don't know if you can hear me.

But if you can, that's twice you've been hurt, trying to defend me—but you'll be okay. We're not going to let anything bad happen to you, I promise. And, um, what I wanted to say was . . . thank you. You were right; I did need to trust someone. And I'm glad I chose you."

Cat stirred a little, her eyelids twitching, throat working as she swallowed. A tiny wrinkle cinched between her dark brows, as if those slight movements hurt. But even if she couldn't consciously hear or understand me, any reaction seemed like a positive development. Encouraged, I kept talking, fumbling for things to say to her.

"Because you seem special to me," I continued, gaining steam. "That you're willing to risk life and limb for someone you barely know, especially given the way you've grown up, the life you've had with your mother. It's . . . you're rare, and not only because you're a halfling. Because you're fascinating, and brave. And I hope I'll get the chance to know more about you."

And I meant it all, I realized with a shock. I might not know her well, but I *was* taken by her; she was utterly unique, unlike anyone I'd ever met. She provoked in me the kind of uncharacteristic stirrings, the craving for a genuine connection that I hadn't experienced since Ivy and I first met. And she hadn't seemed deterred or offended by my own abrasiveness, or anything but intrigued by my blunt demeanor. I wanted to understand her better.

Possibly, I even wanted to kiss her again, sink into the compulsion of that seismic pull between us.

I was still talking to her, keeping up a soothing, steady stream of confidences—it was oddly easier to share sentiments when you were nearly sure the other person wasn't listening—that I barely noticed when Ivy slipped back in.

"Dasha's on her way," she said, setting a light hand on my shoulder, her voice softening. "Listen, you must be exhausted, too. Want me to make us some tea? Get you something else? After we're done fixing her up, we'll need a proper talk, you and me. But that can wait, and until then, why don't you just tell me what *you* need."

"Thank you," I breathed, leaning into the reassuring warmth of her touch, the exhaustion and adrenaline crash I'd been staving off closing over me all at once. "Tea would be wonderful. Let's . . . let's start with that."

"Done. Just give me a minute, I'll get you a snack, too. You look like you could use some chocolate in your life."

By the time Daria Avramov arrived twenty minutes or so later, the lavender-and-chamomile blend Ivy had brewed for me and the ancient chocolate chip cookies she'd dug up in my pantry had taken some of the edge off. Still, it raised my hackles to see Dasha step into my living room in all her haughty, morning-star splendor; although Cat was the fae here, my best friend's ex looked almost equally surreal, like Lucifer walking the mortal realms. Avramovs tended to be aggravatingly stunning on the whole, and Dasha was no exception. While her curtain of glossy hair wasn't quite as pale as Cat's, it was still a satin-sheened, cornsilk blond you didn't normally see on adults, without even a hint of a wave to it where it brushed her waist. With her pale brows and lashes, creamy skin, and huge eyes such a light blue they seemed almost silver, she looked milk-dipped, something made of porcelain. Most Avramovs ran brunette or auburn, but the effect of this total pallor was just as dramatic.

Ivy had called her "Starshine"—which had invariably made me want to gag—but I had to admit, I kind of saw it. It added insult to injury, somehow, that a person who'd hurt my best friend as deeply as she had should look like that, so flawless and untouchable. As if the many hurts of the world couldn't even graze that alabaster surface.

"Hey, Delilah," she said, lifting a hand to me and nodding to Montalban, and I at least took some pleasure from the clear notes of discomfort and diffidence in her tone. Being here wasn't the easiest thing for her, either, but she'd still come immediately when Ivy called. That counted for something, in my book. "I heard you could use some deathspeaker help?"

"Yes." I slid off the edge of the bed, standing to allow her access to Cat. Montalban hopped off the couch to land on my shoulder, fixing Dasha with a beady eye. "A wraith attacked my friend, in the Witch Woods. Do you know anything about wraiths?"

Her feathery pale eyebrows peaked, shock flaring across her delicate face. "I do, in theory. They're considered chthonic creatures, so they fall under our purview. But I've never met one in the flesh, figuratively speaking—not even in our woods, and I've spent a lot of time there. Never heard of any of the family running into one, either, not on this continent."

I stifled an eye roll; Avramovs seized every opportunity they could to reference their venerable connection to the Old World, as if hailing from ancient Russia elevated them to some kind of royalty. Apparently they'd never received the "we're all immigrants here" memo the rest of us had internalized. And of course she'd refer to the Witch Woods as Avramov property, even though they were technically a municipal forest, owned by the town.

"It infected her with ectoplasm," Ivy broke in, all clipped formality, her entire posture radiating distance. "I can feel the taint, but I can't do anything about it, not with green magic. I figured you could, you know, do your thing. Suck it out of her, like a death leech."

"Charming visual," Dasha said dryly, and I caught Ivy's full lips twitching as she tried not to smile. "Beautifully evocative. But I hear you—death does speak to death, so I'll do my best helpful leech impression for you. I *should* be able to draw it out, if it hasn't sunk too deep. May I touch her?"

I nodded swiftly, moving aside to let her kneel next to Cat. She was in all black, from her studded gladiator sandals to her distressed cutoffs to the T-shirt knotted to bare part of her milky midriff, no mitigating color, like a silent movie heroine come to life. But the protective garnet all Avramovs wore blazed red at her throat on its dainty silver chain as soon as she set a hand on Cat.

"Ah, yeah," she said, a faint tremor running through her. She'd closed her eyes, and I could see them rolling from side to side beneath delicately blue-veined lids, like waking REM. "There's an infestation in her, alright, almost like an ectoplasmic venom. Extracting it won't be pretty. It's going to hurt her, and it'll scare you to see it. Do I have your permission to try anyway?"

"Yes!" I blurted out, my insides cinching even tighter. It was never good news when an Avramov encountered something that unnerved even them. "Please. Whatever you can do, please try it."

"Understood."

She drew away from Cat, steepling her hands in the air, fingertips all aligned with one another. Then she began a series of delicate fluttering movements with her fingers, as if she were playing an invisible instrument, while intoning a guttural charm under her breath. For a few moments, nothing happened—then the black veins fissuring from Cat's wound began branching out into repeating patterns, like some dread tessellation imprinting onto her amber skin. Cat began to whimper, a faint mewling sound so achingly vulnerable that I clenched both hands into fists.

"She's in pain!" I protested, but Ivy wrapped a quelling arm around my waist, tugging me close.

"Let her do her work," she said, low and insistent. "She did warn us it would be ugly. Sometimes good, necessary medicine hurts; I know you know that, too. And trust me, Dasha's one of the best at this."

I nodded shakily, chewing on my lip. A compliment like that from Ivy went a long way, especially if she was comparing Dasha to the rest of her family. As natural necromancers, Avramovs were all stellar exorcists; if Dasha excelled at death magic even compared to the rest of them, that was something I could trust.

She'd ignored our exchange entirely, as if the spell she was casting demanded a level of concentration that tuned out anything beyond itself, left her operating on some entirely different frequency. Those twitching, eerie movements of her fingertips had quickened, and the rhythm of the incantation had sped up to match them, until all of it resembled macabre music; some sly, dark song a snake charmer might sing to entice a viper out of its den.

Abruptly, Cat's back arched so hard it looked like she was levitating, half-risen off the couch. Her head snapped back, her mouth falling open so wide it reminded me sickeningly of the wraith's own gaping jaws when it had advanced on me, ready to strike. Then darkness began pouring out of her like some filthy river. Braided skeins of gray and black gushed from her mouth like liquid smoke, coalescing into a roiling globe hovering a few feet above her head. I could see how badly its exodus hurt her, from the pain twisting her face. Though her eyes were still closed, those mewling sounds of complaint had grown into a constant, steady groan, as if she were exerting some wracking effort, too.

As soon as the last of the ectoplasm had slid out of her, Cat dropped back down onto the couch with a thump, a faint hint of pink blooming back into her cheeks. Like she'd begun improving immediately, now that the poison had been drawn out.

Dasha said some harsh word, elongated vowels strung like rope bridges between the sibilant hiss of the consonants. Then she snapped the fingers of both hands hard, flung back her head, and opened her own mouth. The garnet at her throat blazed like a gem-enclosed flame—as though it contained the very essence of fire, the dim, scholarly part of my brain noted with fascination. Maybe it did; I knew from my studies that Avramovs were so keenly attuned to the spirit realm, and therefore vulnerable to all levels of ghostly possession, that they used the garnets to keep themselves grounded and protected.

As soon as Dasha's lips parted, the whorling globe of ectoplasmic darkness hovering above Cat darted over to her. It hung above her face like a thundercloud, then slowly began to drip into her open mouth. Drop by dark drop, until it sluiced into a steady stream, a semi-liquid ribbon.

Though her entire body lurched with revulsion—clearly ectoplasmic soft serve was not delicious, even for an Avramov—she swallowed it down, her throat muscles working with each gulp.

"Fuck, that's disgusting," Ivy mumbled beside me through a suppressed gag, almost startling a laugh from me. As if in agreement, Montalban gave a hacking caw from my shoulder. "Couldn't be me. How in the hell do they *do* that shit?"

"I think it's kind of fascinating," I murmured back, slightly more relaxed now that Cat was clearly out of the woods, and free from the worst of the pain.

"You would."

"Aren't you at all curious why she'd need to *eat* it?"

Ivy shuddered beside me, all but sticking out her tongue. "Girl, I cannot express how much I don't care to know."

With a final full-body convulsion, Dasha swallowed the last of the ectoplasm. She slumped forward with a quavering sigh, bracing herself with a palm on her thigh and swiping the back of her other hand across her mouth.

"That should do it," she said hoarsely, as if the spell had stripped her throat raw. I couldn't even imagine how foul it must have been to consume something like that, something that shouldn't even come into contact with human skin, much less one's insides. "She's still hurt, but now it's only normal injury. Also, should inquiring minds want to know, I'm deeply unhappy to report that wraith venom tastes like chilled cat piss."

"Ugh." Ivy stifled another gag, heading toward the kitchen. "I'm going to get you some water. And please, Dasha, just . . . say no more."

13

Hard Truths

BY THE TIME Dasha felt steady enough to leave, Cat was still asleep. But I could see the new ease in her body, the slackness of her muscles compared to how agonizingly taut they'd been before, the renewed healthy color in her cheeks. While Dasha recovered from the mini exorcism, chugging two glasses of water and a glass of apple juice to flush the taste out of her mouth, Ivy had gently sealed Cat's wounds. The rest, she said, it was better not to push. Without the taint, Cat's system was free to finish healing itself, and sometimes letting natural processes run themselves to completion was the wiser path.

"I'm glad you called me," I could hear Dasha's low voice drifting from the foyer as she prepared to leave, Ivy ushering her out. "And I'm even more glad it was something I could actually help you with."

"Thank you for coming. I . . . I do appreciate it. I needed your help on a friend's behalf, so I asked for it—but that's all it was, okay? It doesn't change anything between us. This is *not* an open door. Do you understand?"

A fraught silence fell between them, and I could almost feel the simmer of Dasha's dissatisfaction, her desire to press the issue.

"Dasha. Tell me you hear me."

"I do. Of course." This time her tone was wary, chastened. "Take care of yourself, Ivy. And if you ever need anything again . . ."

"I won't. But if I do, I know where to find you."

I thought I heard the faintest deflated exhale of Dasha's sigh, followed by the soft click of the door closing. Then Ivy slumped back into the living room, naked pain drawn over her face.

"Phew, seeing her does such a damn number on me," she murmured, resting the back of her hand against her forehead. "You'd think I'd be immune to her by now, but nah. Still throws me for a loop. Funny, though, how much more dependable she is now, compared to when we were actually together."

I chewed on the inside of my lip, awash in remorse for having dragged Ivy—and Dasha, by extension—into this. "I'm sorry you had to call her."

"Didn't have much of a choice. And it was worth it, right?" She glanced over at Cat, still resting easily on the couch. "She looks much better. It's just going to be a matter of time now, until she's back on her feet."

"How long, do you think?"

"I'm not sure how non-human systems react to an assault like this. I expect she'll sleep a lot for days, be very groggy even when she's awake. Make sure you wake her up every once in a while if she doesn't seem inclined to rouse herself, keep her up on her nutrients and fluids. Broth and juice should do it, if she's not up to more."

I nodded, chewing on a knuckle, my gaze lingering on Cat's prone, vulnerable form. The idea of tending to her, taking care of her instead of the other way around, gave me a distinct pang of an emotion I couldn't quite categorize. "I can do that."

Ivy scrutinized me, her liquid dark eyes skimming my face. "Lilah. You *care* about this person."

"You don't have to sound so shocked about it," I said stiffly. "I've been known to exhibit human emotion."

"Oh, don't give me that. You know that's not how I meant it." She set both hands on my shoulders, turned me deliberately toward her. "Lilah, honey. I'm asking you as your friend. Your best friend, someone who loves you. What's *really* happening here? Who is she, why is she here? And who is she to you?"

My jaw tightened so hard I could feel my neck muscles straining with discomfort; even my chest clenched up, as if my ribs were shrinking like corset stays being laced around my insides. I knew Ivy wouldn't go to Uncle James or Emmy without my permission, but I also knew that if I shared everything with her, I'd be facing the full force of her judgment, her pressure to approach them myself, come clean, and ask for help. And if things went south, I didn't want her involved in this, implicated in any way that might make her culpable for any fallout.

"I can't talk about it with you," I said, with a terse shake of the head. "I just—I can't, Ivy. You have to trust me on this."

"Trust you on this," she echoed in disbelief. "Even though you won't trust me. Because you're *that* afraid of needing help, of being weak in any way, that you'd rather trust this stranger with whatever's happening to you than me."

"Ivy . . ."

"No." She held up a hand, her lips trembling with contained emotion. "No, Lilah, you listen to me. You're shutting me out, even though I've been through *every* miserable minute of this with you. I've held you, I've walked you through lost memories, I've put all my own extremely real fucking problems on the back burner to be available to you. Because you needed me that badly, and you had to come first. That's how it is, sometimes, with people you love. It isn't always equal."

"I know what you've done for me," I said, dropping my gaze. Unable to look her in the eye, sodden with guilt and self-loathing for everything I'd taken from her. Everything I'd accepted. "And you know how grateful I am, for all of it."

"Then do the hard thing! The thing *I* need you to do, for once," she snapped. "And I need you to talk to me, share this with me, just let me in. Of course it's easier for you to trust some outsider, some person who doesn't even know you—who doesn't matter to you like I do, even if you're starting to consider caring about her. Which I know is an entire process with you."

She was right; I couldn't deny it. It *was* easier to trust Cat, to allow myself to depend on her precisely because she wasn't a mainstay in my life, a fixed star in my constellation. Once this was all over, she'd eventually disappear; simply, conveniently be gone. Whereas Ivy would always remain, a constant reminder of how desperate and weak I'd been, how endlessly needy of her.

How could I possibly ask for even more of her, after everything she'd given already?

"I can't," I whispered, my voice fracturing. "I just . . . I can't do that."

"No," she replied woodenly, hands lifting off my shoulders. "It isn't that you can't—it's that you won't. Just like Dasha wouldn't, when I needed something from her."

Against all odds, an even deeper pit managed to open in my stomach. "Please don't compare me to her."

"You're right. It's not fair. Dasha has issues of her own, but hers, I understand at least in theory. You, though? I've loved you for years and you still baffle me, Lilah. You'd rather ask a complete stranger for help than let yourself believe that me and James and Emmy would do right by you—that we wouldn't see helping you as some kind of eternal debt you'd owe us. That's how little stock you put by us all, how little respect you have for us. No matter how we all try to accommodate *your* needs, to love you unconditionally."

That pit yawned in my stomach, a dark chasm lined with jagged teeth like spires. "That's not true."

"Oh, it is. And it's fucked up and selfish and sad as hell." She backed away from me, heading to the door, her eyes glistening bright with restrained tears. "Have it your way, then. Let her be the one to hold you up, if that's what you want, because I won't be any part of this anymore. You're on your own now, Lilah. Just the way you like it."

I waited until I heard the door close behind her, the furious clatter of her feet down the staircase, before I let myself dissolve into a blistering flood of tears.

FOR THE NEXT week, Cat mostly slept, just like Ivy had predicted. At some point, she roused enough to let me lead her like a child from the couch to my bed, where I thought she'd be more comfortable. I couldn't abandon Tomes to take care of her, so I took a lunch break each day to make the quick walk home, for long enough to help her to the bathroom and coax her into spooning chicken soup and lemonade into her mouth before she lapsed back into that restorative slumber. The intense way she slept through both days and nights reminded me of a sick animal; the way that cats and dogs turn inward, focusing on healing so completely that they check out of consciousness for as long as it takes.

To the degree that anything registered with her, she seemed to like Montalban's presence, as if my familiar were an extension of me. So I left her at home to watch over Cat during the day, for company if nothing else.

I'd never in my entire life taken care of another person that way, and it made me feel oddly, almost painfully tender toward her. It also gave me a satisfying sense of evening out the scales, as though in tending to her this way I was making up for what she'd done for me, at least in part.

It didn't escape me that this was exactly what Ivy had meant when she'd flung her accusation of selfishness at me. As much as it hurt to admit it, she hadn't been wrong about the fundamentally transactional way I viewed relationships. Defense mechanism that it was, I couldn't deny that it was profoundly selfish, too.

If I let myself think too much about what she'd said to me and the bitter way we'd parted, the loneliness and sense of abandonment—both of which I knew I deserved—threatened to overwhelm me. Instead, I focused on nursing Cat back to health, working with Nina on restoring the wards, and keeping a constant watchful vigilance, should something manage to bypass my protective charms and sneak into the store to try to eat me. Without Cat's warrior's skills at my disposal, I'd be left to my own devices in mounting a defense, so I reviewed the more aggressive elemental and banishing spells I was strong enough to cast on my own, so I could be ready to unleash one at a moment's notice.

It was a lot to grapple with; almost enough to distract me from the fact that the person I cared about most in the world wasn't speaking to me.

Fortunately, for nearly a week, a blissful amount of nothing happened. Going about business as usual was so lulling that I'd almost let down my guard when, just as Nina and I were closing up shop that Thursday evening, a basilisk tumbled down the chimney.

These days, the Tomes fireplace was just for show; we had central heating, and the hearth hadn't been fired up in living memory. We used the mantelpiece to display artifacts for sale, and a watercolor by a local artist of Lady's Lake at night hung above it on the pebble dash wall. So when the thumping and slithering started up in the walls, along with a hissing sound like a frantically boiling teakettle, both Nina and I froze in place, exchanging perplexed looks.

"What is that sound?" Nina said, flicking a wary glance at the hearth. "Do you think a bird's trapped in the flue?"

"I do not think it's a bird, no, although that would be a fantastic change of pace," I muttered, lifting my hands in readiness as I ran through potential defensive spells, panic flaring in my stomach. "I do think you should leave. Right now."

"Why would I do that? Whatever it is, I could—"

Before she could finish, a thoroughly bizarre monstrosity came swooping out of the fireplace like a bat out of hell—if the bat were a wonky-looking cross between a cobra and an oversized chicken, luxuriously feathered in stripes of emerald and jade. It was almost more awkward than monstrous, a gouging beak and fangs juxtaposed against stubby wings and silly little chicken feet that protruded from the curves of its serpent's body.

But there was nothing remotely funny about the hungry gleam in its slitted yellow eyes, the way it twitched its snake's head to fix its glare on me.

"Basilisk," Nina spat in a brusque tone I'd never heard from her before, both authoritative and domineering, as she swept over to place her slight frame between me and the fireplace. Exactly like Cat would have done. "Delilah, take cover."

I was so stunned by the protective gesture, and by the fact that she even knew what the cryptid was—I had recognized it, too, but I'd been immersed in woodcuts of mythical creatures since I was a baby scholar, not an activity I imagined went on much at Yon Castle Camelot—that I stayed put, gaping at her back. Nina flung her hands up and incanted a complicated elemental charm, even as the basilisk half slithered, half flew toward her, still emitting that semi-ridiculous teakettle hiss, its fangs dripping acid that scorched the floorboards where it fell.

Then a bolt of silvery sparks arced elegantly from Nina's extended hands, and the basilisk petrified in midair, turning into a stone statue of itself.

It hung there for a moment, suspended like a very ugly ornament gifted by your least favorite eccentric aunt, then plummeted to the floor. Upon impact, it shattered into shards with such explosive force that Nina flung out a shining, gossamer-fine bubble of a shield to keep any of the splintered fragments from impaling us. The shards bounced harmlessly off it, peppering the ground instead.

"What . . . ?" I managed through a sawdust-dry throat. "How . . . ?"

"It's an elemental creature," Nina replied, as if I'd successfully formulated a full question. "Sometimes they're called cockatrices, too. They correspond to earth, so you have to petrify one to kill it properly."

"How do you even know that?"

"I *do* read," she said tartly. "Also, I have some experience with elemental creatures. They can be by-products of Blackmoore magic, though this one had nothing to do with me. I haven't been channeling anywhere near the level of magic required to trigger the manifestation of an elemental."

She focused on me, frowning a little as she ran a practiced eye over me for any injuries, as though she dealt with this kind of emergent situation on a daily basis instead of drafting memoranda, or whatever it was that lawyers did. "Are you alright?"

"Fine," I mumbled, lost in thought. "But it shouldn't even have been able to get in here. I have the whole store warded every which way against paranormal intrusion . . ."

Except for the chimney, I realized ruefully. Since we didn't use the fireplace, I'd forgotten about it completely as a point of ingress to the store.

"I felt that," Nina said, her eyes narrowing. "But why, Delilah? You've never had those wards in place before, and you didn't ask for my help with them. And you're steadier, much more stable with your casting. Something's different with you. It's been different ever since your *visiting scholar* showed up."

"Maybe I decided we needed some additional protection," I shot back, bristling at the skepticism in her voice, still too jangly with adrenaline to mount even the pretense of courtesy. "In case next time, something even worse than you decides to obliterate me and my store like a fucking hurricane."

Anguish and fury flooded her face, her dainty jaw setting hard even as her lips quivered.

"What is it going to take?" she said roughly, spreading her hands. "What is it you want, to finally forgive me? I'm doing everything I can think of to make it up to you, Delilah. I'll cast spells for you, play errand girl, petrify fucking elementals if you need me to, *whatever.* The one thing I can't pull off is undoing the past. The triple goddess knows, I would if I could. But I *can't.*"

"Then stop trying," I snapped, turning away from her, eager to get out of Tomes and back to my heavily warded apartment before anything else took a stab at me. And to escape from Nina, and all that suffocating need for absolution I couldn't find it in myself to grant her. "Stop forcing it. Because forgiveness isn't in the cards for us, and that's never going to change."

14

Binary Stars

WHEN I GOT home from Tomes, still a little quivery from the averted basilisk disaster and the confrontation with Nina, I found Cat not only fully awake but dashing around my apartment playing tag with Montalban, who was having the time of her life chasing Cat around. I leaned in the doorway for a moment, watching them, delighted to see Cat so clearly recovered— no trace of scarring on what I could see of her chest above one of my borrowed crop tops.

A smile tugged my lips as Montalban dive-bombed her in a thrash of black wings, trying to entice her into giving more chase. Magical as she was, I sometimes forgot that my sweetheart was still a raven; a silly, sweet, playful trickster who loved pulling pranks on both people and other animals.

"You're back! And behold, I've roused! Can we *please* go somewhere?" Cat exclaimed when she caught sight of me, her tawny cheeks warm with exertion. My familiar echoed her delight, fluttering toward me in a joyful rush before settling on my shoulder. "I feel like I've been out of commission for a million years, and if I don't move, I'll spontaneously combust. Not that hanging out with Monty hasn't been the best, but if I have to do another set of push-ups just to burn some of this energy off, I am going to *perish* of boredom."

"Sure we can—and I'm glad you're feeling better. But maybe give me a moment to catch my breath first."

She peered closely at me as I moved past her and sank shakily onto the sofa, sobering as she took note of my still-trembling hands. "Delilah. Did something happen while I was sleeping? Another attack?"

"A basilisk broke into Tomes. But I'm fine, don't worry," I assured her, seeing the panic flash across her face. "It didn't get far. Nina was there—she petrified it for me."

"Clever," she acknowledged, jaw setting. "I should have been there, though. That's supposed to be *my* job."

"Not your fault." I heaved a sigh, tipping my head back against the cushions. "And annoying to have to be grateful to her, but I agree; she handled it well. I'd prefer not to think about it anymore tonight, in any event. And I'm with you. I'd rather be somewhere besides here, too."

"Somewhere safe, if that's an option. I might have raging cabin fever, but I don't want to expose you to anything even worse than a basilisk tonight."

I only had to think about it for a moment. There was one Thistle Grove treasure she hadn't seen, easily the most beautiful spot in town, and we were likely to be safer from any paranormal assailants near its sanctified waters than we would be anywhere else in Thistle Grove.

"I know just the place," I told her. "You can borrow one of my suits."

AN HOUR LATER, Cat and I stood by Lady's Lake, the water's immensity laid out like cosmic glass before us. Montalban wheeled in circles high above the water, her cries piercing the still night air. One of Thistle Grove's metaphysical quirks was that this mountaintop lake seemed much larger than it should have been—and Hallows Hill itself felt much higher once you were actually up here than its formally measured height. The clustered lights of the town below glimmered through the ring of pines that circled the lake, like tiny bonfires burning in a far-off distance. And the lake itself . . . As gorgeous as it was during the day, at night Lady's Lake was a revelation, a vision that made you want to fall to your knees in spontaneous prayer. Overfull of stars as Thistle Grove skies always were, there seemed to be even more of them reflected in the water; whole diamond galaxies glittering on the blown-glass surface, seemingly untouched by the warm, sweet-scented breezes that eddied around the lake.

Tonight was one of the aurora borealis nights, even though we should have been nowhere near far enough north to catch such regular displays of northern lights. Lacy frills of technicolor green danced in the sky above us, their feathery reflections rippling in the water. And all around the lake, flowers clustered everywhere; the spiky Scottish thistles for which the town was named, flaring bright purple even by the frosted light shed by the moon and stars.

The moon was near full and heavy as pale fruit, a silver apple hung on the black bough of the sky.

The overall effect was so transcendent that when we first arrived, Cat had simply stared in awestruck silence, those uncanny green eyes reflecting the galactic glory of the landscape in front of us. This tiny mountaintop universe, the underwater firmament that served as the avatar Belisama's citadel.

"How could you ever get used to this?" she whispered, turning to me. The moonlight limned her platinum hair, turned it even more striking against the warm tint of her skin and those sooty black lashes and brows. She looked even more ethereal up here, like something that belonged by this otherworldly lakeside. "I thought I knew what real magic, beauty, looked like. But this . . ."

"We don't really get used to it, I don't think. I always come up here when I want to remember who I am. How special my little world is; how lucky I am to be a part of it."

"You are," she murmured, her throaty voice catching as she looked back to the water. "You really are. And I'm glad you know it."

"You know what's even better than staring at it?" I asked, tugging my tank top over my head to reveal my black one-piece. "Getting all. Up. In there."

She burst into low, melodious laughter, staring at me in disbelief. "We're allowed to swim in it?"

"We are, unless you need a formal invitation," I added, shimmying out of my cargo shorts and leaving them puddled with my top as I strode toward the water—a surge of wildness building in my chest, the same sense of freedom that always came over me up here.

Without waiting for her, I broke into a sprint, whooping as I launched myself into the water. It parted around me like warm milk, a smoother, silkier texture than any other water I'd ever felt. The lake maintained a balmy temperature almost year-round, except in the chilliest depths of our short winters, but midsummer was always its sweetest time. I opened my eyes underwater like I always did, to see the wavering reflections of stars suspended above me on the surface like trembling sparks.

Then I came up for air, only to be showered in a tremendous splash as Cat cannonballed in beside me. She surfaced a moment later, sputter-laughing as streams of water sluiced down her face, running a palm over her head to slick back her short hair.

"Well, that's it," she declared, grinning at me, beads of water clinging to her lips. I had an almost overpowering urge to swim over to her, suck them right off her mouth like dewdrops. "I'm never getting out. It really does feel like rolling around in magical catnip, all obvious jokes aside. And, fuck, it smells *incredible* in here. Like . . . incense, maybe, and ambergris, maybe a little bit like fallen leaves and firewood? How is that possible? That is not, in my experience, your standard freshwater smell."

"That's what Thistle Grove magic smells like," I said, startled that she could detect it—most normies couldn't, from what I knew, even if they'd lived their entire lives here. Even some witches were less sensitive to that distinctive, Halloween-tinged perfume than others. But, then again, Cat was half-magic herself; it stood to reason that it would register with her. "And it's strongest here because this lake is our power source. The wellspring."

"Well, I love it." She dipped her head back to let her short hair splay out along the surface of the water, floating like a corona of pale seaweed fronds. "Where does this magic come from, do you know?"

I hesitated for a moment, still not wholly comfortable with the fact that I was considering trusting an outsider with the deepest and most recent of Thistle Grove's secrets. But Cat didn't feel like a stranger to me anymore; she felt both like a protector and like someone who'd been vulnerable with me in her own right, who'd been dependent on me in a way no one else ever had.

It felt, oddly, like being on perfectly equal footing with someone for the first time in my life.

"There's a statue of a goddess submerged at the bottom," I said, Cat's eyebrows peaking with shock. "Semi-sentient, it seems—able to interact with some of us, to a degree. As if part of the real goddess's consciousness resides in that stone. We didn't even know about her until recently. And we still don't know how she came to be there to begin with."

"A *goddess*." Cat shook her head, incredulous. "Chicago might be rife with supernaturals, but I don't know that even we've ever seen a deity come through. This town keeps throwing the wildest kind of curveballs. Just when I start thinking I've gotten a handle on it, everything shifts. Including you."

"Me?" I echoed, startled. "What do you mean?"

She licked her water-beaded lips, the way I'd desperately wanted to just moments ago; still very much wanted to, if I was being honest. "Are there any shallows here? Somewhere we can just sit a little, while we talk? I don't mind treading water—especially this water—but it is a little distracting."

"Sure," I replied, my heart leaping to nestle into the hollow of my throat. "The bank slopes more gently over this way, makes a nice spot for lounging."

She swam over after me, both of us sitting in the shallows with the lake's warm silt seeping around us like wet clay, the water lapping just above our waists. I twisted my hair into a long braid and squeezed the water out of it, draping it over one shoulder like a damp rope. For a long moment, we sat in the lovely balm of evening silence, pierced only by the soft calls of night birds, whirring cicadas, and the periodic splash of Montalban diving into the lake, either just for fun or with some tasty catch in tow.

"I wanted to thank you," Cat began, flicking me a brief, slantwise look. "For enlisting your friend—and her friend—to help, after the wraith. And I . . . fuck, I don't do this very often, and I'm fairly shit at it. But I really am grateful that you'd go to such lengths for someone you hardly know. I know it wasn't an easy call for either of you to make."

"You remember Dasha being there?" I said, taken aback. I'd assumed that Cat had been completely unconscious, with the wraith's ectoplasmic venom surging through her system.

"I remember snatches of it. The extraction of the venom, most definitely," she added with a delicate shudder. It bunched the muscles of her strong shoulders in a very distracting way, and tensed the carved lines of her abs visible above the water's surface. I'd loaned her one of my bikinis instead of a one-piece, and though it hadn't been intentional—I wasn't *that* thirsty—I was certainly happy about it now, with so much of that honey skin bare and taut in the silvered wash of moonlight. "That hurt so damn much I doubt it'll be slipping my mind anytime soon."

"Right," I mumbled, wondering if she remembered what I'd said to her before that, while we'd waited for Dasha to arrive. The confidences I'd spilled at her bedside in an effort to help her hang on to life. "It was pretty gruesome to watch, too."

"Oh, I bet. And then your friend was angry with you, because of me." She shot me a sympathetic look from under lowered dark lashes. "I remember that, too."

"Her name is Ivy," I murmured, blinking back the salty sting of tears. "We used to be together, years ago, but now . . . we're just best friends, now. Or we were, before all this. She's not wrong, though. I *am* selfish. I *do* keep her shut out, because being dependent on her feels like some kind of punishment. It was why we didn't work out in the first place; she felt like I never really allowed myself to let her in."

"How can you say that about yourself?" she asked, reaching out to graze her knuckles down my bare arm, following the winding trail of my tattoos. The sensation felt like it gathered all my physical awareness and drew it through a needle's eye, until it emerged, almost excruciatingly keen, focused entirely on where her skin brushed mine. "Call yourself selfish, after what you said to me while I was close to dying? After the way you took care of me? You didn't have to do that. Just like you didn't even have to save me in the first place, after the wraith bested me in the woods."

"Any decent person would have done as much," I argued.

"Not at the Shadow Court, they wouldn't," she said, with a rueful little laugh, another of those blithe shrugs that concealed such a wealth of pain. "Many there would've just let me die. Common decency is a hell of a misnomer, given how uncommon it is— especially to the extreme you took it. So, no, I don't buy this 'Delilah Harlow is a selfish bitch' party line."

"Well, it is different with you," I admitted, feeling like a hard knot inside me was cleaving at this confession, breaking forcefully apart like a peach pit. "You didn't grow up here; you haven't always known me. And people here don't . . . Well, that's not fair. People *in general* don't tend to like me. I'm too abrupt, too direct, too short-tempered. Too impatient with unnecessary niceties. Just too rude, the way my sister Genevieve always says."

"Fuck your sister Genevieve," Cat muttered under her breath, ardently enough to startle me into a laugh. "She sounds like an idiot."

"She is who she is. She can't help it, any more than I can. And it hurt too much, being constantly rejected even when I tried, did my best to be better. To be different. But there are workarounds. I taught myself not to like people, either; not to need them, if I could possibly help it. To find fulfillment inside myself, in my work and my witchcraft. In the traditions my family's been carrying out through centuries." I smiled up at the sky, where the circling silhouette of my familiar occasionally blotted out a snatch of stars. "And in my connection with Montalban, now."

"You taught yourself to be self-sufficient," Cat said, so low it was almost a whisper. "An island unto yourself. Growing up in the Shadow Court, especially with my mother . . . I know something about that kind of forced independence, too."

"And it crystallizes, right, over the years," I continued, in a desperate rush to get it all out now that someone seemed to finally understand what I'd spent so long not quite being able to articulate. "Into a shell. Like an exoskeleton. And it's bristly and tough, this spiny carapace that sits around you. That you don't know how to take off even when you wish you could."

This time, she stroked my arm with an open palm from shoulder to elbow, her fingertips trailing languidly down my wet skin, sending a spiral of chills wending all the way down my side and coiling at my center. With her other hand, she caught my chin, gently turning my face toward hers until we were locked eye to eye. Like two binary stars, chained to each other as they wheeled together through the dark expanse of the universe; not the same but similar, caught in each other's undertow.

I drew a shuddering breath, snared by the intensity in those pale fae eyes, the way she looked at me like she saw past every veneer. Down to the softest, most vulnerable core of me that I always did my best to hide.

"Did you mean it?" she asked intently, her luminous gaze shifting between my eyes. I wondered what they looked like to her, what my own dark irises reflected back. "The things you said to me before Dasha got there, when you thought I might die?"

"Of course I meant it," I said, swallowing, unable to look away from her even if I'd wanted to. "You've put yourself on the line for me twice now. You *are* rare, and it certainly isn't only because you're half fae. And you're definitely fascinating, and clearly generous, and braver than anyone else I've ever met. And—"

With a soft whisper of a sigh, she tipped my chin up and angled my face toward her, then covered my mouth with hers, blotting out whatever else I'd been about to say. I drew in a sharp breath, instantly aflame at just the contact with her lips, still cooled and slick from lake water. When they parted to let her tongue stroke against mine in a searing sweep, I exhaled shakily into her mouth, overcome by such a giddy surge of lust I felt like my head might swim away, float off into the ether like a lost balloon.

With a low hum of pleasure, Cat slung her other arm around my neck, drawing me closer until we were pressed chest to chest, one of my legs tangling through hers. As the kiss deepened, her other hand stroked feathery lines down the length of my neck and arm, fingers lacing around my wrist. Then she sank her teeth hard into my lower lip and pinned my hand behind me, trapping it with hers against my lower back.

I gasped so sharply it almost made me shudder, a throb of hot desire pulsing to life between my legs.

"Yeah?" she whispered, still nibbling at my lower lip, drawing it between her teeth,

"Yeah," I confirmed shakily, head spinning. Wanting her all over me, everywhere at once.

As if she could read my mind, her mouth grazed over my cheek to settle on my earlobe, sucking and nipping, then licking slow circles over the delicate spot between my ear and jaw. It felt so good, so perfectly like what I wanted, that I slid my free arm around her hard waist, clinging to her like an anchor. Slow, unhurried, she licked her way down my throat, a long, scorching slide of her tongue that brought her to the juncture between my neck and shoulder. There, she settled, in a blazing rush of open-mouthed kisses and sharp-edged bites. Sliding her arm free from around my neck to cup the full swell of my breast, squeezing hard through the elastic fabric of my swimsuit.

"Fuck, Delilah," she moaned against my skin, her hand firm and insistent against my breast while I quivered like a drawn bow, almost panting from desire. "You feel so fucking perfect. Wanted to do exactly this since I first saw you at Tomes."

"I'd probably have let you," I admitted. "Even then. We have a little storeroom in the back. And there's always the attic."

She chuckled against my neck, hoarse and low. "Then I'm even sorrier I had to wait this long."

"Should we . . ." I closed my eyes, struggled to catch my breath. "Should we maybe get out of the water?"

She pulled back, enough to give me a wide, ferocious grin, the predatory gleam in her eyes only stoking the flaring heat in my belly. She was looking at me like something edible, something she wanted to devour.

"Yes, let's," she agreed, rising and pulling me up along with her in one easy motion. "I want you out of that suit, and it'll be easier dry."

Minutes later, we'd toweled off and settled onto the soft picnic blanket I'd brought; I might not have loaned her the skimpier swimsuit on purpose, but I'd had *some* idea of what I wanted to happen once we were up here under the stars. True to her word, she peeled the suit off me with deft hands, then unlaced her own bikini ties and let them fall away. We lay side by side, facing each other. Bare and goose-bumped in the soft caress of the breeze, the lake's incensey perfume rolling over us.

She watched me for a long moment, trailing her fingers over my collarbone and down my chest, around the weight of my breasts and the long line of my torso. Skimming my waist and hip, the outside of my thigh.

"You're so goddamn gorgeous," she whispered, her lips a breath away from mine and eyes at half-mast, heavy-lidded with desire. "Your eyes, your lips, that amazing Rapunzel hair. Like some kind of forest nymph."

"Dryad," I corrected her, unable to help myself, "would be the correct term."

"*Pedantic* dryad," she corrected back. "And don't even get me started on the unspeakable glory of your tits."

I giggled against her mouth, snaring a tiny kiss. "Thank you. Means a lot, from someone who looks like a Valkyrie."

And she did look like a warrior in repose, a beautiful one. Her entire body was lithe and hard, broad in the shoulders and lean through the hips; every muscle defined beneath that golden skin, her breasts small and pert, nipples dark and hard as pebbles. I reached out to touch her, mesmerized—and she caught my hand mid-motion, then flipped us over until I lay on my back with both arms pinned over my head. She hovered over me, smiling wickedly into my eyes.

"Oh, no," she murmured, shaking her head in mock reproach. "Me first. That's how this works."

"If you say—"

Her mouth settled over mine, and anything I might've wanted to add vanished, melted from my mind.

She kissed me hard and deep and slick, the back of my head pressing into the soft, grassy ground beneath the blanket, her free hand toying deftly with my nipple, rolling it hard between her fingertips. When she finally slid down my body, releasing my arms, I kept them above my head, my whole body arching as she took my nipples into her mouth, alternating between the right and left in slow, languid rhythm. Sucking and licking until the keen connection between nipple and clit seared inside me like a vein of liquid fire, pulsing relentlessly between my thighs. I could hear myself moaning, high-pitched and desperate with desire, one of my hands buried in her hair, the other still flung up above my head.

"Please," I begged her, parting my legs to wrap them around her hips, writhing up to grind my pelvis against hers. "I need . . ."

"Please what, Delilah?" she demanded when I hesitated, giving my nipple a bite that made me cry out. When she drew away from my breasts, the cooler tickle of the breeze against my heated skin felt like the most exquisite kind of torment. "You need what?"

"Your mouth on me," I whispered, my heart battering against my ribs. "And your . . . and your fingers."

"I'll think about it," she said coyly, flicking a devilish glance up at me before bending back down. Setting her mouth in the space between my breasts, where my heart beat a frenzied rhythm directly against her lips.

It felt like an aching eternity of need, more foreplay than I thought I could survive. I felt galvanic, electrified, every inch of my body so sensitized that anything she did felt like the sweetest torture. She licked a slow and deliberate path over my rib cage, drawing circles with her tongue around my navel until my moans pitched even higher, my hips writhing against her, my hand clutching at her hair. When she finally settled between my thighs, slinging my legs over her shoulders, I almost cried out of sheer anticipation.

She kissed the soft insides of my knees, then nuzzled her cheeks against my inner thighs, rubbed her damp hair against the delicate skin until I whimpered her name, pleading for more.

"Okay, then," she murmured against me, and I could hear the straining expanse of her own desire roughening her voice. "Since you ask so nice."

When her lips sealed around my clit, silken tongue flickering over it in searing, insistent patterns, I half screamed, my fingers digging into the blanket's soft fabric and bunching it tight in my clenched fists. It felt so good that I abandoned all pretense of control, any sense that this was something I was supposed to lead or manage. There was only the building swell of sensation, an increasingly urgent series of peaks and valleys, so delicious it was almost unbearable.

When she plunged her fingers inside me to the knuckle, began working them in a curved, beckoning rhythm that felt like it had been tailored to fit exactly what I craved, I couldn't stand it any longer.

"Cat," I half moaned, half sobbed. "I'm . . . I'm going to come, I . . ."

"Do it," she ordered, working her fingers harder, tongue lapping hot and sweet against my clit. "Come for me, Delilah. Right now."

I usually came with my eyes closed, lost in the overload of sensation. But this time, the orgasm was so shatteringly strong it managed to take me by surprise even though I'd known I was on the cusp. My eyes flew open, head tipping even farther back as waves of pleasure radiated outward, toward my belly and down my legs, curling my toes. Thistle Grove's diamond stars glittered in my eyes like a slow-motion explosion, an echo of the delicious cataclysm unfurling inside me.

When it finally subsided, my entire body melted into a jellied puddle. "Oh, fuck," I exhaled on a shuddering breath, little aftershocks zinging through me, making me twitch. "Flames and stars, I don't . . . I don't even . . . I don't know what just happened to me."

"Bitch, *I* just happened to you," Cat chuckled, still dropping scattered kisses on the insides of my thighs. "But if you're still not sure, don't worry. You're about to find out a few more times."

"Cat, I really don't think I can," I protested feebly, so spent and mellow I felt spreadable, like something you could eat on a scone for high tea. "That was beyond intense. There's no way I have it in me to repeat that."

"So here's the thing about fae . . . we don't think in absolutes, or impossibilities," she whispered, running the tip of her tongue along the seam of my swollen folds, drawing a sharp moan from me. "So why don't you be a good girl, and don't tell me what you can't do. Because when it comes to me, I'm pretty sure you're in for a hell of a surprise."

15

Pedantic Dryads

SHE WASN'T WRONG.

I came three more times, until I'd moaned myself hoarse, before Cat would accept the possibility that I might have had enough for now. Even then, we weren't through with each other; I may have turned into jelly, but I still wanted to touch and taste her for myself, take my turn to coax her into losing that ironclad grip on her own control. Even though my whole body still trembled, I'd sucked at those hard brown nipples until she hissed my name, traced every contour of muscle on her belly with my tongue, spent a stretch of timeless bliss with my face nestled between her legs. She smelled like wildflowers everywhere, and going down on her made me feel like a human hummingbird, something granted permission to sample the most enticing nectar.

Braced on a still-shaking arm, I sucked at the salty-sweet center of her, my own fingers buried in her dripping heat. Following her whispered and precise commands, bringing her to the brink until I learned exactly what she liked, what it took to send her crashing over the edge.

When we finally collapsed next to each other, both breathing hard, Cat let out a low, smoky laugh, chuckling at the star-strewn sky.

"What?" I demanded, my throat still raw, poking at her side. "What's funny?"

She drew me closer, until my head rested in the crook of her shoulder, my leg slung over both of hers. The warm breeze swept over our bare skin with an almost silky touch, like some gauzy shawl being fondly drawn over us in lieu of covers; as if Lady's Lake, or the Lady herself, approved of what had transpired here between us.

"Oh, I was just thinking how much I had no idea what I was in for when I headed this way," she murmured into my hair, dropping a kiss onto the top of my head. "And it's a rare occasion, when something happens that takes me by this much surprise."

"Or someone," I corrected. "To quote a recent acquaintance, *something* didn't just happen to you. *I*, specifically, happened to you."

"Yes, you did, you totally irresistible, pedantic dryad." Her voice softened, and she ran a hand tenderly down the back of my neck, twining her fingers through my hair. "And I'm so glad you did, even if you did just reduce me to an *acquaintance*. I don't think that's usually defined as 'person with whom you just had a stunning amount of lakeside sex.'"

I rested against her for a long moment, almost afraid to articulate the question that had flared to life right behind my sternum, like a blazing nugget of phosphorus.

"Fair point," I started, licking my lips nervously. "But then again, what else do I call you? I know you stayed for the monsters, to begin with. But . . . but now."

"But now," she agreed. "A different matter entirely."

"Is the Shadow Court expecting you back? Arachne must be, and certainly your mother. Does this . . . do we . . . is there some expiration date here I should know about?"

She sighed, a deep, almost mournful sound, her chest expanding under my cheek. "I have a confession to make, Delilah. Something I haven't been completely honest about."

My already tight chest clamped down even harder, shortening my breath. "What do you mean? What haven't you told me?"

"When we first talked about the Shadow Court, I said I loved it," she began, and I could hear the hesitation in her voice, that deep, hidden sea of vulnerability swimming just beneath. "And I do, to a degree. It's a very intense place to live, and I fit there infinitely better than I did in my mundane life. And I did tell you that Liusaidh's a difficult person, that being her daughter and working with her has always been demanding."

"So where's the lie?" I asked, more tersely than I intended. "Or omission. Whatever you're calling it."

She laughed a little at that. "Where is the lie, indeed. For starters, when I said my mother left me with my father to keep me safe from the Shadow Court, until I was old enough? That was only true in part. The real truth—the truer truth—is that she had no interest in raising a child, even though she wanted one. She didn't want to bother with the boredom, the chore of it. So her plan was always to let my father handle it by himself, and then to come claim me when I was older."

"And she *admitted* that to you?" I said, horrified. Not that the sentiment itself completely shocked me—I imagined even the most devoted mothers found their young children dull sometimes—but to say that openly to your own daughter after having abandoned her for years, let her flail her way through a hostile environment she'd never been meant to navigate alone? And to let someone else carry the burden for you, do all the heavy lifting until you felt ready to claim your living prize?

This Liusaidh of Arachne sounded like a righteous psychopath.

I didn't realize I'd said it out loud until Cat laughed again, the low rasp of it thrumming against my ear. "She more than likely is, by human standards," she said. "Even by fae standards, she's considered . . . sharper than average."

"And she thought you would *forgive* her for that?" I demanded, still reeling. "For leaving you stranded for fifteen years with only your normie father to depend on, because actually raising a child would have been inconvenient and annoying for her? And then turning around and stealing you from him?"

"Well, she knew I'd have no choice but to come around. Who else did I have in the Shadow Court, besides her? And I couldn't go back, not without putting my father in danger; now that it was known that I existed, who I was, I became valuable. Possible leverage against the leader of Arachne. Even if I ran away and tried to live with him, smooth things over, our lives would never have been safe."

"So she forced you to rely on her. Strong-armed you into it, essentially."

"Don't get me wrong," she replied wryly. "I fought her at first. I wouldn't speak to her for months after I arrived at Court, and I *did* try to run away a half dozen times, which was ridiculous, of course. She always caught me before I even reached the city limits.

I only stopped resisting once she explained to me in excruciating detail what would happen to my father if her enemies ever discovered his identity and whereabouts."

"Cat . . ." My insides twisted, knotting around each other. I rubbed my cheek against her shoulder. "I'm so sorry. I can't imagine."

"It wasn't all so bad. Liusaidh is, well, impossibly charming and magnetic, larger than life. Funny, wry, brilliant in so many ways. She's lived a very long time, has a million stories to spin, like a modern Scheherazade. And she took my training into her own hands, made sure we spent enough time together that she'd lodge under my skin eventually. Worm her way into my heart, whether I wanted her there or not."

"So you love her now," I said, unable to keep the skepticism from my voice, tinged with fury on young Cat's behalf. "Even after all that manipulation. Even after the way she used you and your father, like pawns."

"It's complicated," she said, after a long silence. "I can't deny how alike we are, and how much she does love me, in her very particular way. Part of her choice was pure pragmatism—the Shadow Court *is* a dangerous place to grow up, and would have been doubly so for a daughter of hers. And she didn't force my allegiance to Arachne, either. She chose to give me broad training and education instead, so I could align with one of the other clans if I wanted to. They aren't bloodline-driven, the way it is here. You can choose where you fit best."

"What else could you have become?" *Especially after she shaped you into a mini her,* I thought, but didn't say. Even I sometimes managed to recognize a moment that called for a filter.

"I could have pledged to Belladonna, maybe. Healers, poisoners, our version of doctors; I like magical flora, too, like you do. Or I could have chosen Delphi and become an oracle, a soothsayer for hire. There are seven clans, plenty of places where a half cat sith with my various talents might have slotted herself in." She tapped the spider by her eye, tracing its outline. "This could have been a deadly nightshade blossom, or a spiral. But I chose the spider for myself."

"Right."

She shifted against me, picking up on the distress roiling beneath my surface, my unhappiness with her choice. "Is it really that off-putting to you, that difficult to understand? You cast a baneful spell, Delilah, just so you could follow a destiny determined by *your* bloodline. So you could get back the kind of mind that allows you to be a master keeper. Isn't that true? Is it really so different, for me to have chosen to follow in my mother's footsteps?"

"The difference is that my uncle James is *good*," I said, a touch more ferociously than called for, protectiveness bristling in my chest. "And so was my nana Caro before him. I'm following a line of dignified, noble people who care about history and knowledge and preservation, who love books and this town. Not someone like your mother. Someone who sounds like she doesn't care whom she hurts to get what she wants."

"She doesn't care, most of the time. You're right about that." She relaxed a little against me, brushing her lips over my temple until some of the tension bled out of me, too. "And I'm in no big rush to be back in her domain, even if it is home. Which brings us back to your question—how long am I here for? The answer is, as long as I'd like to be. I'm a free agent; I may report to Arachne, but I only take orders from them under specific circumstances."

I nodded, lips pressed together, that lump of phosphorus still burning needily in my chest. "So there's no one else, back home? Waiting for you?"

I could feel the curve of her cheek against my temple as she smiled into the star-pricked dark above us. "No one's currently pining away for me in Chicago, if that's what you're asking. I've had my fair share of lovers at Court, yes. And possibly some who might argue they're still technically mine."

My stomach twisted at the thought, an unaccountable spike of jealousy lancing through me—especially given the way she'd worded it, like those lovers had all belonged to her, but never the other way around. I had no real claim on her, I knew that, regardless of what had happened between us in the short time since she'd gotten here. And how did fae—even half fae—approach relationships, the concepts of monogamy and fidelity? Maybe it ran counter to their essential natures. Cat herself might not have been anywhere near as alien as her mother sounded, but some part of that callousness, that distance from human empathy, had to be embedded in her DNA, too.

It didn't mean that I didn't *want* a claim to her, though. That I didn't already crave her company and closeness, that the idea of her leaving didn't feel like a dark, aching void excavated in my middle.

"But they'd be wrong," she whispered into my curls, winding her arm tighter around my neck. "Because this is where I want to be. Right here, as long as you need me, to protect you and help you solve your mystery. And as long as you want me here. Is that enough of an answer for you?"

"It is," I affirmed, nestling back against her, inhaling that wild-flower perfume of her skin. That green fire in my chest subsiding. "For now."

〉 〉 〉 ● (((

AFTER OUR NIGHT by the lakeside, I did something I'd never done before—I took time off work, to spend uninterrupted with Cat. As my reasoning went, after the basilisk visitation, it was safer at Tomes without me there, anyway. And Nina had the list of wards that needed casting, so she could carry on with the restoration even in my absence while Uncle James looked after the store.

If I tilted my head and squinted at the idea, I could almost trick myself into believing I was being upstanding and cautious instead of hugely self-indulgent.

Regardless, I called in sick for three days; Uncle James was so earnestly sympathetic to my "stomach flu" that I couldn't help but feel a stab of guilt at my desertion, before Cat briskly dispatched it for me with her mouth and hands. We spent the time rolling around in bed, gorging on delivered food, and playing with Montalban. It felt like a precious bubble, a winking, stolen gem of a moment set outside of time. Amazingly, nothing appeared to hunt me; maybe because we didn't set foot outside my apartment, which was so heavily warded it was practically the fun-size version of a magical stronghold.

I'd never felt so close to someone before, especially after we talked for hours, about Cat's life at the Shadow Court and mine in Thistle Grove. She was insatiably curious about our history and traditions, and I wound up playing storyteller much more often than she did. Laying out the family lineages and magical talents, sharing gossip (mostly gleaned from Ivy, since I wasn't exactly an integral component of the Thistle Grove rumor mill) about the scions and their various shenanigans. Explaining how the Grimoire had been written by my ancestor Elias Harlow from the four families' collected spells, the way it served as both a collective resource and a rule book for our community.

"Which is the next one?" she asked, head propped up against my belly as I told her about the Wheel of the Year holidays we celebrated in Thistle Grove, as per the Grimoire. "The way you mark them sounds like something I'd love to see for myself."

"It's Lughnasadh," I said, running her platinum hair through my fingers. Thick as it was, her hair felt impossibly fine when gathered up, like spider silk. "Sometimes called Lammas, but not by us."

"I've heard of it. Some Court members mark the day, especially the ones of Celtic origin, like my mother. It's dedicated to Lugh, yes, the divine blacksmith?"

"That's right. It's on August first, and marks the midpoint between the summer solstice and the fall equinox. We celebrate at Honeycake Orchards, since it's a harvest holiday; there's fresh-baked bread, corn on the cob, about a million fruit pies. Decorative scythes everywhere, and lots and lots of mead and wine. Closes with a huge circle cast by all of us to give thanks for the year's bounty."

"Sounds delicious," she murmured, turning to nibble tantalizingly on my stomach. I squirmed beneath her, but she only pressed her cheek more firmly against me, keeping me in place. "Just like you."

"Stop it," I squealed, awash in tingles—though something tugged at my mind. Something about the juxtaposition of "harvest" and "delicious," as applied to me, specifically. "I'm not for eating."

"You're not?" She blew a raspberry against my belly. "I'll be the judge of that, thank you, after three whole days of taste tests. And according to my criteria, I've determined you to be *very* edible."

I sat bolt upright against the headboard, abruptly dislodging her. She made a disgruntled sound, propping herself up on a forearm to fix me with a puzzled look.

"What? What is it?"

"Edible," I repeated to myself, mind flashing through a series of blinking connections that, in hindsight, seemed blindingly obvious. Goose bumps sprang up along my skin, stippling the disturbing crimson of the flowers that wound around my arms, the cryptic runes that marched between them. "Cat, that's it!"

Her brow crinkled with confusion. "Delilah. What are you talking about?"

"The monsters that have been after me," I started, ticking them off on my fingers. "The succubus, the dhampir, the wraith, the basilisk. What do they all have in common?"

She tipped her head, thinking, until comprehension dawned. "They're all suckers. Cryptids that consume different types of essence. Even the basilisk feeds on human blood, though the fact that its own blood is venomous is the more prominent piece of lore."

"Exactly. And they were drawn to me in particular—so intensely attracted that a handful of them managed to stumble into this town, even though Thistle Grove must be protected against their incursion somehow. But my pull was stronger. Which means . . ."

I met her wide eyes, tendrils of fear crawling like ivy up my throat as I remembered the way Montalban had stared at me when I'd first come home from having cast the Light That Calls for

Blood. That reflected ruby glimmer in her bright black eyes, vivid and disturbing as a captive drop of blood, as if she saw and reflected something that glowed deep down inside me. The way the eglantines had taken a sudden new interest in me in the Sweetbrier Enclave with Ivy; how I'd woken to the shades in the Witch Woods swarming around me in the aftermath of the spell.

"Which means the spell must have left something inside me," I finished shakily. "Something they wanted to consume."

16

>)) ● ((

Inner Tomes

I**S IT GOING** to hurt?" I hated myself for even asking, the piti-
ful note of cowardice curdling my voice like soured milk. Montalban ruffled her feathers in sympathy, making a rueful little *glook*
sound next to my ear.

But there was only warm compassion in Cat's thick-lashed
eyes, no trace of judgment. We were sitting across from each other
on the cerulean-and-cream Turkish rug in my living room, its
lavishly fringed border framed with tiny flowers; a gift my globe-
trotting nana Caro had brought me back from one of her jaunts to
Ankara. Cat had been cupping three small spools of yarn in black,
red, and white in her palms, but she let them rest in her lap as she
reached out to take my hands.

"Not at all," she replied, shaking her head. "Remember, this is
just a different, deeper version of the psychic link we've already

shared. And you felt my presence, right, but it didn't hurt last time."

I nodded, tucking my lips behind my teeth. "It did feel jarring, though."

"By design, because I wanted it to. Needed to shake you out of a succubus stupor, remember? This time, you'll be sharing the experience in me—it'll be immersive for both of us."

"This is my head you're talking about," I cautioned, not loving the way she was making this telepathic sojourn into my brain sound like some zany adventure. We'd agreed that it was the best path forward—to allow her to peer properly into my mind, see if she could discover what the baneful spell had deposited inside me that held such allure for sucker cryptids. Or, rather, Cat had floated the suggestion, and I'd agreed to it only reluctantly, because I didn't see any viable alternative. Even now, she looked a little keyed up, her eyes glistening with anticipatory thrill. "Not a carnival ride."

"Of course. But, all due respect given to the fact that we're going trekking into your head, not mine . . ." She leaned across the space between us, closing the distance with a kiss. "I still think this is going to be more fun than you might expect. Trust me on this."

"I do, but I'd still rather you weren't quite so jazzy about this whole thing." I glanced down at the yarn in her lap, cocking an eyebrow. "Remember when you were screwing with me that first day at Tomes, and mentioned weaving as your 'favorite craft' right before you stole my deck? I'm feeling some of that same energy now."

"Hey, I was being a certain kind of honest that time, was I not?" She tipped me a little mock pout, then held up one hand, waiting for me to rest my palm against hers in midair. "This time, we're both on the same page—no trickery. Remember to keep your breathing even; the same open, meditative flow you'd want for casting. Even with magical assistance, I won't be able to fully dive in without your consent."

"Make like an open book, I got it," I said, still a little testy, pressing my clammy palm against hers. "Let's just do this, Cat, okay? Before I lose my nerve."

"I hear you." She gave my hand one last squeeze, then closed her eyes. "Here we go."

I kept mine open for another moment, just so I could see what she was doing, which was twining the yarn around our joined hands in complex crisscrossing patterns, binding us together with what looked like an impossibly complicated multicolored web. I'd never seen a spell that looked like this before, like a cat's cradle steeped with magic; but, then again, I'd never seen a fae cast any kind of spell. Especially not one of their own workings, not intended for human witches to either wield or understand.

And this one clearly wasn't. Cat's weaving hand moved too quickly for me to track, as she dropped the spools and picked others up, winding them around our clasped hands. As if they were the earth itself, and the yarn a web of tiny ley lines that would let her magic flow through and between us. Her motions were rapid and hypnotic, and despite my misgivings, a deep feeling of relaxation washed over me; decadent and engulfing, like being dipped in some creamy sweetness. The way, I thought to myself as my eyes slid closed, nougat or praline must feel when enrobed in ganache.

The thought was so dreamlike and vivid—I even had a mental flash of a candy nugget slipping under the ripples of a glossy chocolate surface—that it acted like a transition, a seamless segue. One moment, I was staring into the swirling black behind my eyelids . . .

The next, I was standing at the counter of Tomes & Omens, as if Cat had performed a portal spell.

But it *wasn't* Tomes, at least not the version of it that existed in real life. Even though I felt like I was really, physically there, this Tomes was overgrown with ivy and flowers; woody, green-leafed branches sprouted from the shelves, as if the shop had been grafted onto a forest. Magical flora and fungi grew everywhere, pushing their way out from between the books; the blossoms pulsing with color and radiance, their massive leaves drooping over the shelves below. Their cumulative fragrance was almost overpowering, a heady herbal and floral mixture that expanded in my lungs like a dizzying cloud.

Awestruck, I started forward, brushing my fingertip over a fuchsia orchid's lip—and it opened for me as if it had been waiting for my touch, unfurling to reveal a center of glowing, molten gold.

"The recipe for spriteslip healing unguent," I whispered to myself, with a bright spurt of understanding—or *knowing*, rather, as if I'd physically touched a memory. "That's what this one is. They're all recipes!"

I made my way through the shelves, touching flowers and mushrooms, utterly enthralled to discover that the entire catalog of botanical medicine and magic I carried in my head had overgrown the bookstore.

Then the birdcalls came.

My head snapped up, jaw dropping open. Flocks of birds flapped and wheeled and drifted high into the distant gloom of the ceiling; whole legions of them, like a moving mosaic of brilliant plumage. Many, many more than could have fit into the actual store. More even than would have fit into all of Thistle Grove's wide skies. Some were modeled after mundane specimens I saw in the waking world, though even those were bigger and more beautiful than any real bird I'd ever spotted. Others were avian creatures lifted from myth: rocs and griffins and phoenixes.

The only one I couldn't spot, I noted wryly to myself, was a basilisk. Probably because my mind wouldn't allow such an invasion here. And Montalban was absent, too; this deep into my mind, maybe not even my familiar could follow, not without the kind of direct invitation I'd extended to Cat.

"Fucking stunning," Cat breathed from right behind me, as if she'd been at my shoulder this whole time, or as if I'd summoned her with a thought. "Pedantic dryad, *indeed.*"

"Are you doing this?" I demanded, wheeling around to face her, gesturing at the flamboyance flourishing around us. Unlike Tomes, Cat looked exactly like she had in the real world; her angular face bare of makeup, my borrowed T-shirt slipping off her muscled shoulder. "Making my mind look like . . . *this*?"

She shook her head, a corner of her mouth ticking up. "You think I could possibly dream up something like this? No, Delilah. This is what your thoughts look like—what *you* look like, when it comes down to it. Because what are we, if not the sum total of our thoughts and memories?"

"But what do you think the birds are?"

She gave a coy shrug, her gaze flicking up at them as they flew above us, in Vs and lines and spiraling murmurations. "Why don't you call one down and see?"

I lifted my hand, reaching toward that tremendous flock, my focus drawn to a peregrine falcon with glimmering gold-and-silver plumage. As if it sensed my attention, it came diving down, landing painlessly on my extended forearm. As soon as its massive talons curved around my arm, the rhyming couplets to Aurora Rising—a powerful elemental spell from the Grimoire I'd never even attempted to cast myself—floated to the forefront of my awareness.

"They're spells!" I exclaimed, turning to Cat. "Each one of the birds is a memory—*my* memory—of a spell I once read and memorized. So that must mean all these books . . ."

"Exactly." She smiled, her eyes sweeping over the crowded shelves. "They're all your waking memories. The complete collected works of Delilah Harlow."

I looked around the flower-festooned bookstore, brow knitted. "But that would mean all of this belongs here. That it's native to me, not some by-product of the blood spell."

"Whatever's hidden inside you might be elsewhere. Somewhere more secluded, maybe, separate and apart from the rest of you." She frowned, nose wrinkling in thought. "Is there a place like that in Tomes, in the real world? If so, we'd be looking for its equivalent here."

"Yes," I said, my mind leaping immediately to the attic. "Upstairs, where we keep the witch community's private records and treasures, collected over the centuries. We can get up there from the back of the store."

"We're in your domain, so . . ." Cat gestured me forward, like a cavalier, with a sweep of her arm. "Lead the way."

She trailed me through the flower-webbed shelves, so familiar and foreign at the same time. As we neared the winding open staircase in the back that led up to the attic, the quality of the light changed. Where the front of my inner Tomes had been a wash of soft periwinkle, violet, and green emanating from the flora, a ruby flush tinged the back, the red deepening as we came closer to the stairs. Looking up, I could see the same bloody glare outlining the silhouette of the attic door above us. As if some brilliant scarlet light source pulsed behind it, seeping out through the cracks surrounding the door.

I cast Cat an apprehensive look, a wave of trepidation breaking over me. "We have to go see, don't we?" I asked her, swallowing hard.

"We do," she replied, reaching out to thread her fingers through mine. I knew that in real life, our hands were already clasped, bound together with her yarn. But her warm touch felt just as real here, and deeply reassuring.

Whatever was up there, I could stand to face it knowing she'd be next to me.

We clattered up the stairs together, me leading the way, Cat on my heels. In front of the door, the light was so bright and violent it nearly turned my stomach; the exact garish hue I remembered emanating from the Witch Woods' soil, when I'd let my blood drip into the ley line nexus. I paused in front of the door, balking at the idea of throwing it open. I knew somehow that it wouldn't be locked, would instead swing open at my touch.

Eagerly, almost, as if it had been waiting for me to come.

"You can do this," Cat urged, giving my hand a tight squeeze. "I'm with you, all the way."

I nodded shakily, swallowing through a parched mouth. Then I reached out and gave the door a push.

It swung open just as easily as I'd anticipated, opening into an attic that was now a nearly empty room. The shelves of town and family historical records, spellbooks, and unique arcana had all been stripped away, until nothing remained but bare floorboards and the dormer windows—a featureless black looming beyond their glass, an emptiness that looked darker and emptier than mere night.

And where the malefica shelf would have stood in the real world, a massive sphere of scarlet light rotated like a bloody globe, an orb of pulsing magma. The throbbing light it shed spilled throughout the room in irregular ways, as if it were creeping toward us along the floor, halfway between incorporeal and material.

It emanated sound, too, a droning hum that hadn't been audible below, masked by the rustling of leaves and the chorus of birdcalls. But up here, it had an unsettling, electric energy, like the thrum of power lines.

"What the fuck is that?" I whispered, appalled. "All that red. It looks *alive.*"

"It isn't just red, Delilah," Cat corrected, sounding halfway between fascinated and horrified herself. "Look beyond. Look *through* it. There's something suspended inside the sphere."

Squinting, I stared into the center of the globe. As soon as I shifted my focus, my gaze pierced effortlessly through all the vermilion light—and I saw that there *was* something embedded deep within. Something like a jagged shard of onyx floating in the sea of red. Its shape evoked crystal, but it flickered in and out like something immaterial, and its darkness was absolute. A matte black like a sucking void that drew in and obliterated all other light. Like a sliver of a black hole, carved into the shape of a shard.

Now that I was concentrating on it, I could see that the red sphere surrounding it was hollow. It wrapped around the black shard like an encasing shield, or an isolating forcefield keeping the slice of onyx locked away.

Abruptly, Cat let go of my hand and took a few slow steps

forward, her fingers stretched out toward the light, curiosity blazing over her bold face.

"Cat!" I managed in a strangled whisper, too afraid to follow. I wanted to stay as far away as I could from both the red sphere and that terrifying darkness it encapsulated—while I wasn't an expert on doomsday crystals floating in my own head, the fact that it looked like black kryptonite couldn't possibly indicate anything good. "What are you doing?! Don't *touch* that!"

"It's not going to hurt me," she soothed, tossing me a reassuring look over her shoulder. "I know it feels like we're really here to you, but we aren't—this is like a diorama, or a stage. Only a very convincing representation of what's in your mind. When I touch it, I'll really be giving it a psychic sweep, enough to understand what it is. But I won't be touching it in reality; it won't be able to do me any harm. Okay?"

"Okay," I agreed, but only reluctantly, heart still hammering. Part of me deeply, powerfully didn't want to know, to even consider what either of these arcane manifestations were. I'd have given anything to pound back down the stairs and take shelter in the Tomes below, that safe, enchanted bower of luminous flora and fauna and books. "Just . . . be a little careful, please."

"Oh, you know me." She flashed me a smile, tipped a devilish wink. "'A little careful' is practically my middle name."

Then her hand plunged into the vermilion light, its pulsing wash painting her face a disconcerting bloody red.

Prepared as she'd been for this psychic exploration, Cat gasped anyway, her head falling back. "Oh, fuck *me*," she muttered, her teeth clenching. "That . . . that should not be possible."

"What is it?" I called out, shrill with panic. "Cat, what are you feeling?"

"Not now," she managed, waving me off with her free hand. "I have to get through it. To feel what's beyond."

Teeth gritted, she plunged her hand deeper, the muscles of her arm cording with strain, her feet braced against the floor as she pushed forcefully against the light. As if that scarlet coagulation was resisting her, somehow, hampering her progress toward the crystal at the core.

Then, with a final effort, she penetrated it, her fingers grazing the dark shard at the center of the globe.

"Oh," she whispered, giving a full-body shudder as her fingers trailed over its facets. Her face a topography of wonder bathed in pulsing scarlet, laced with incredulity. "Oh, I *see*."

"What is it?" I demanded, halfway pleading. "Cat, just talk to me."

Slowly, she withdrew her hand and backed away from the globe, turning to me. I stepped into her arms, winding mine around her neck, torn between wanting to understand and not wanting to hear any of it.

Because whatever impossibility she'd felt, it was going to change things irrevocably; I knew it in my marrow.

"The red sphere is the ley line nexus," she said, pulling back to shake her head with that wonderstruck disbelief. "The *entire* thing, all of it. It's trapped inside you, shaped into an isolation shield. And that crystal? That's a piece of the oblivion glamour still stuck inside your mind. Like a splinter of a spell."

17

))) ● (((

Blueprint Vibes

I STILL DON'T understand," I repeated woodenly, curling my hands around my mug of hot chocolate, in hopes that some of its heat might seep into my clammy hands. It was shaped like an ivory pumpkin, the handle a dainty curling vine and leaf. The foamy surface was sprinkled with cinnamon in a series of interlocking hearts—a flair of artistry that I couldn't have appreciated less, given the circumstances.

As soon as I'd opened my eyes, Cat and I had blinked back into our own bodies—both of us unexpectedly drained from the mental expedition, me so exhausted and depleted I was trembling. There'd been next to nothing to eat at my place, as usual, so we'd made the short walk to the Wicked Sweet Shoppe on Yarrow for a badly needed infusion of sugary calories.

But I'd barely managed more than a few sips, acidic nausea churning in my stomach. Fear had rimed my insides like blooming frost, belying the summer heat outside the dessert shop's window, decorated with fluttering coils of tinsel, clouds of cotton candy, and bouquets of spun-sugar flowers. It sat in my gut like an ice block, taking up too much space to allow for food.

"Here's what I think," Cat offered, taking another bite of her cookie; she seemed much less thrown than I was, even though she was the one who'd experienced the revelation. Maybe profoundly terrifying shit like bloody orbs and onyx crystals were much more common where she came from. A journey into someone else's floral yet also fucked psyche? Must be Tuesday! "You cast the Light That Calls for Blood, which was meant to heal any damage done to your mind by accessing the power of the nexus, in exchange for an offering of blood. Clearly, the spell didn't work like it should have. Maybe it wasn't strong enough, given that you don't have just damage, residual scarring. An active piece of the oblivion glamour itself—that dark crystal—is still in your mind. Like lodged shrapnel."

I glanced around by instinct, to make sure no normies were around to overhear us. But there was only the bored teen barista with rainbow hair intricately braided away from her temples, slumped behind a counter display of fudge, truffles, and assorted cakes and pastries. So engrossed in her phone and clearly disinterested in our quiet conversation that I didn't bother with casting a privacy charm; spent as I was, even that relatively small piece of magic seemed unduly taxing.

"But how?" I demanded. "And why is it still in there? The glamour was lifted, undone. Why did any of it stay behind?"

"You said that when Nina tried to steal Belisama's stone, she struck you with an oblivion glamour supercharged by the divine favor she'd been granted." I nodded, chewing on a knuckle; I'd been reticent about what had happened to me, but it was one of the things I'd finally shared with Cat during our days of pillow talk.

Cat tapped her lower lip, thinking it through as she spoke. "Possibly that rendered her spell so powerful that even once it was reversed, some part of it found purchase. Like a thorn. And even that splinter was enough to disrupt your mind, too embedded to be healed even by a baneful spell."

"So what do you think happened instead?"

"I think the ley line nexus reacted to your blood, somehow," she said, her eyes flicking back and forth as she stared into the distance over my shoulder, piecing her thoughts together. "So strongly that it attempted to offer an alternative solution—to create a barrier between the disruptive splinter and your mind. So you could function as you once had, with all its power harnessed inside you to keep the residual oblivion locked away."

"But it's a *nexus*," I argued, shaking my head helplessly. "Taking that much raw magic inside me should have killed me. So why aren't I dead, Cat? Why do I feel completely fine—better than fine, even? I lost a ton of blood casting that spell, and I didn't even have to get medical attention after Ivy helped. And I've had more energy, felt more like myself than I have since the glamour happened."

"You're right; you shouldn't have survived that. I've never heard of a transference like this, the shifting of a whole nexus from earth to person." Cat twitched her chin at my red tattoos, the runes winding around them. "I think some bizarre alchemical or metaphysical reaction must have happened."

I pitched my forehead into my free hand, massaging my aching temples. "Like what?"

"I don't know. Something that elevated the blood magic into an even more complex version of itself. If I had to guess, I'd say that having been born a Thistle Grove witch lent you some unusual affinity with that nexus—possibly with all the ley lines that converge here. So, when it poured inside you, it mingled with your living essence; became something part itself, part you. And then the spell sealed it shut inside you by inscribing itself into your skin with runes, turning your ink red."

"To mark me as a living, walking ley line nexus, presumably," I said, bitter as coffee dregs . . . as if I had any right to be. As if I hadn't brought all this onto myself, driven by the miserable, sludgy fuel of hubris and desperation. "In case I wasn't enough of a cryptid beacon already."

"Right. That's what makes me even more sure that some commingling between your essence and the nexus happened. The suckers are drawn to you because they can feel it inside you. Consuming you would let them partake of it, too. Can you imagine a power boost like that, for something like the dhampir or the wraith?"

I shuddered, goose bumps erupting all over my skin. "Frankly, I'd rather not."

Cat glanced pointedly down at my now-lukewarm hot chocolate, the untouched slab of oversized cookie beside it. "Eat, Delilah. You need it."

I took a grudging bite of the cookie and washed it down with the chocolate, though I could barely taste either.

"So what now?" I asked, forcing the gritty lump down past the sudden obstruction in my throat. "What am I supposed to do? How can I go to my uncle with something like this, or to Emmy? This is so much worse than I even thought. I didn't just cast a baneful spell from a forbidden grimoire; I desecrated Thistle Grove. Fucking *stole* part of its magic."

"It's not a great look for you," Cat admitted, shrugging when I fixed her with a glare. "What? I'm backing you up here, because you aren't wrong. Obviously, I don't know your family, how forgiving or flexible they are. And you didn't do this on purpose; it's not like you were *trying* to suck up a nexus like a boba pearl through a straw."

I half choked on my next sip of hot chocolate, scrunching up my face. "That is a truly terrible simile."

"Hey, never claimed to be a poet. I'm just saying, I can see why you'd hesitate to take this to them."

"Then what do I do?" I demanded, the bubble of held-back tears bursting, spilling down my cheeks. "I can't *live* like this, with monsters knocking on my window and falling down the chimney. And I can't just expect you to guard me for the rest of your natural life, however long that even is."

"I can think of worse ways to spend at least the next half century or so," Cat replied with a small, quirked smile. Despite the circumstances, warmth welled in my chest, threaded with a silvery little thrill that she'd find the idea of staying with me for some longish haul so palatable. "But you're right. There are deadlier beasties out there than what we've faced so far—even if they do seem to be slipping in one at a time instead of in a horde, fortunately for us. But we can't keep playing Whac-A-Mole forever."

"And you've already gotten hurt twice. I can't let that happen to you again."

She drummed her fingers on the tabletop, thinking. Wicked Sweet featured an eclectic mishmash of vintage furniture under a bright tangle of fairy lights hung overhead, and ours was a rickety bistro café table with an elaborate wrought iron base that rocked a little from that brisk rhythm. Kitschy wooden signs hung on the walls, informing us in cutesy cursive of imperatives like *Life Is Short, Eat Dessert First!*

It felt, frankly, a little on the nose. Given my circumstances, I probably *should* start considering eating all my desserts first. Maybe even transition exclusively to desserts.

"What if you came with me?" she said, locking her intent verdigris gaze with mine. "To the Shadow Court. We have brilliant adepts there, magical practitioners who are even more skilled than I am at psychic work. And some of them are ancient fae, with many more years of experience than your family or any of the other witches here. They've been around for centuries; one of them will know of a way to safely remove the nexus from you and pry that oblivion fragment out of your head."

I thought about it, gnawing nervously on the inside of my cheek. "Cat, I can't. You know I can't. Whoever we ask for help will want to know about me; what I am, where I come from, how this even happened. I'll wind up serving them Thistle Grove on a platter. And no offense, but from what you've said, members of the Court aren't the kind of people—or creatures—I'd want getting wind of my home. Especially not your mother."

"*I* know about Thistle Grove," she reminded me with a tilt of her head, still keeping me pinned with that direct gaze. "So that makes one member of the Shadow Court who's done nothing but help you."

A sudden flash of apprehension seized hold of me, hot and prickling, like an internal sunburn. I'd essentially spent the last few days telling Cat everything about this town; because I liked her so much, and it had felt like sharing myself with her, showing her the parts of me that mattered most. It hadn't even occurred to me that she might be able to use this information as some kind of Court currency down the line.

"Cat," I began, trying to wrest the swell of panic under control. "You wouldn't tell Liusaidh or anyone else at Court about me without my permission, would you? Or about Thistle Grove? You wouldn't do that."

"Of course not," she soothed, reaching across the table to slide a warm, strong palm over my hand. "Everything I learned about this place—about you—was told in confidence. I wouldn't break your trust that way."

I nodded, forcing myself to relax. Cat had nearly died for me, and after the days we'd spent together, the things we'd told each other, I trusted her. I *did*. But that didn't mean I had to trust the place that had made her.

"I can't," I finally said, with a resolute shake of my head. "It's too risky for Thistle Grove. There has to be something else I can do, some other way to fix this on my own. There's literature on ley lines and nexuses back at Tomes that I've never read; I can start there. And now that I know how the vestigial oblivion glamour is affecting me, maybe I can do my own research on how to eradicate that, too. I can't be the *only* person in all of history something like this has happened to."

Cat nodded slowly, eyes still roaming my face, uncertainty emanating off her. "I wouldn't bet on it. Everything about this gives off a very edge case feel, that once-in-a-millennium type of vibe. But believe me, I understand your reservations. And if anyone can solve this for themselves, it's you."

"I appreciate the vote of confidence." I massaged my temples, venting a frustrated sigh. "Especially given how epically I've been fucking everything up to get us here in the first place."

"Something else we might consider—I still haven't had a chance to look at the *Opes Sanguinis* for myself, or read the spell you used. It might spark something, a better idea."

"That's right." I pushed back, beginning to rise. "So let's just—"

"Oh, I think not." In a flash, she lunged over the table and grabbed my arms, gently pressing me back down into my seat. "First, you finish the consumption of restorative calories. Then, we discuss next steps."

"You are not the boss of me. *Ma'am.*"

"Maybe not." She smiled, a slow, voluptuous curving of those fine lips so suggestive it made my cheeks ignite, despite everything. "But I think we can agree I tend to generate some very compelling ideas. And persuasive plans of action."

"Are you talking dirty to me while I eat sugar cookies on command?"

"Well." She caught her lower lip between her teeth, smiled through it. "I guess you could say I'm not *not* doing that."

"If you think double negatives count as flirting, I have unfortunate—"

My voice trailed off as I caught sight of a purple shimmer sparkling to life behind Cat, right near the middle of the store, swirling in midair like the shaken glitter inside a kaleidoscope. As I watched, it whipped up into a column of bright violet smoke—a purple so pretty and vivid that, to my botanist's eye, it immediately registered as "probably poisonous."

Then it vanished, to reveal a female figure nearly seven feet tall.

A long serpent's tail lay curled in coils beneath her, its iridescent scales scattering up the lithe stretch of her lower belly before they melted into taut green skin. A faint, glimmering trail of them traversed her muscular abdomen, circling it in spiral patterns, ending in a shining, lacy, sculpted spill of scales over her high breasts, like built-in lingerie. Her hair was a tumble of auburn and dark brown, glossy as chestnuts and coiled around her head—but its strands *writhed*, as though each separate lock might be alive, part tentacle, part hair.

A silver circlet sat low on her forehead, its inset opal pulsing above huge almond-shaped eyes with orange irises and slitted pupils, set in a face that was a stomach-dropping mix of woman and snake. Carved cheekbones jutting above gaunt cheeks; vertical slits in lieu of a nose; plush lips a deep emerald against the paler jade of her skin.

The fact that she was close to beautiful, an alien grotesqueness that somehow neighbored on stunning, only chilled me that much more.

A musty smell drifted from her, dry and dusty and clearly reptilian, triggering every scrabbling prey instinct in my own lizard brain. In turn, her own nostrils flared wide as if she'd caught some enticing scent, her head cocking sharply before swiveling to focus on me.

"Oh, fuck," I muttered under my breath, already rising, my chair scraping back with a whining screech. My heart felt like it had ballooned into a triple-sized version of itself, a frantic, fleshy lump heaving itself against my ribs. "Cat, behind you! A lamia!"

A lamia, because I hadn't thought to ward the dessert shop. I'd been exhausted, there hadn't been any supernatural assaults in days, and it had somehow slipped my mind that Wicked Sweet was neither Tomes nor my magical fortress of a home.

And now here we were, because of yet another of my stupid, egregious mistakes. Faced with yet another deadly creature torn from the pages of a mythological bestiary.

From what I remembered, lamia preferred the blood of children; based on the lore, I'd been under the impression that this was, in fact, their exclusive diet. But from the intent way she'd homed in on me—those reptilian eyes narrowing, lips parting in a smile that revealed a set of glistening snake's fangs so long their vicious tips sank into the pillow of her lower lip—they clearly weren't the picky eaters the myths made them out to be.

Cat sprang into action, whirling to face the creature, her double-sided blades appearing in her hands like battle magic. But before she could move, the normie barista rushed out from behind the counter, brandishing her phone—a look of sheer delight stamped over her thin, overly contoured little face. Beneath the spackled makeup, she couldn't have been more than sixteen or seventeen, and the way she was admiring the lamia glowed with the kind of childlike wonder I associated with much younger kids.

And she was about to get herself killed.

"Holy *balls*, you look amazing!" she squealed, fake-lashed eyes alight as she positioned her phone to take snaps of the increasingly bewildered lamia, who'd screwed her unnerving face into a distinctly human expression of bemusement and disdain. Like, *What in the divine shit is this dimwit mortal even* doing *right now?*

Apparently even cryptids didn't appreciate the Insta paparazzi crew.

Caught up in her phone, the barista clearly hadn't witnessed that brief gush of violet smoke, or the way the lamia had manifested in the store. That would've been an obvious display of magic, the kind of thing that triggered the town-wide oblivion glamour automatically, inducing a vague, perplexed haze before erasing the relevant memory. Instead, this unfortunate normie thought she was seeing a person decked out in elaborate costume and makeup—a sight, in her defense, not all that unusual in Thistle Grove.

"That's gotta be the best cosplay I have ever seen," she gushed, holding her phone high above her head to capture a different angle. "Giving those fucking *blueprint* vibes, girl! Like, who are you supposed to be, though? I don't—"

With a disgruntled hiss, the lamia flicked her tail in the girl's general direction; more a swipe at an irritant than a concerted attack, like a horse swatting away an obnoxious fly. But the tip of her tail caught the girl directly in the sternum, and even without any true malicious force behind it, it was enough to lift her off her feet and sweep her into the counter, the force of the impact shattering the glass.

With a shrill scream that stopped as if it had been severed as soon as she struck the display case, the girl tumbled to the floor.

Dislodged pastries rained over her sprawled form like some macabre homage, blood trickling from her nose. The disjointed arrangement of her limbs suggested broken bones—if not something worse, from the way her skull had knocked against the ground.

The sight of her, that sheer vulnerability—the bright spill of rainbow hair spreading around her head; how excited and urgently alive she'd been, only moments before; the way she'd bothered to sprinkle cinnamon hearts onto my hot chocolate for no reason at all—ignited a white-hot rage in me. Like the fiery tongue of a solar flare, or the initial licking blaze of a star that had been hovering on the precipice of going supernova.

Even as Cat rushed toward the lamia with glinting blades at the ready, I spread my feet and braced myself, incanting one of the most aggressive spells I'd been rehearsing during Cat's recovery, when I'd thought I might have to fend for myself alone.

At my behest, a river of what looked like quicksilver coursed across the floor, rushing toward the lamia. It forked around Cat, avoiding her entirely, then sluiced back into a single stream right in front of the cryptid. As soon as it touched her, it pinned her to the ground, that reflective flood surging up the stacked coils of her tail and her human-looking torso, until it had spread all the way up her throat.

Its advance was so don't-blink-or-you'll-miss-it quick that before the lamia could eke out so much as a single screech of protest, it had closed over her head and crystallized her in place.

Where she'd stood, there was now a sculpture that looked like it had been poured from glass. It captured the lamia down to the last fine detail—her arms flung out in alarm, lips parted and fangs exposed, eyes wide with shock—but instead of scales and skin there was only a glassy surface that reflected the store. Like some bizarre novelty mirror no one sane would want to bring home.

If I was being honest, I might have admitted to taking *some* inspiration from Nina's handling of the basilisk.

"Damn," Cat exhaled, letting her blades drop. "Well done."

"I'm *not* done," I snarled through gritted teeth, that inferno of rage still crackling through me, setting my nerve endings alight. I swept over to the lamia, picking up one of the bistro chairs on my way. Then I raised it high and brought it down on her head with all my might—shattering her brittle form into a shower of broken glass.

18

Fault Lines

OSSING THE CHAIR aside, I rushed over to the fallen barista and dropped to my knees next to her, picking up her limp hand in search of a pulse. I let out a shuddering breath once I finally felt her heartbeat ticking under my fingers, even if thready and irregular. I didn't like how clammy her skin was, either, pale and beaded with the chilly sweat that accompanied shock. But at least she was alive. That was something.

More than I deserved, at any rate.

"Delilah," Cat said a moment later, a strong hand settling on my shoulder. "This isn't our problem. It *can't* be our problem."

"What the hell do you mean, it's not?" I ground out. "It's by definition our problem—or mine, at least. I forgot to ward the store, Cat. I just . . . forgot. That's how that shitty motherfucking blood snake got in here in the first place."

"And now said motherfucking blood snake is a pile of broken glass on the floor," Cat pointed out. "How are you going to explain *that* to the paramedics when they get here? What exactly are you going to say happened here, besides you, me, and a wicked sweet helping of aggravated assault and battery?"

"The paramedics are on their way?"

"I already called 911—they'll be here in under ten minutes. And there's nothing else we can do for her, anyway. You need to cast an oblivion glamour on her, make absolutely sure she doesn't remember either the lamia or us. And then, Lilah, we need to clear the fuck out before anyone finds us here."

I knelt for a moment, struggling with myself. I was responsible for this girl; I felt the cavernous echo of that certainty resonating all the way down to my soul. If it hadn't been for my carelessness, my abysmal, unforgivable lapse of judgment, this helpless normie wouldn't be here, broken and bleeding on the glass-strewn floor, beneath saccharine signs urging us to do such compelling things as *Stop and Lick the Brownie Batter*.

"I forgot, too, Lilah," Cat said, pitching her voice softer, sensing the roiling depth of my distress. "I could have reminded you to cast wards, and I didn't, did I? We were both tired, and tired people make mistakes."

"Not like this," I said, with a furious shake of my head. "Not bad ones like this."

"Well, you won't help her by wallowing, or getting tossed in jail while the police decide what to do with you—and with me, for that matter, since I'm obviously not leaving you. And you're not a Thorn. Unless I'm misunderstanding how your magic works, you can't knit her bones back together for her. Or mend whatever might be going on in her skull."

Cat was right, as much as I bristled at that inhuman pragmatism, the lack of an instinctive empathic response to someone else's hurt. But I *wasn't* really a healer, not without my magic-imbued tinctures and unguents. There was almost nothing I could do for her—and even if I did let myself get led away in handcuffs to the poky little building that passed for Thistle Grove's police station, the only thing I'd be achieving would be putting our police force at risk of anything that might manifest in search of me while I was trapped behind bars.

Bowing my head, I brought my hands together above the girl's forehead, and whispered as gentle an iteration of the oblivion glamour as I could muster. Making sure she'd remember all of the afternoon before Cat and I arrived, but nothing after, which wouldn't ring any alarm bells with her medical team. With a traumatic head injury like this, some memory loss would be normal, expected.

"Alright," I said, standing reluctantly, my head swimming from the exertion of having cast even that relatively small glamour. "Let's go home. I need to pack."

Something indecipherable sifted across the bold planes of Cat's face, like a fine thread of wind whisking through prairie grass. "Wait, what?"

"You were right," I said grimly, striding toward the door as she fell into step beside me. Trying to harden myself against the sound of the girl's labored breathing behind us, the fact that we were leaving her all alone on the glass-strewn floor until the paramedics arrived. "I can't stay here. I can't keep carrying on like this, exposing other people to danger. It's too stupid, too selfish. So I'll throw my things together, get Montalban, and then I'm coming with you to Court."

))) ● (((

"So THIS IS what it really looks like up here," Cat said, gaze skimming over the crammed contents of the Tomes attic. I'd been trying to impose some semblance of order on it since I'd begun taking over for Uncle James, but I'd been dealing with centuries of accumulated books and artifacts, and a long series of previous keepers much more interested in the acquisition of knowledge than its organization. "A lot more stuff and dust than in the version you're carrying around in your head."

"Fewer blood globes and sinister floating crystals, though. Points for that."

Cat had wanted to stop at Tomes before we left town, to fetch the *Opes Sanguinis*; my huge duffel bag and the one small roller suitcase I owned were packed and waiting for us below, along with Montalban, roosting in her travel cage. I'd balked at the thought of removing one of Tomes' books—hadn't I already done enough damage to not only my town, but specifically my family's legacy, without tacking on book theft?—but she'd insisted that whichever Court adept took on the task of clearing out my mind and removing the nexus would want the spellbook at hand. They'd need an understanding of the specific spell I'd used to establish the baseline, she'd said, along with the rest of the grimoire for context. I could always return it once I came back.

I'd reluctantly agreed, only because it made a compelling amount of sense. I'd have wanted a reference point, too, if I were going to be rummaging through some random afflicted witch's head. And if this worked, I'd hopefully be home before anyone missed it, or me, anyway.

"What all is up here?" Cat asked, as I moved to the malefica shelf. "It doesn't feel the same as downstairs. More . . ."

"Magical?" I offered, lifting my cupped palms for the key-summoning spell. "That's because it is. We store all the rarest and more powerful spellbooks and arcana up here, along with records of any magical or founding family–related events since the town's inception."

I murmured the charm, and the three filigreed keys winked into existence, hovering with their usual glimmer before they dropped into my waiting hands.

"Cool," Cat remarked, lifting an eyebrow. "But is it strictly necessary to be snatching invisible keys from thin air? Or is it at least seventy-eight percent for effect? Be honest."

"It's *mostly* practical. The alternative is walking around carrying them on my person at all times—they're for the baneful spellbook shelf. Wouldn't want anyone else to be able to get their hands on them."

I fit the keys into the series of locks and chanted out the unlocking charm, steeling myself for that low, malevolent susurrus I'd heard the last time I opened the malefica bookcase. But the books were oddly quiet, emanating an aura of restrained hostility—as if they could sense a stranger's presence here, and wanted even less to do with Cat than they had with me.

But the *Opes Sanguinis*, when I found it and drew it from its slot on the shelf, felt precisely, awfully the same. Slimy and unnerving, somehow both malignant and aware. Touching it felt like a terrible reminder of everything I'd done, the ruinous trail of mistakes I'd left in my wake. The enormity of my poor judgment staggered me—would have overwhelmed me if I hadn't known

Cat was right there, as she'd been from the beginning, committed to supporting and helping me.

"Can I see it?" she said softly, as if she could sense the groundswell of my emotion. "You don't look like you're enjoying holding it."

I turned to her, blinking back a sudden sear of tears. "You're right about that," I said roughly, pressing the book into her hands. "Touching it . . . it's horrible."

I expected a similar shudder of revulsion when her fingers closed around it. But if anything, the book simmered down at her touch, went oddly quiescent. And the look on her face wasn't a mirror of my own disgust; it was closer to the opposite. In fact, I could see the strangest, faintest glimmer of something like relief in her eyes, distant but luminous like the first tendrils of dawn gathering on the horizon.

Then it vanished, and she was watching me with a furrowed brow, concern etched across her sharp features. "You okay? Ready to go?"

I nodded, biting at the inside of my lower lip. "Yes," I whispered, though my voice unraveled just a little. "I guess I have to be. And Cat . . . thank you."

"Oh, Delilah, for what?"

"I don't know. Everything, I guess. Being here for me at every turn. Fighting monsters on my behalf, like some kind of knight errant. Offering to help even more, to take me to Court." I pressed my lips together, tucked them behind my teeth so I wouldn't fully cry. "I just . . . no one's ever stuck by me like this before, Cat. Even Ivy couldn't go this far for me. So I want you to know how much I appreciate it. How grateful I am for you."

I dropped my eyes, struggling with the words I wanted to say, each of them heavy as a stone. Too heavy for me to keep inside, but almost equally grueling to speak aloud.

"I know it's so early between us," I said, low and hoarse. "Believe me, I know. This . . ." I let out a soft, incredulous laugh, shaking my head. "This has to be the most un-me thing I've ever done in my entire life. But I *have* to say it; I have to tell you. I think I'm falling in love with you, Cat. Or, at least, I think that I'm going to, soon. And I need to know . . . is that okay with you?"

She stared at me for a moment in utterly blank silence, those exceptional eyes shifting between mine, the dim light of the attic lamps igniting their green depths with an eerie, sprite-like glow. As if to underscore the difference between us, how beautiful yet inhuman a part of her was. That silence expanded between us, pooling and then gelling until it turned both chilling and pervasive, the pit of my stomach going cold in response.

"Cat," I whispered, my mouth so dry I could hear myself swallow. "Say something. It's . . . it's okay if you say no. I just need to hear it from you."

Her face fractured like a fault line, something like grief mingled with guilt seeping through the cleft it left behind.

"*Fuck,*" she spat, half under her breath, as if she were speaking more to herself, the book clutched fiercely to her chest like a life vest. Like something she was using to keep herself afloat. "I can't fucking do this, can I? I can't go through with it, after all."

"Cat?" I tilted my head, reached for her; fighting a rising tide of panic, as if a storm were brewing in my insides. *Red sky at night, sailors' delight,* my mind chimed inanely at me. *Red sky at morning, sailors take warning.* "What are you talking about?"

Before I could touch her, she turned sharply away from me and collapsed into the pilled brown couch shoved into a corner of the attic. But in slow motion, somehow, as if she were wilting. Bowing under the crushing weight of whatever had broken over her.

"I lied to you," she said, toneless. Book clutched to her chest, eyes pinned to the floor. "I lied about a lot, Delilah. A whole fuckload of a lot."

"What," I said, hollow, more statement than question. The attic felt like it was tilting vertiginously around me, like I might lose my footing without even taking a single step. "What do you mean?"

"There wasn't any succubus," she said, still scrutinizing the floorboards. "I mean, there was, obviously. But I wasn't tracking one in Chicago; I had no idea one was going to attack you until it did. And I doubt she used any kind of future sight to find you, either—she probably just happened to be close to Thistle Grove when you cast the spell. I came here because of *you*, Delilah. Because of you, and this fucking book."

"But . . ." I shook my head, trying to understand, "how did you even know I had it?"

She relinquished her hold on the grimoire with one hand, burying her fingers into her hair, giving it a short, brutal tug. "It's a long story. Long and convoluted and fairly shitty, like most of mine tend to be. The short of it is, Arachne isn't a clan of monster hunters like I told you. Nothing so upstanding as that, I'm afraid. What we are is mercenaries of every stripe, known for subtlety. Swords for hire, assassins, thieves, procurers . . . name your need. And I'm not just sworn to Arachne, Delilah. I'm Liusaidh's second-in-command."

"Even if . . . even if that's true." I took a deep breath, trying not to spin wholly out of control. My mind felt like a room in which someone had forgotten to close a window before a storm, fierce winds whipping through and overturning furniture, tossing books and papers haphazardly to the floor. "What does any of that have to do with me?"

"My mother owes a favor to a very old fae," she replied, her fine mouth twisting. "The head of the Shadow Court. He goes by Steven Ahto in the mortal world, but that isn't his true name. He's terrifying, the oldest, most cunning creature I've ever met. I don't know what happened between him and my mother, but even *she's* afraid of him. So when he called in the favor—tasked her with finding the *Opes Sanguinis*, a grimoire of fae blood spells that had disappeared from the Court's library—she assigned it to me. Her daughter. Her trusted second."

"So the *Opes* is a fae spellbook," I repeated, trying to wrap my mind around any of this, even as my insides crumbled like a sandcastle besieged by the tide. That explained why the grimoire came with none of the usual attributions to spellsmiths or aggregators; it hadn't been written by or for human witches. I remembered the chorus of alien whispers that had started up when I began casting the spell, its unnervingly unfamiliar language, the way it had left a metallic, rusty taste in my mouth like no other casting ever had. It had probably only appeared to be written in Old English as camouflage, to conceal its true origins.

But how had I even been able to cast a fae spell in the first place?

"When did all this begin?" I asked her. "When did you start looking for it?"

"Almost a year ago. I have no idea why Ahto wanted it just then. The library is massive; it could be no one had even noticed it had gone missing before he needed it. I'd been chasing down dead ends, turning up fuck all. So I also cast a finding weave just in case, to cover my ass. I set it up to ignite at regular intervals, perform a sweep every week or so—it would alert me only if someone used a spell from the book, rendered it active and therefore findable. You can't magically locate an inert grimoire."

"But you arrived in town before I ever even used the *Opes*," I challenged, still not wanting to believe any of it. "How can that be?"

"Remember what I said about scrying?" she said miserably. "When I was pretending that tracking the succubus led me here? That part was true. A finding weave can look ahead, but only by a little—and the tremendous flare of energy you released when you cast the Light That Calls for Blood triggered it. It gave me just enough information to be able to track you here before you actually cast the spell, but not any more than that."

"So that's why you stole that deck to create a psychic link between us that first day. It wasn't for my protection against monsters you didn't even know would be coming for me—it was so you'd know when I *did* cast it." I remembered the brief flash of her I'd felt in my head while I was engulfed in the bloody deluge of the spell in the Witch Woods. "Why bother waiting? Why not just, I don't know, kidnap me or something as soon as you got here? Torture me, make me tell you where the grimoire was?"

Her nostrils flared, mouth tightening. "Those would be my esteemed mother's methods, not mine. I prefer . . . not to work under such conditions."

"Oh, a mercenary with *workplace standards*," I spat at her, rage boiling up as I suddenly remembered the times she'd casually mentioned examining the grimoire, always framing it as a favor to me. "How OSHA compliant of you. How *honorable.*"

"I don't recall ever once claiming to be honorable," she replied, with a listless shrug. "So at least we can't count that as a strand in my tangled web. And I knew the grimoire had to be here somewhere, but I assumed a witch would know how to keep something like that well hidden, so why bother with brute force? The finding weave can only scry a short stretch into the future, anyway. All I had to do was have a little patience."

"Then why didn't you come as soon as I'd cast the spell?" I demanded. "Why wait until the succubus attacked me?"

"Because the expended energy when you cast the Light was *enormous.* I wanted to know how a human witch was even able to cast a fae spell, and what it had done to you—I wanted to see what would happen. The succubus showing up only confirmed my suspicion that something beyond the pale had transpired at the casting."

"So why admit you were fae in the first place? And why lie about Arachne's business, bother with the whole monster-fighting charade?"

"You'd have noticed the difference in me yourself, eventually— better to build up goodwill by offering you part of the truth up front. That's how effective deception works." She flicked a shoulder in a shrug. "I needed you to trust me, to be willing to hand over the *Opes* once it was time. You're not really very hard to understand, Delilah. When it came to my allegiances, I knew you'd need at least the appearance of integrity to sway you. And then came the dhampir, the wraith . . . it was increasingly clear that you yourself had become somehow special. I was hoping we might get to the bottom of it here, before I brought you to Court."

"Before you . . ." I repeated, a terrible knowing opening up inside me like a sinkhole. "You always intended to bring me back with you, didn't you? Long before you suggested it today."

"Yes," she said simply. "One way or another, you were coming with me. The book would have fulfilled my mother's obligation to Ahto, but you? A witch who had somehow affected an entire nexus, who drew creatures like a beacon? A witch who came from a magical town we'd never heard about, fueled by a sunken goddess in a lake? You would have been a colossal prize, a gift to him. A way to raise Arachne, and especially my mother and myself, in his very fickle esteem."

"And you would have really done it?" I asked, sickened. *"Given* me to him, like I wasn't a person at all? Just a thing, something you could use?"

She looked away, a muscle in her square jaw jumping under her skin. "Courtiers live and die by Ahto's regard, Delilah. I couldn't pass up that kind of opportunity. And it's not like he would have hurt you; you'd have been valued as a precious resource. He'd have . . . he'd have treated you well. Or at least, carefully."

Abruptly, all the will I had to stay standing evaporated in a puff, a wave of fatigue and enervating sadness washing over me. Moving slowly, as if my bones had become achingly brittle, I lowered myself to the floor and knelt, my feet splayed behind me.

"How could I not have seen this coming?" I whispered, putting both hands over my face. "Why did I ever even trust you? How could I have let myself, once I knew you were part fae? Even fucking Nina Blackmoore knew something was off with you!"

"Don't blame yourself too hard," she said, both bitter and wry. "It wasn't completely your fault. I wove an enticement weave for you. The bracelet, the one I wore that first day? It was made for you, designed to lower your defenses. To make you more receptive to me."

"So you, you *brainwashed* me?" I let out a harried, half-hysterical laugh, so stunned by the depth of her treachery, her immense betrayal, that I almost didn't know what to do with myself. I had trusted her; I'd trusted her with *everything*, with more of me than anyone else had ever gotten. And everything between us had been lies stacked upon lies, built on an ever-shifting foundation of quicksand. "Just like the succubus did."

"Not like that. If you hadn't been primed to be responsive—if you hadn't found me attractive all on your own—it would never have worked. It just softened you, that's all. Made you more open, more willing to do what you'd have wanted to do anyway."

"If you think splitting hairs is going to make me hate you any less for manipulating my senses without my consent," I said through gritted teeth, lifting my head with an effort, each sharp word tasting like poison, "then you're lying to yourself even more than you have to me."

She flinched at that, as though I'd really wounded her. As if she were even capable of being hurt. "I don't think that. You have every right to hate me—how could I expect anything else? And I . . . fuck, I'm sorry, Delilah. I'm so, so sorry. Please believe at least that much."

"Why would I believe anything you said to me, ever again?"

"Because I didn't have to tell you any of this," she said levelly, regaining a fraction of her composure. "You were ready and willing to come to Court with me, of your own accord. If I'd just kept my mouth shut like a good soldier, we'd have been there by midnight. You would have presented yourself to Ahto of your own volition, unsuspecting."

"Then why drop the act? Why tell me anything now?"

"Because—as it so fucking inconveniently turns out—I *care* about you!" she burst out, so agonized my head snapped up. Her eyes were shimmering with tears, their glaze casting her eyes an almost garishly eldritch green. "And I can't have this, you, on my conscience. I do have one, no matter what you might think. Enough of one, at least, that I just . . . I can't do it. I can't let him have you, not even for Arachne. Not even for my mother."

I looked away, unable to stand any evidence of her pain. She didn't have any right to it, not after what she'd done to me.

"Was everything lies?" I asked her, low. "What you told me about your father, the way you grew up? The way your mother stole you, how you felt about her? And all those . . . all those hours, in bed with me?"

"No," she said shortly, pain flickering over her face. "Every word of that was true. Every touch. And, Delilah, I didn't lie about the rest of it, either. The way you took care of me . . . no one else has done that for me, ever. I've never felt what I feel for you, not for anyone else. If I had any real choice, please know that I'd choose this. Being with you."

Whatever buttress was still holding fast inside me abruptly gave way. Even now—even after everything—the fact that I was about to lose the only person I'd ever fully opened up to gutted me, left me feeling like all my innards had been hollowed out. Not even this hard, sparkling new hatred that had sprouted inside me, sharp and jutting as a cluster of quartz, could compete with that sweeping sense of loss.

"But you're still leaving," I croaked, swiping my hand over my face. I'd started leaking tears without even realizing it, and I succeeded only in smearing wet and salt all over myself. "You're really going to go back, to *them*."

"I have to," she said in a ragged whisper. "You don't understand. If I don't deliver at least the *Opes* to Ahto, he'll kill Liusaidh. It's that kind of debt she owes him. And she's my mother, Delilah. I do love her, even if she can be terrible."

"But, after that. What if I said . . ." I gritted my teeth, feeling so far beyond pathetic I barely recognized myself. "What if I said I wanted you to come back? Despite . . . despite everything?"

"You do not want that," she said quietly, rising from the couch with one lithe movement, her own skim of tears still shining in her eyes. "That girl, at the dessert shop? She's hurt because of me, not you. I knew you hadn't set wards, and I didn't remind you on purpose. I couldn't be sure, but I was hoping something would come for you. Give you that final, extra push, to convince you to leave with me."

"No." I shook my head, still blubbering into the back of my hand. "You wouldn't . . ."

"Sacrifice a mundane, for something that needed doing?" She shrugged, arms crossed tightly over the grimoire. "Apparently I would. Apparently I'm not that encumbered with a conscience, even if the scrap of it I have won't let me see you hurt."

I let my head fall forward, too overwhelmed to withstand any more revelations from her. "So you're terrible, too," I said, faintly. "Like your mother. You said Arachne were swords for hire, assassins, thieves. Which are you? Or are you all three?"

"I won't murder for money," she said, mouth tightening. "But yes, I will fight for it. Mostly I've been a very talented procurer. I have a gift for convincing people to part with precious things. Usually with minimal bloodshed, even."

"You know, all things considered, maybe you're worse than your mother," I mused, in an acidulated tone, "because part of you is human. Part of you should at least *want* to be better than this."

"Maybe it does—and maybe that part of me is why I'm going to tell you one more thing. As a farewell gift." She paused on her way to the attic door, shifting her weight. "I think I *do* know why you still have that splinter of oblivion stuck in your mind. Tell me, did it get worse when Nina started working at Tomes to help you restore the wards? When you started seeing her so much more often?"

With an effort, I cast my mind back to when my symptoms had exacerbated. "It *did*, actually. How could you know that?"

"Because I felt it. It's your own will holding it in place, Delilah. The scar tissue of your trauma. I'd bet that initial lodged splinter was tiny, an insignificant shard that would have melted away on its own. But your fury, your loathing of Nina—those emotions fed it, until it grew into something potent. And now, the fact that you can't forgive her is what's keeping it stuck."

"So all I have to do is, what, find some forgiveness in my heart for her? That sounds invented. Like fairy-tale bullshit."

"I expect it'll probably be slightly more complicated than that, but at least you know where to start." She hesitated for another instant, lingering by the door. "I won't tell them anything. Not about you, or Thistle Grove. I'll spin some other tale for Ahto, about where I found this forsaken book. So you don't have to worry about Courtiers darkening your door. I swear it, upon my life. For whatever it's even worth to you."

I blinked at the floor, then swung my head up one last time. Feeling dazed and staggered, drunk on too many conflicting drafts of emotion. "How do I know you're not lying about that, too?"

"A very good question, Delilah Harlow." Cat smiled, desperately, infinitely sad, twitching one shoulder in a resigned shrug as she eased the door open. "I guess you'll just have to take my flimsy word for it."

19

Your People

IBARELY REMEMBERED slogging back to my apartment, with my luggage and Montalban in tow. The hurt was colossal, catastrophic, like some natural disaster had been unleashed on my insides and allowed to rage untrammeled. I'd shed my spiny carapace for Cat, peeled it off and set it aside. And she'd lied and lied and lied, and then left me, anyway.

My newly tender, unshelled self wasn't sure how I would survive so much deceit and manipulation. Especially given how completely I'd let myself fall for it.

I sobbed on my bedroom floor for hours, crying myself hoarse—leaving poor Montalban so miserably distraught that she'd been fussing over me incessantly, picking up strands of my hair in her beak and pressing her head frantically into my cheek, grief-stricken that nothing she did seemed to offer me any solace—before I finally broke down and texted Ivy.

You were right.
I'm so sorry.
I need you.
Please come. Please.

And she came; of course she came. Even after the way I'd disappointed her, Ivy Thorn didn't have it in her to hold a grudge when even her prickliest, most difficult best friend pled for help. I fell into her arms as soon as the door swung open; collapsed into her, let myself sob into her shoulder with a fierce, shameless, unrestrained fervor I'd never given into before.

"I'm so sorry I chose her," I kept repeating through tears. "When you were right there, *asking* me to trust you, telling me I could. I shouldn't have—"

"It doesn't matter," she soothed, palms pressed flat to my back, supporting me even though I was nearly half a head taller. "I shouldn't have said some of what I said, either. Everyone got a little too heated. We'll talk it through later, honey. We both owe each other some grace—though, yeah, more you than me. For now, let me make you some amnesty tea, and then you're gonna tell me exactly what went down with that alley cat."

"THAT VICIOUS, LYING *bitch*," Ivy spat when I finished telling her everything, so uncharacteristically venomous I twitched a little where I was lying with my head nestled in her lap. The promised amnesty tea had been drunk, and was now sloshing warmly in my stomach. I was so thoroughly cried out I felt almost clean, as though I'd been scoured of the sharpest and most violent of my high emotions. It wouldn't last—this was just a temporary oasis of emptiness—but the pain had been so intense I was grateful for even a momentary reprieve. "I never trusted her shifty ass."

"You never even really *met* her," I pointed out. "Not when she was conscious, anyway."

"I'm a Thorn, honey. Taking someone's moral temperature is our thing. And I healed her, remember, which means I had to go wading knee-deep in her highly suspect vibes. I'm telling you, she even *felt* slippery."

"That's . . ." I wrinkled my nose, laughing thinly despite myself. "Ew."

"Just calling it like it is." She paused, running her fingers pensively through my curls. "Partial credit to her, though. She at least halfway did the right thing, in the end. Came clean with you, snatched only a spellbook that it sounds like we're well rid of anyway. That does count for something, if you ask me."

"But will she keep her word? Not tell anyone at Court about me, our town? Ivy, I couldn't stand it if something happened to Thistle Grove because of me."

She smoothed my hair, humming thoughtfully. "We'll cross that shitty bridge when we come to it, and hopefully we'll never have to. No sense in borrowing trouble. And in the meantime, I think you know what I'm going to say next."

I sighed deeply, heaved myself upright. "I may have some unfortunate idea."

"It's past time to go to your uncle, Lilah. You know it is." She fixed me with a clear, unflinching gaze, her dark eyes warm in the lamplight. "Now that you know you're capable of it, it's time to start trusting the right people. *Your* people."

))) ● (((

IN THE YEAR since I'd all but taken over Tomes, I'd started thinking of Harlow House—the Harlows' modest family demesne, a handsome but unassuming colonial in an otherwise normie residential neighborhood—as my second home. Or third, presumably, since I spent more time at Tomes than I did anywhere else. In any case, a place I felt much more comfortable than my own parents' house.

I'd certainly never been as shaky and off-kilter here as I was tonight, my jangling nerves at stark odds with the comfortable atmosphere of the eclectic, cozy library. Soft light trickled from the charming punched-tin ceiling fixture and spilled warmly over the Chantilly parquet, glossy chestnut bookshelves, and mismatched slouchy furniture chosen for comfort. Even the hearth seemed somehow inviting despite its unlit darkness, the mantel scattered with lovingly framed photos of James, Cecily, and Emmy. Even a few shots of Emmy and me when we were little and apprenticing at Tomes together, half adoring, half hating each other as we jostled for James's favor.

Or thought we did, anyway. The more I got to know him as an adult, the more I thought it much likelier that he'd always made ample room for both of us, and that any competitive energy had been generated only by the friction between my cousin and me.

Seeing Uncle James now, watching me with those unfailingly kind brown eyes, pierced my heart. He sat across from me with an ankle propped on the knee of his other lanky leg, lamplight shining off his beatnik glasses. Even on what I assumed had been a quiet evening before I'd roused him from bed well past midnight, he was in wingtip shoes, neatly pressed slacks, and one of his formal sweater vests, as if some urgent librarian's duty might call at any moment. The shared blood between us had always been manifest; he had a commonality of feature with my mother that I'd inherited as well, along with dark curls and the cream-and-cinnamon freckled coloring that I echoed. In my pettier moments, it hadn't escaped me that I looked more like his daughter than Emmy did.

And even with all that, with everything he'd given and taught me, I'd still let him down so egregiously.

"I'm sorry to have come so late," I said, twisting my hands in my lap. Though I'd already apologized when I called him, and once again when I showed up on his doorstep, cowed and miserable. "It's just, this couldn't really wait. I'm glad I didn't wake Aunt Cecily."

"Ly, sweetheart, you know it's no trouble," he said in his soft, rumbling tone, like a good-natured bear that had taken a particular liking to you. He was the only person who'd ever called me Ly, and now it only stoked my guilt to hear it. "Go on, now. Tell me what's upset you."

I took a shuddering breath, pressing my fingertips under my swollen eyes. There was no masking how hard I'd cried, and to be honest, I didn't particularly mind. After years of tucking my softest feelings away, it felt almost a relief to finally be this exposed. As though the effort of keeping all that vulnerability locked in had been a physical weight I'd carried, bowing my back, and I could finally stand up straight.

"I made a mistake," I said, through an aching throat, wishing I'd let Ivy accompany me here, or that I'd at least brought Montalban.

But I deserved to make this atonement to my uncle alone, unsupported, whatever the outcome. "A very bad one. And I . . . I think I need your help fixing it."

Slowly, haltingly, I walked him through everything that had happened—the collapse of the Marauder's Misery spell, my breakdown, my casting of the Light That Calls for Blood. His bushy, silver-threaded eyebrows shot up when I admitted to having used the *Opes Sanguinis*, but he refrained from comment. I explained the effect the spell had exerted on me, the way it had transferred the nexus into me and turned me into a beacon for dangerous, thirsty monsters even as it shielded me from the effects of the oblivion splinter lodged in my mind.

And I told him all about Cat; her origins and her ulterior motives, the way she'd finagled my trust and stolen the *Opes*. Sparing myself no damning detail.

"She swore she wouldn't reveal anything about me or Thistle Grove to the head of the Court. But I have no reason to believe her, and if she does . . . it'll be my fault, Uncle James. I'll have brought them all down on our heads. And that poor girl, the normie barista at Wicked Sweet . . ." I gave a shuddering exhale, lips quivering. "She's hurt because of me, too, because I forgot to ward the store. I remembered tonight, though, don't worry. I warded Harlow House against everything I could think of, before I even knocked on the door. I'm just, I'm so sorry. I'm *so* sorry, about everything."

When I lapsed into depleted silence, he didn't respond, leaning over to brace his forearms on his thighs, large hands dangling between his knees. His neck bent, so I couldn't read his face. Fear ratcheted up in me like someone turning a crank, trepidation boiling up my throat. How could he possibly forgive me, now that he knew everything? Out of everyone in Thistle Grove, the next Harlow keeper should have known better than to do any single one of the things I'd done. Much less all of them in turn.

When he stood, I thought for sure it would be to ask me to leave. To get out and never darken his door again, banished from not only my role but my family.

Instead, he opened his arms, waiting quietly until I rose and crossed the room to him, unable to believe it. Uncle James wasn't much of a hugger—none of us Harlows really were—and knowing that bruised my heart all the more.

"Really?" I asked, my voice cracking as I looked up at him. Tall as I was, even I had to crane my neck to meet his eyes.

"Of course, Ly," he said, face creasing with concern, tinged with pained disbelief that I'd question something so apparently manifest to him. "Always. Sweetie, you shouldn't even have to ask me that. You come first, no matter what. Everything else, we can sort out together. Elbow to elbow, master and apprentice, as is proper and right."

When I stepped into his arms to accept his brief but crushing hug, his scratchy sweater vest pressed against my cheek, pungent with coffee and ink and old books. He smelled like Tomes itself, even more than I did, as if all the years spent there had steeped into his very being. The massive swell of relief that rushed up inside me felt like it might melt my bones. Whatever I'd expected, it hadn't been this unconditional pardon; the kind I'd assumed he'd reserve for a daughter, not a curmudgeonly niece. It reminded me of what Ivy had said, about my unwillingness to trust exactly the people who were the most likely to catch me if I fell, because I was so specifically afraid of their rejection.

I'd given my uncle far too little credit, like I always did.

Because I'd been perceiving him through the fundamentally flawed lens of my own fear and insecurity.

With a final squeeze and a kiss dropped on the top of my head, he released me. I all but floated back to my cushioned sofa chair, feeling the first glimmer of real hope I'd felt since Cat had closed the attic door on me.

"First off, you don't have to worry about Maddy," he said. "That would be the barista, Gretchen's daughter—Gretchen Miller, who owns Wicked Sweet. She sent out an alert to all of us with storefronts on Yarrow, to keep a lookout for the 'unsub,' as she put it, whatever that means," he added, long nose wrinkling in bemusement. "I suspect she's partial to a certain kind of television. She was still at the hospital when she emailed, but Maddy's expected to make a full recovery. Nothing worse than a concussion and some broken bones."

"That's really it?" I swallowed hard, remembering her—Maddy—pale and tiny and so damaged on the floor. "But she looked terrible."

"The resilience of youth. And now that we know the incident had to do with us, I'll confer with the elders; Gabrielle Thorn might be inclined to slip in for a visit, possibly confer a little healing on the sly. We wouldn't normally intervene in ungifted affairs, but in this case, I'd say it's our responsibility to right the balance a bit."

I nodded, grateful they'd make an exception. I knew it was unreasonable to expect the Thorns to behave like modern saints, conferring secret healing on the town's masses; we couldn't run the risk of becoming a place known for unexplained medical miracles, even the minor kind the Thorns could achieve. And it wouldn't have been fair to expect that of them, when they had their own lives to lead.

"I'll speak to them about the cat sith halfling, as well," he continued, settling back into his chair. "There, I think we'll have to hope for the best and prepare for the worst. We do have the Avramovs and the Blackmoores at our back, so even if some confrontation should happen down the line, we'll be far from defenseless." He cracked a small smile, shaking his head. "If anything, I imagine Elena's heart will beat a little faster at the mere prospect of conflict. The Avramovs might be speakers to the dead, but there's no quelling that old warrior blood."

"And what about me?" I asked, subdued. "I used baneful magic; I violated the keeper's oath to cause no harm with knowledge."

"Oh, Ly, we all have lapses. Myself included." His eyes sparkled with something shockingly like mischief. "When I was apprenticing with your nana Caro, we came by a rare chthonic grimoire, and I developed a bit of a fascination with it. I even snuck it out of Tomes one afternoon, and went conjuring undead cockroaches in the Witch Woods, because . . ." He shrugged, spreading his hands. "Frankly, I still couldn't tell you. Possibly ghost bugs sounded cool to a sixteen-year-old hooligan with a half-baked prefrontal cortex?"

My mouth dropped open as I struggled to square my straitlaced uncle with the image of a teenage troublemaker summoning up ectoplasmic creepy-crawlies. "Uncle James. You didn't really do that."

"Oh, but I did. Things got a bit out of hand; the swarm threatened to overrun the town, wreak whatever havoc it is that undead insects are inclined to wreak. Like you, I cried uncle."

I grimaced, like, *touché.* "Okay, ouch."

"Well, less literally, maybe. Our dear departed Stasia—Elena's mother, still the Avramov elder back then—had to banish them for me. She managed to give me a blistering dressing down *while* casting the banishing spell, about what she thought should happen to stupid little boys who meddled in magics they didn't understand."

"What happened after? What was your punishment?"

"I had to forgo my lessons at Tomes for a week, nothing worse than that. What I did was simple curiosity, not a genuinely malicious act; everyone understood that. And in your case, sweetie . . ." His broad face crumpled in sympathy. "Who could blame you for stooping to desperate measures, after what you've been through? If anything, we're the ones who failed you. No wonder you turned to the wrong kind of magic."

"But how was I even able to do it?" I asked. "Not even Cat could answer that. How could I cast a fae spell at all, or absorb an entire nexus without that much magic killing me?"

He sat back in his chair, steepling his hands in front of his chest. "I *may* have some insight there. But Ly—and this is a serious matter—if I share it with you, you have to promise me it stays between us. And not merely a promise, but a lakebound oath."

I caught my breath, the back of my neck tingling with anticipation and a whisper of fear. A lakebound oath meant swearing not only on the lake's magic, but your witch's soul—the tether that connected you to that wellspring of power. If forsworn, it meant you'd lose the birthright of your magic, your place as a Thistle Grove witch. It was invoked only under great duress, when the other party demanded ironclad assurance that you'd abide by your word.

If Uncle James insisted on a lakebound oath in exchange for this information, that meant it must be a *very* big deal.

I cupped my hands in front of my chest, summoning a small,

captive spark of magic to bear ceremonial witness. "I, Delilah Charlotte Harlow, swear upon my magic, my undying witch's soul, and Lady's Lake itself, that I won't breathe a word of what you tell me tonight."

Warmth rushed through me, a shimmering helix of heat that swirled in my chest for one bright moment before fading. Once it vanished, so did the dancing spark between my hands.

"Good," Uncle James said with a brisk nod, that devilish smile that surfaced only on rare occasions flashing across his face. "Because I've been *dying* to share this—and I haven't yet decided how much to divulge to the other elders. But it's only fair that you know, given what you are. What *we* are."

A bright flare of understanding streaked across my mind. "It has to do with Belisama, doesn't it? The statue in the lake?"

"It does. You might have noticed I've been traveling more as of late, since you've taken over so much of the Tomes day-to-day." He leaned toward me a little, avid excitement glimmering in his eyes. "But you may also have noticed that our acquisitions don't particularly reflect the increased activity on my part. I'm not bringing in very many new books, am I? Nor have I sold any notable amount over the past six months."

I had noticed the lull in his activity, but dealing in rare and antiquarian books was like that, sometimes, an organic ebb and flow. I'd been happily picking up his slack, anyway, so I assumed he'd merely been letting me have my head.

"It's because I've been investigating," he went on, that rampaging scholar's flame still lighting his eyes. "Following a very old, deeply buried trail. Once Nina uncovered the existence of the statue in the lake—the source of Thistle Grove's power, the goddess Belisama's avatar—I knew it had to be intimately connected to us, to the Harlows. Elias was, after all, the first of the founders to discover the lake. And we, his descendants, are the ones with the power to sift its tremendous magic into something other witches can use. Put together, it meant a clear connection. Some shining thread that binds us to her."

"To who?" I asked, struggling to keep up as he gained speed, spurred on by the thrill of his discovery. "To *Belisama*?"

"Yes. The goddess herself. The answer didn't lie in Tomes' records, or I'd have stumbled across it already. But there's a world of knowledge out there, beyond what we've curated for ourselves. So I began following the links, unspooling all that tangled thread; skipping from the Italian Matera Valley to Bordeaux to Linlithgow. The trail led back to Scotland, where our family's from."

And not just us, I thought to myself with rising wonder. Also the spiky purple flowers that lined the lake, that gave the town its name—Scottish thistles.

"I found a story there, in one of Edinburgh's great libraries— in a section most ungifted scholars never even learn of. I dredged up an account of a great war between the lesser gods, one that left Belisama grievously wounded. Knowing she was close to divine death, she entrusted one of her devotees with continuing her legacy." He cocked his head eagerly, reliving the tantalizing process of piecing the clues together. "But what did that mean? What did 'her legacy' entail? It took months to stitch it all together, find all the relevant accounts."

"Elias," I hazarded, not understanding the full picture, but seeing this one facet rise from the murk like true gold sifting loose from dross. "The devotee. It had to have been him."

"It was." He grinned at me, with a mentor's pride in my quick grasp. "Belisama had an enclave of followers in Linlithgow, it seemed. Our family seat. And Elias was one of the last remaining faithful, a fervent devotee of a pagan goddess whose flame was on the wane. She appeared to him, entrusted him with some essential piece of her. I don't know what it might have been; the text referred to it only as a 'soul pearl.' She's a goddess not only of light, but of lakes and rivers, as I'm sure you already know. Her plan was to submerge herself underwater for centuries, perhaps millennia. However long it took her to heal."

"So what was he supposed to do with it? With the soul pearl?"

"Hide it somewhere safe," James explained. "Somewhere secluded but also powerful, a naturally magical haven. Scotland was much too small for what she ultimately intended, so he looked beyond it, across the seas to the New World. Somewhere far away, where none of her enemies or their followers could possibly find this last, crucial piece of her."

"But the lake was already magical when he found it," I argued. "So wouldn't her statue already have been here, too, when he came? None of that makes sense."

"Because it's the wrong order of operations!" Uncle James exclaimed, with a gratified flourish. "That's what the founding story *says*, but it's not what really happened. Lady's Lake *wasn't* magical before—Elias was the one to seed it with the soul pearl, once he came upon a piece of land so naturally rich in ley lines and their nexuses. It could be he never even knew what it looked like in its final form, after it sank so far down and took root."

"And the other families? How did they know to come here?"

"That part of the legend is true; the other founders felt the lake's siren song from a distance, the new power flooding from it. It would have felt like a safe haven to them, somewhere they could freely practice their own magic in the wake of the witch trial scourge. This would have been by design; Belisama *wanted* more witches here. Because—and this is the brilliant part"—another of those rakish grins, so unlike my buttoned-up uncle, that seemed to reveal a much younger version of himself preserved under the aging surface—"an entire community of witches going about their magical lives would eventually form something like a sacred perpetual-motion machine. Each spell cast over the years would function as a little prayer, funneling yet more power into the piece of Belisama that lies here."

"Like a positive feedback loop," I murmured, marveling at the intricacy of the plan, its many fine-tuned, interlocking gears.

"Exactly like that!" he said, pointing a finger at me. "Days, weeks, centuries of spells, always yielding more power. Which would, in turn, help the real goddess endure and heal."

I sat, reeling, absolutely stunned. That all of Thistle Grove could be such a cleverly constructed clockwork mechanism, an entire town designed around helping to heal an ancient, injured goddess.

Talk about intentionally planned communities.

"You said she wanted him to seed her somewhere secluded, far from Scotland and her enemies," I said, seizing on the first inconsistency that came to mind. "But wouldn't the pull of a lake that drew the other founders here in the first place also attract dangerous attention?"

"Of course it would. Once they'd formed their pact—sworn allegiance to this new town, and to keeping its true nature as a haven for witches secret in the years to come—one of the first orders of business was a town-wide spell the founders cast together. A massive deflection glamour, shielding the town from any supernatural interlopers that might endanger the lake or its magical inhabitants. A predecessor to the oblivion glamour, which was intended only to prevent the town's eventual ungifted settlers from becoming privy to its real magic."

"So that's why no malevolent supernatural entities have ever been sighted here," I elaborated, inwardly congratulating myself on having gotten it right—there *was* an additional glamour in place, just not one intended to keep normies in the dark. "None, that is, that we didn't summon or conjure ourselves."

"That's right. The light of that severed nexus floating in you would have interfered with it—enough to draw a select few who were probably in the neighborhood anyway, allow them to come through and track you down."

"I'm still not completely understanding how this explains what I was able to do," I said, glancing up from my lap, where I'd been staring intently at my hands as I followed Uncle James's logic. "We're Elias's descendants, which, what, makes us Belisama's devotees by proxy? And that's why I was able to cast a fae blood spell and extract the nexus?"

"Almost, but not quite. Now we arrive to the reason I swore you to secrecy by lakebound oath." He leaned toward me, arms slung over his thighs. "Elias wasn't *just* Belisama's devotee, Ly. He was also her descendant, an heir to a bloodline that was once half-divine. Which means all of us Harlows carry a living piece of her divine spark, amplified when we're near the lake. That's why you were able to cast a spell not even intended for a human witch. That's why you were capable of lifting up an entire nexus, and surviving it as it took up residence inside you."

Disbelief and awe vibrated inside me, thrumming like some enormous struck gong. This explained so much, such a tremendous amount. Not only why Harlows were able to sieve Belisama's divine magic into useable fuel for human witches, but also why we were so keenly attuned to the magic of the town; its distinctive smell and feel so inherently familiar to us, as recognizable as the scent of our own skin. This was how Emmy had been able to take on the role of the Voice of Thistle Grove, as all Harlow elders had before her.

Because our connection to the lake, and therefore to the town itself, literally ran as thick as our own blood.

We were the magically weakest of the families only because we were so completely preoccupied with filtering that ceaseless flow of power—because we were the living conduits that fueled the spell-to-prayer engine that was this town. The walking prayer beads that kept Belisama alive, in whatever underwater refuge she lay hidden and healing.

"So where is she?" I managed, through the haze of wonder. "The original Belisama, the goddess in the flesh? Do you know?"

James shook his head, trawling both hands through the coarse, curly ruck of his hair. "I can't be sure. Even much of what I've shared with you isn't a die-cut certainty—more a very educated guess, a tale spun of conjecture backed by the most reliable sources I could find. But I suspect she lies in one of the deeper Scottish lochs, the ones that have never been plumbed."

I snorted an incredulous laugh, as a ridiculous idea occurred to me. "James. Are you saying she's in *Loch Ness*?"

He chuckled himself, tilting his head. "I wouldn't rule it out. A sleeping goddess would certainly attract the kind of phenomena Loch Ness is infamous for; it would explain some of the more un-usual sightings that have been recorded there over the years. But really, she could be in any one of them. It doesn't matter, and it's probably best that we don't know."

"So why do you think it was those particular three who were drawn here?" I asked, changing direction as another question occurred to me. "Caelia Blackmoore, Margarita Avramov, and Alastair Thorn. Why did they, specifically, heed the lake's call? They couldn't have been the only witches around in early eighteenth-century America."

"That, I don't know. Perhaps Belisama has some affinity with them as well—she did grant a Blackmoore her divine favor, rather than one of us." He shrugged, spreading his palms wide. "Or perhaps it was something about their skills, the way our various magical talents mesh with or complement one another. Who could know a goddess's plan or mind? Maybe it's as simple as the fact that they were the closest, in the moment when the seed pearl came to fruition. I couldn't tell you, Ly."

I rubbed my chin, uncertainty gnawing at me. "But if you think there's a chance they might be her chosen, too, then why the hesitation about telling the other elders?"

"Even if they aren't, this town belongs to all of us; my gut deems it wrong to keep this from them. But it does beg the question, doesn't it, of why this knowledge wasn't preserved in the first place. The writings of Elias's that I found secreted in the Harlow House attic—the ones that allowed me to make the final leap to fully understanding who we are . . . Why didn't Elias include them in the Grimoire, if he wanted this passed down? Why did I have to dig so very hard?"

He slipped off his glasses and massaged the bridge of his nose, in a habitual gesture I found as familiar as one of my own.

"I'll confer with your nana Caro and Emmy about it, of course. And Cecily already knows; I could never keep something like this from her. But it'll stay between the five of us until we decide."

"Thank you," I whispered, a fresh rush of gratitude surging up in me. "For trusting me with something so huge."

"Who if not you, my apprentice, the future keeper?" He smiled, adjusting his glasses yet again as they lost their hold on his nose. "But before all that, why don't we put our heads together and focus on the more pressing problem at hand. The issue of you."

20

))) ● (((

Hale and Whole

BANEFUL MAGIC MIGHT not have been the answer, but I was almost as surprised to find that the alternative involved sitting in the Mandrake Salon, The Bitters' shabbily decadent ballroom, my butt slowly going numb from the chilly marble floor.

I sat in a circle with Ivy, Nina, Emmy, and Talia Avramov, Emmy's partner of two years, the peeling ends of the maroon velvet wallpaper wafting toward us like reaching fingers in the ghostly breeze that moaned around the room. A steely-eyed portrait of the deathly gorgeous Margarita Avramov herself surveilled us from above the fireplace, the scorn on her aristocratic face like a sneering, preemptive dismissal of Uncle James's and my plan. *This shall* never *work, thou unwashed, lackwit peasant,* her heavy-lidded sloe eyes seemed to say. *How ludicrous of you to even try.*

Maybe the real Margarita had been more sweet-tempered and encouraging than my mental image of her, but somehow I doubted it. Even Montalban, perched on the red-veined gray marble of the mantelpiece, was peering up at her with clear uncertainty.

"Do we absolutely have to do this here, of all places?" I muttered to Emmy, darting a wary look up. The chandelier looming above us—a Gothic travesty of spike-tipped iron encased in centuries of melted candle wax, swinging slowly and malevolently over our heads like some doomsday pendulum—looked like it might crash down and impale me if I so much as breathed in a way that might be perceived as an insult to the Avramov name. "It's not exactly the most therapeutic environment. The Dread Lady Avramov looks like she'd rather be ordering someone to lop off our heads than witnessing a healing ceremony."

"Oh, she wouldn't," Talia assured me cheerfully, tipping me a little wink with one ice-colored eye, and I narrowly avoided blushing. Raven-haired and lush-lipped, my cousin's partner was one of those ravishing women who made lesser mortals trip over their own feet, even if you'd attended preschool with them. Inspiring the kind of awestruck lust that Cat had also ignited.

The thought of her came accompanied by a sharp, unhelpful stab of pain, until I forcefully quashed it. This was no time for indulging pangs of breakup-due-to-treachery-most-foul.

"Not that Margarita was anti-decapitation, per se," Talia clarified, just in case there was any confusion on this front. "Definitely *enthusiastically* pro, under the right circumstances. But she likes you; she'd want this to go well."

I squinted at Talia, wondering why she sounded so sure, like she'd only recently chatted over coffee with an ancestress who'd shuffled off this mortal coil at least three hundred years ago. Then again, given the casually mundane way the Avramovs handled their undead business, it was entirely possible that she had.

"You know why we're here, Lilah," Emmy added. "You and I might be doing most of the heavy lifting, but Talia's work will be the crucial step. We want her to be in a safe, necromantically conducive environment—one where no paranormal creatures would dare to tread, as a bonus. And I think we all agreed we'd take a pass on the Witch Woods."

I nodded, licking my lips. "I know. I'm just bitching about it because I'm nervous. And, uh, kind of terrified that this won't work."

Emmy started a little; she'd probably never heard anything that amounted to such a clear admission of vulnerability from me. Then her face softened into a smile, moss-green eyes narrowing with sympathy. Her curling honey-brown hair was long enough now that she'd pulled it back into a neat bun to keep it out of the way, just like I had, and for once it felt as though we looked like the cousins we were.

"It will," she said, decisively. "Because *you* came up with it."

Stomach churning, I glanced over at the simple bronze censer that already burned at the center of our five-person circle, fine wisps of smoke winding around one another from the smoldering herbs. I'd ground up a blend of mugwort, myrrh, yarrow, star anise, honeysuckle, and rosemary, with a little sprinkling of dried Lady's Lake thistles on top. Most of the herbs were chosen to enhance openness, foster psychic receptiveness between the five of us. And though I hadn't told them this, the thistle was meant for me and Emmy; to symbolize our special affinity for the lake, and facilitate Emmy's connection to the town as the Voice of Thistle Grove.

Her task—at least, magically—would be the hardest; she needed all the ancillary support I could give her.

Nina's would be the easiest—she was here only because I needed her to be, for my own role in the ceremony. The rosemary, an herb intended to sweeten tempers, foster forgiveness, and heal old wounds, was for the two of us. But given what lay between us, a trench I'd dug and dug at until it widened into a seemingly unspannable chasm, would it be enough?

I caught Nina's eye, across the circle from me. If anything, she looked even more nervous than I did, her narrow face pale and drawn, her normally meticulously styled hair in a simple blond braid over one shoulder. Almost as if the success of this undertaking were as integral to her as it was to me—and for once, I wondered if maybe it was. Maybe I'd been misjudging her for a very long time, minimizing the sincerity of her remorse, the pain her own guilt was causing her. Yes, she'd hurt me badly, in a terrible lapse of judgment—but at the time, she'd been chasing and protecting something precious to her. Something that was as paramount to her as the recovery of my mind had been to me, when I tossed caution to the wind and chose to cast the Light That Calls for Blood.

Maybe, when it came right down to it, we were closer to two peas in a pod than moral opposites.

In the spirit of mutual understanding, I attempted a wobbly little smile at her, possibly my first. The astonishment that lit up her face *was* gratifying, in a very virtuous way; maybe there was something to Genevieve's insufferable schtick about the "pleasure of being polite."

Then she smiled back at me, sweet and tremulous, a flicker of answering hope shining in her brown eyes. "I know I don't have to do anything but sit here, really," she said, her earnest gaze shifting between my eyes. "But if something does occur to you . . . if I can help . . ."

"I'll tell you," I said, and meant it. "But I think, mostly, I just need you to be here. So, are we good? Everyone ready to do this, before we catch ass frostbite from this floor?"

A startled chuckle threaded through the circle—did everyone besides Ivy *really* think I was so humorless that a joke sticking the landing actually surprised them?

I'd have to work on that.

When the bright belling of laughter faded away and everyone nodded in turn, joining hands to close the circle, my stomach felt as though it had turned into a raw, tangled skein of naked nerves. Then a pulse of warmth spread through me from my left where Ivy held my hand; a sweet and somehow sticky heat, like holding a spoonful of honey on your tongue. I knew that, on her other side, Talia would be feeling it too—and Nina and Emmy as well, like a binding current that ran through all of us, or a spiritual glue.

"You've got this," Ivy assured me, low. "Because we've got you, too."

I closed my eyes, taking long inhales of the smoking herbs, breathing them deep into my lungs. The mugwort fizzed through me, its smell pungent and familiar; it was one of the most commonly used occult herbs, helpful for almost every type of casting. I imagined its power gathering in my forehead, my third eye opening, blinking to life between my brows. And I imagined, through the empathic connection forged by Ivy's magic, that all five of us were of a piece, indelibly conjoined. A close-knit assemblage that I could trust would follow wherever I led them.

Just this willingness to connect with and trust the other four, to believe that this collaboration would help me, was the first step in the improvised spell Uncle James and I had devised together.

Sensing the commencement of the ceremony, Montalban flew over from the fireplace and lit on my shoulder, offering me her support.

"Imagine yourself walking into Tomes," I instructed, keeping my voice calm and even. "The bell above the door chiming an alert at your arrival. Imagine yourself stepping into that familiar space; a space we've all walked through, many times. A space you know."

I gave them a moment to erect an image of Tomes in their mind, build it according to their own specifications. It didn't matter if it wasn't accurate; the notion of perfect recall was an impossibility, anyway. Experiential memory was inexact, a patchwork sewn from disparate, subjective pieces of sensory interpretation. A private hallucination that each of our brains dreamed alone, as its own version of reality.

And we were witches, skilled at superimposing the shapes of our wills onto the world. We'd been taught how to visualize effectively ever since we were old enough to cast—so I knew that whatever images were burgeoning in those four other minds, their ideas of Tomes would be vividly and expertly drawn, if not rendered in quite the fine-grained detail I could imagine myself due to my familiarity with the store.

"Now imagine flowers," I guided, inhaling more of that fragrant, herbal smoke. "Big, heavy blossoms of all kinds, the most exotic you've ever seen. As if a hothouse had somehow been grafted onto Tomes."

Ivy made an involuntary sound at that, curious but pleased.

Having grown up on an orchard with greenhouses, she could probably imagine it in especially fine detail.

"They're huge and vibrant and colorful," I continued. "Shining pollen in their centers, their petals glowing with light. They're bursting from each bookshelf, peeking out from between the books, growing wild across the shelves. Imagine their massive heart-shaped leaves, their fibrous stems. And imagine large, strange mushrooms popping up between them, too, like something out of *Alice in Wonderland*."

"No shit," Talia muttered hazily, under her breath, as though she hadn't foreseen this development. I smiled to myself, because this was good. It meant her vision was so tangible and well developed that unexpected turns could still take her by surprise.

"Each one is a memory," I explained, so they'd understand—so they'd feel as if they were really there, in that diorama of my psyche. Since none of us were telepathic half fae, this re-creation was the next best thing; the closest we could come to being connected in a way that would grant both Emmy and Talia access to my mind. "Each represents a magical recipe I know by heart. And if you think, 'Cut the shit, Delilah, there are *way* too many for that,' well . . . you're probably not even imagining enough."

"Blowhard," Ivy mumbled next to me, laughter in her voice, and Nina snorted a soft, suppressed giggle in response. The humor was good, too, helpful. I could feel the way it bound us even closer, wove us more tightly into a cohesive whole that responded to my lead.

"Now think of birds," I instructed. Montalban cawed emphatically, as if to remind everyone what birds sounded like. "Flocks and flocks of them wheeling under the rafters; some of them out of myth—rocs and griffins and phoenixes. Others are real, but the prettiest and biggest robins, swallows, and peregrine falcons you've ever seen. These are memories, too—except they're spells. All the spells I've ever learned."

Slowly, deliberately, I led them on a tour of my inner Tomes; winding between the shelves, having them stroke flowers and leaves and call down birds. Until I was sure that they held the image of it unwavering in their minds.

Then, it was time to take them with me to the attic.

Once I'd walked them up the spiral staircase, I described the bloody nexus globe, the dark crystal floating inside it. From the series of gasps my description elicited, whatever they were envisioning was just as disturbing as what actually lived in my mind. I opened my eyes for a moment, just to center myself—shocked to see that a small, translucent red sphere had appeared in the middle of our circle, a black shard floating inside.

It didn't look exactly like it had in my head, because, again, this wasn't the psychic foray Cat had been capable of. Instead, I was looking at a projected amalgam of what the five of us had pictured—and apparently, thanks to Ivy's empathic bond, our shared vision was powerful enough to manifest an illustration of what all of us were seeing.

"Emmy, walk to the nexus globe," I directed her. "Sink your hands into the light, and think about being the Voice of Thistle Grove. You are this town, and this town is you—and the missing nexus is something you can fix, a wound only you can heal. Focus on channeling it through yourself, shifting it back to the Witch Woods where it's supposed to be."

"Got it," Emmy said, and the absolute conviction in her voice— her clear confidence in herself and her ability to mind-meld with the nexus globe—reinforced my own belief in what we were doing. Creating our own little positive feedback loop.

I couldn't feel what she was doing, but I could see her begin to glow, shedding the sapphire light that always accompanied her, calling on the connection between herself and Thistle Grove. But something was certainly happening; the projection of the globe hovering between us began fading, losing coherency. Then it brightened for an instant, pulsing bright vermilion—just as bright, searing pain burned through me. A thunderclap of a migraine that started in my head and then traveled down my neck and arm to where Emmy's hand clasped mine.

Still, it was nothing like the fearsome, shattering pain that had come with actually casting the spell. This was a survivable ache; almost pleasant in a sense, the way that a deep massage working out tight knots both hurt and felt good, a necessary pain.

And when I looked down, I saw that the red had leached out of my tattoos. Even as I watched, the lines of runes melted away, fading to nothing. We'd done it, successfully reversed the baneful spell that had held the power of the nexus locked in my head.

Almost immediately, I could sense the lurch in my brain, a shift back to that mental unsteadiness caused by the oblivion glamour shard. But now that I knew what it was, I had none of that old instinctive fear response, the all-consuming terror that I might forget at any moment. It was possible that my own trauma, the constant fear I had of yet another memory slipping out of my grasp, had been contributing to the shard's power over me as well as keeping it lodged. Emotions always affected working with magic; it made sense that my erratic state had made things even worse. It was also probably why Ivy's mantras and affirmations had sometimes helped, acted as a calming, palliative force.

Next to me, Emmy was breathing in short, shallow gasps—taking the nexus in must have hit her hard, too. She was a Harlow just like I was, and being a descendant of Belisama as well as the Voice of Thistle Grove would allow her to hold the nexus like I had, until she moved it back to its proper place. But that didn't mean it'd be easy for her. This was why we'd decided that Talia would be the participating Avramov instead of Dasha, who might have been better equipped for the role. As Emmy's partner, Talia would lend Emmy the grounding of emotional support through just her presence.

The fact that my cousin had chosen to do this so willingly, take on this suffering both on my account and on behalf of Thistle Grove, made me feel truly terrible about all the times I'd judged her so harshly in the past, questioned her dedication to her family and this town.

Regardless of the charged history between us, this Emmy, as she was now, deserved nothing but my admiration and respect.

"I'm holding it," she said, pain pulling her voice taut. Her sapphire glow had begun to pulse, alternating between blue and red, as the power of the nexus vied with her connection to the town.

"You okay?" Talia asked, tense. "Sure you can handle this?"

"I can do it. But, Ivy, could you take the edge off a little, please? Holding it in place hurts like a bitch. I know how to shift it back into the woods where it belongs—I can feel the appropriate channel—but the pain . . ." She gritted her teeth, sucking slow, deliberate breaths through them, trying to master herself. "It's interfering with my focus."

"On it," Ivy murmured. Through our connection, I could feel

the warm glow of her healing magic course through all of us, that heady river of sweetness melting into us like magical CBD. Emmy heaved a relieved sigh, her stiff shoulders relaxing a fraction.

"Much better, thank you," she murmured abstractedly. "Give me a minute. This is going to take some time."

We all waited, swimming in our shared focus and bound by Ivy's empathic bond, so attuned to each other that I could hear our breathing had synced up. Time felt fluid and formless; when the scarlet globe abruptly winked out in the middle of the circle, and Emmy's light skewed back to that pure, clean blue, I couldn't tell if minutes or hours had elapsed.

"It's done," Emmy said, with a flush of triumph. "The nexus is back in place in the Witch Woods between its three ley lines, exactly where it should be."

"Amazing work," I said to her, squeezing her hand. She squeezed back, hard. "I know that must have been excruciating. Believe me, I know. Thank you, Emmy."

"You're my cousin," she said simply. "And this is my town. There's no need for thanks."

"Well. I'm grateful anyway."

Beside me, I could hear her smile. "Then you're welcome anyway."

In the middle of our circle, the black crystal now floated on its own, shucked from its scarlet shell, glinting as it spun in slow revolutions. "Talia, you're up," I said. "Now that Emmy's removed the nexus shield, I need you to exorcise the oblivion splinter. Think of it as a ghost of the spell it once was. A restless shade that has no right to be squatting in my mind."

"On it, Captain," Talia said, a faint frisson of excitement

threading her voice. If there was anyone who craved a challenge, especially one involving some exotic breed of ghost, it was an Avramov. And oblivion glamours were Avramov spells; she'd have a natural facility with it that other witches wouldn't. "I have it in hand. It's sharp as shit, and very, *very* cold—but it's also, somehow, immaterial. Like . . . like an idea of crystal, instead of the reality of one. Or, like you said, its ghost. That's it, yeah. I can feel how this should go."

As she worked, murmuring the words of an exorcism spell under her breath, I brought my focus to bear on my own emotional state. If Cat had been right, it was the scar tissue of my own trauma, my anger at Nina, that was keeping the shard lodged in my mind like such a stubborn burr. Talia wouldn't be able to excise and banish it unless I dislodged it first.

"Nina," I began, opening my eyes again so I could look at her, her clear brown eyes already on my face. As I watched her, I kept the parallels between us foremost in my mind, speaking them aloud to her. "You know how angry I've been at you—and I was right to be. But there's always been more to it than that. The thing I was ignoring—the thing I understand, now—is how similar we are. More alike than different. We've both made awful mistakes, the life-changing kind that hurt other people very badly. And both our actions were, at least in part, justified."

A tremor passed over her face, and she gave a small, tight nod, clearly struggling not to cry.

"And you've worked so hard to atone, to make it up to me," I continued, emotion welling in my own throat. "You've been so patient and respectful, and you almost never pushed back, even when I was being horrendous to you. You showed up for me and

Tomes, and you did it with the kind of grace I wasn't capable of. You tried to have enough for the both of us."

She didn't reply, but she tilted her head to the side in wry acknowledgment, like, *Yes, you were indeed a raging bitch and I still respected you.*

"And here's another thing I know," I went on, my voice fracturing a little. "Withholding forgiveness from you—keeping it so close to my heart, like some talisman—was my own attempt at control. A clumsy fumble, a way to grapple with what was happening to me, exert at least some of my own will over it. So I know I bear some responsibility here too, for how much I suffered. If I'd been more open—if I hadn't doubled down on hating you—I might even have recovered months ago."

She bit her lip, wide-eyed and tremulous. "Maybe that's true. But you had *every* right to hate me. We both know it was my fault infinitely more than yours. And I'm sorry, Delilah. I am so completely sorry for what I did to you."

"I know you are," I whispered, some taut thread snapping in me—bringing with it a sense of huge and long-awaited unspooling, as though a tightly wound coil inside me had finally come loose. "I do. And I'm sorry, too, for the way I treated you."

I could see that the projection of the shard was stuttering, winking in and out of existence like something was interfering with its reception. It was still clinging on, but only feebly. Which meant I'd almost arrived at where I needed to be, to fulfill my own role in this working, my obligation to both Nina and myself.

"Almost there," Talia muttered, her voice a little strained. "It's fading, yielding to me. Slowly. Another minute, and I'll have it in the bag."

"You can do this, boo," Ivy whispered, squeezing my hand. "You *need* to do it, for you."

I nodded, because I could feel it too; I could feel that it was time to let go. I locked eyes with Nina again, her mouth quivering like a child's, her entire face trembling. On my end, I felt almost serene; as though I'd finally stumbled across some reclusive oasis after a long, hard trek, a haven that had always been within my reach.

"Neither of us will forget what passed between us," I said. "And we shouldn't, because some part of it was, maybe, valuable. The kind of lesson both of us could stand to learn. But I vow to you that there won't be any more holding on, no more needless grudges. As witnessed by this sacred circle—and by Emmeline Harlow, our Victor of the Wreath and the Voice of Thistle Grove— Nina Blackmoore, I offer you my full and genuine forgiveness. Do you accept?"

"Of course I do." Her tears spilled over, flooding her lower lashes and glistening on her cheeks. "Thank you. Oh, Delilah, thank you for that. And I . . . I forgive you, too."

As soon as she spoke the words, the black crystal disappeared, vanishing between one blink and the next. That lurch of discomfort, that disorientation lurking in my mind, went with it, and I could feel myself become me again.

Delilah Charlotte Harlow, a Harlow witch and the next master keeper, distant descendant of a sleeping goddess.

Delilah Harlow, blessed with closure and free from bitterness.

Delilah Harlow, finally hale and whole.

21

))) ● (((

Rainbow Harvest

I T RAINED ON Lughnasadh, for the first time since I could remember.

Thistle Grove weather tended to cooperate beautifully for the Wheel of the Year holidays, so even this rain was light and warm, the kind that fell softly against a backdrop of buttery sunshine and produced dramatic rainbows. No one seemed to mind it. Some of the gathered witches used water deflection spells like invisible umbrellas, while others pulled up their robe hoods or went in for normie umbrellas, because why not. And some simply embraced the misty spray, strolling around Honeycake Orchards in damp robes and with glistening faces, treading gleefully through puddles as they ate slabs of fresh-baked brown bread—bespelled to stay warm, spread with sweet, grassy butter and drizzled with honey or sprinkled with coarse salt. All washed down with goblets of beautiful Honeycake mead and red wine.

The rain complemented the decor too, glinting off the scythes thrust into the ground and wound with dried sunflowers and sheaves of wheat, and sheening the tumbles of gourds and summer squashes piled on the picnic tables—Ivy's handiwork. Courtesy of all those weddings and baby showers, my best friend had a keen eye for arranging a centerpiece.

I liked the rain, myself. There was a cleansing and just slightly melancholy feel to it that dovetailed with how I felt. As if this day of abundance and giving thanks had been tailor-made for me. And now that I knew how closely my family was connected to the goddess in our lake, and to the coursing lines of magic that underpinned the town itself, I wondered if maybe it had.

Maybe Thistle Grove itself could feel my contentment as well as the lingering ache that still occasionally throbbed beneath, and had modeled itself after me.

It had been two weeks since Cat had left—and two weeks since I'd healed myself, with my little coven's help. No more monsters had prowled into Tomes in search of me, nor had any threatening Shadow Courtiers come to call; I was starting to slowly, cautiously believe that Cat had kept her final promise.

Otherwise, life had settled back into the well-worn grooves of my usual routines. Now that I felt like myself again, with the tension bled from Nina's and my relationship, we'd become a formidable team. With her help, I'd managed to restore nearly two-thirds of the remaining wards on our list. At this pace, we'd be done well before Samhain and the accompanying tourist swarm.

We'd also taken to spending time together just for fun, a development I wouldn't have foreseen in a million years. Sometimes Nina brought me to the Shamrock for happy hour, which meant a steady stream of Morty's artisanal concoctions on the house.

Other times we went hiking up to Lady's Lake—or, rather, she jogged and I walked briskly, because the appeal of running for fun had always eluded me—just to sit together and chat. I'd never heard the details of her stint as a demigoddess, or the spontaneous witch bond it had incited between her and Morty, which they'd both chosen to keep even after Nina relinquished her goddess's favor. For the first time, I found myself feeling for Nina, truly grasping how difficult it must have been; the near-impossible choice she'd had to make between her own integrity and her noxious family. And without that serrated friction sawing at us, I was free to enjoy her wry and occasionally acidic humor.

Weirdly enough, the pricklier bits of her reminded me of me.

I'd also spent hours with Uncle James, reading the accounts he'd gathered about Belisama and Elias for myself, awash in wonder. He'd told Emmy what he'd learned soon after he told me, but between the four of us—Emmy had immediately wanted our grandmother Caro's take—we still hadn't decided whether to loop the rest of the families in. Taking some more time to mull it over likely wouldn't hurt, but the lightning storms above Lady's Lake had only intensified as summer deepened, drawing to a close to make way for our long fall. It had left us all wondering if there'd been some change to the statue, or to the actual goddess herself, wherever she lay.

If something new was afoot in town, or Lady's Lake itself, the entire witch community would need to know sooner rather than later.

Taken together, it all left me with very little time in which to dwell on Cat. But I did catch myself thinking about her, despite everything she'd done, how deeply she'd wronged me. Even so, I still found myself starting a little every time the Tomes bell chimed *ahoy!!* inside my head, a tiny part of me hoping it'd be announcing one Catriona Arachne Quinn.

"Don't you look pensive on this fine, if damp, harvest day," Ivy chirped, jarring me out of my thoughts as she appeared next to me with a fat slice of jammy bread in hand, having correctly guessed that I hadn't properly fed myself yet. "Buttered bread and strawberry-rhubarb jam for your thoughts? A much fairer exchange than pennies."

I accepted it, taking a huge, delicious bite, sweetness and sour bursting across my tongue above the silky smear of the butter. The bread was impossibly perfect, too, chewy and faintly flavored with molasses. "Mm, definitely fair," I agreed, even as I eyed the ruby-red beads of jam glistening on the butter with a touch of unease. "Though I might have acquired a lifelong wariness of anything red."

"Understandable," she said solemnly, looping her arm through mine. "If inconvenient. A lot of the best foods do tend that way."

"It'll be good for me, then. Exposure therapy."

We wandered the orchard for a while under the soft, hallowed song of the apple trees, weaving through clusters of mingled Thorns, Blackmoores, and Avramovs engaged in loud wine-fueled conversation, the festive glow of the harvest holiday bringing down the barriers that still sometimes stood between the families.

"So? What were you thinking about?" Ivy prodded.

I heaved a gusty sigh, before taking another spectacular bite. "Oh, you know," I said, mouth full. "Her."

Ivy nodded in sympathy. "Blows, yeah? But can't really blame you, either. Sometimes it's like that with the vicious pretty bitches. Getting all under your skin and staying there."

"I just hate it, that I still miss her," I elaborated, feeling both the pleasure and the growing pains of talking to Ivy this openly, letting myself be vulnerable in front of her. "It makes me angry at myself, like it's this brand-new character flaw I don't know how to address. How can I even feel that way, given what she did to me? Shouldn't I *want* to forget her?"

"Humans are complex creatures, honey," she said, squeezing our linked arms against her side. "Being of two minds about someone is okay. Inevitable, sometimes. You're allowed—expected, even—to have competing emotions about someone who was such a complicated presence in your life. I mean, look at me. I still catch myself hoping to snag a glimpse of Dasha in any crowd of us. Even though I *know* I shouldn't want to see her. I do my best to keep my guard up, but I can't deny a part of me is always on the lookout for that obnoxious hair of hers."

"So? Has Starshine Avramov graced us with her radiantly nec-romantic presence today?"

"Oh, yeah, I clocked her like ten minutes in," she admitted, and both of us cracked up. "In my defense, she doesn't exactly make herself scarce when she's in the orchards—she's clearly still look-ing for me, too. Waiting on me to change my mind. It . . . does not help."

"Are you going to tell me what happened between you two?" I pressed gently. "Now that I'm not an oblivion-riddled mess who needs all the attention, all the time?"

"You were never that kind of attention-seeking, and you know it. And yes, eventually I will," she allowed, shooting me a small, fragile smile. "Talking about it still feels too much like reliving it. So maybe I'll need a little more time to process first."

"I hear you. Not like I don't know how long it takes sometimes, to feel like opening up. And I'll be here, whenever you're ready."

"Hell yeah, you will. Where else would you be?" She turned to smack a kiss onto my cheek, with that trademark waft of sweet pea, vanilla, and shea butter. The beautifully familiar way my best friend in the world always smelled. "Are you going to join for the closing circle? It's about that time."

"Lead the way, friend."

ONCE THE CLOSING ceremony was officially over, I took part in one of my own favorite harvest day traditions—wandering through Honeycake's sunflower field and clipping some of the heavier blooms, which were imbued with not just magic native to the orchard, but also the accumulated power they'd soaked up during the celebration. Still wet from the earlier rain, they nearly fizzed with potential as I picked the finest of them and tucked them into a basket slung over one arm, keeping the magical balms and tinctures I'd brew them into foremost in my mind, instilling them with my intention. As I did so, I also murmured thanks to each flower under my breath, and to the Thistle Grove soil, rain, and sun that had nourished them, to the forces of divinity that had allowed them to flourish here. And to the Thorns for giving me free rein to roam their demesne, allowing me to pick some of their bounty. To hold my own intimate thanksgiving.

I was so wrapped up in this semisacred, private ceremony that I almost missed the hint of wildflower fragrance drifting through the warm, grassy air of the field. I'd only just begun to register it when a smoky voice sounded from behind me.

"Delilah."

I wheeled around to face Cat, who stood with hands clasped by her waist in a way that somehow managed to silently communicate remorse. The sight of her hit me like a sucker punch; for all that I'd been thinking of her earlier, she was the last person I'd have expected to find here.

Late-afternoon sun lit that shock of white-blond hair, kindled a fine honey gleam in her bare arms and shoulders. She wore the first non-combat-ready clothes I'd ever seen on her—a simple hunter-green sundress that set off her unearthly eyes, the skirt skimming the tops of her muscular thighs, its halter top tied behind her neck. She had gladiator sandals on, too, their black thongs winding around her strong calves.

My gaze flitted instinctively to her wrist in search of yet another bespelled bracelet, but she'd worn no jewelry at all, presumably to put me at ease.

A rueful smile quirked the corner of those black-cherry lips. "No beguilement weaves this time, promise. Only me."

At some point, some prankster Thorn had enchanted the sunflower field to respond to emotions by singing a cappella versions of emo rock, and as if on cue, the sunflowers broke into a haunting yet ridiculous rendition of "Kryptonite" by 3 Doors Down. Something along the lines of watching the world float to the dark side of the moon, knowing it had something to do with you. Beautiful and sacred as these flowers were, they could be a little ham-handed with their symbolism.

"'Only you' is entirely bad enough," I said tightly, shifting my heavy, sunflower-laden basket higher on my arm. "How did you get into the orchards? Honeycake's under a normie deflection glamour for the ceremony. And how did you even know to find me here?"

"I'm not a normie, remember?" Her mouth twitched—could it really be nerves?—and she reclasped her hands, fidgeting a little.

"And you told me yourself, when you were describing the way you celebrate Lughnasadh here. You said you liked to finish the day off in the sunflower field, all alone. Reaping flowers for your potions, giving thanks, anticipating fall." Her gaze flicked warily between my eyes, assessing how all this was landing. "I thought it was beautiful."

"Oh, cut the shit." I turned away from her, started back down the path—knowing she'd follow me, unsure if I wanted her to or not. My heart was drumming in my chest, battering with a welter of emotion I couldn't identify, much less sort. Fury and indignation were at the forefront, along with a slice of apprehension; she and I were alone here, after all.

And beneath those, there was a shining sliver of something else I didn't yet want to consider.

"You were just pumping me for Thistle Grove information when I told you all that," I added. "We both know you were."

"Yes," she admitted, trailing on my heels. I could hear the rustle as she skimmed her fingers over the sunflowers' bobbing heads, and part of me wanted to snap at her to keep her thieving hands off flowers that didn't belong to the likes of her. "But I . . . I also just wanted to hear about it, at the time. About you."

"Like I said before you left"—I reached for a promising bloom, slid my shears from the basket—"why would I ever believe anything you had to say?"

"Because I kept my word. I gave the book to Ahto, just like I said I would—but I told him nothing else. Nothing about this town, or you. I said I'd retrieved the *Opes* from some amateur blood witch out in Ohio, who had no idea what she even had."

"Blood witches are a thing?" I paused for a second, thrown

enough that I momentarily forgot how angry I was at her. "Blood witches in . . . *Ohio?*"

"Blood witches are, indeed, a thing—in rural Ohio, not so much. That's why Ahto bought it. The more ridiculous the story, the more likely that it's true. People intuitively recognize that truth is often stranger than fiction. A useful feature for professional liars like myself."

"And I'm supposed to just take your word for it, that you kept mum about everything."

She lifted a shoulder, tipping her head. "Had I let anything slip, you'd know. Courtiers would have flooded the town already—not something you'd have missed, believe me. But no one's come, have they? And they won't. I guarantee it."

"Besides you, you mean." I turned back to face her, vibrating with rage. "Why *are* you here, Cat, and today of all days? What more do you want from me?"

She licked her lips, now clearly besieged by nerves. It rattled me, to see her so genuinely wrongfooted, so wary of making a misstep that would alienate me. "I've broken with Arachne, Delilah," she blurted out, tapping the corner of her eye. Where the tiny spider had once spun its intricate web, there was nothing but a little silvered patch of scar. "I left the Shadow Court. See? She's all gone."

"What do you mean, you left?" I could pretend I didn't feel it, but there it was—a bobbing little buoy of ecstatic hope in the sea of disbelief, the ocean of conviction that this was yet another of her tricks. "How could you just do that? What about your mother?"

"People do leave the Shadow Court," she explained. "It's an enclave, not a prison. It just feels like one, sometimes, to those of us who've grown up there—who feel like we have nowhere else to go, no other world that could contain or accept our strangeness. And yes, my mother was . . . very unhappy with my decision, after all she'd invested in me. But I'd functionally just saved her life, by finding that grimoire for Ahto on her behalf. In a sense, she's beholden to me now, and fae take that kind of obligation very seriously. She couldn't very well repay me by attempting to strongarm me into staying."

"So you're really done?" I pressed, skeptical that it would be so easy. "Completely free of them?"

"Well, no. It being Court, I did have to compromise a bit," she admitted wryly. "I agreed to freelance, as it were. Take assignments if I wanted them, on a case-by-case basis. But I made it clear that I wouldn't be living in the city anymore, and that I'd be the ultimate judge of what I chose to take on." She smirked a little, shrugging. "I do still have to make a living, somehow, and my skill set isn't exactly transferable."

"Why didn't you just do this before, if it existed as an option? Why wait until now?"

"Because I thought the Shadow Court was it for me. The only place I was ever likely to belong." Her eyes softened, their otherworldly green mellowing. That pulse of attraction between us throbbed like an invisible tether, one that was becoming increasingly difficult to ignore. "But, Delilah, I'm so deathly tired of it all. The endless power plays, the violence, the lies on top of lies. Just shadows of real things, all the way down. Nothing to hold on to. And then there was this town, like the answer to a question I hadn't even known I was asking. A town complete with a haunted-as-shit forest and the most beautiful magical lake I'd ever seen, equipped, apparently, with its own goddess. Tell you what, we do not have one of those in Lake Superior."

She paused, flicked up an eyebrow, like, *Do I have permission to continue?* The thought of her beseeching me like this—waiting on me to decide if I wanted to hear the rest of this particular fairy tale—sent a sharp thrill zinging from my belly to my chest.

After a long, purposely fraught moment, I finally gave her a tiny nod. At the very least, I wasn't going to make this easy on her.

"And in this town—this bewitching, peaceful place I could already see myself living in—there happened to live an incredible, brilliant, freckled dryad with a gorgeous mind," she continued, eyes warming even further. "Along with, it must be said, the most glorious rack of all time. I mean, we're talking *unreal.*"

I burst out laughing, despite myself. "Seriously? You *had* to bring in the tits?"

She clapped a hand to her own chest in mock affront, a smile twitching at her lips. "It would've been remiss of me not to pay proper homage. Not a good way to get in with the locals, I hear. At least not for a transplant hoping she might, eventually, put down roots here."

I nodded slowly, considering. A slow, simmering joy had begun building below my ribs, somewhere in the vicinity of my solar plexus. But I had to tread carefully here, without undue haste. To protect not just myself but my town, this special place that had been built by my own semidivine ancestor.

"If you do stay," I started, holding up a hand as delight stole over her face like a sunrise, "if you do, there'll be a price. I'll have to let the elders know you're here—and you, in turn, will have to tell us everything about the Shadow Court. Its inhabitants, their magic, their business—anything we could use, should one of them ever track you here. As an insurance policy."

"I'll do all that, happily. Because, Delilah, I want this to be my place, too." She cleared her throat, those bold features tightening with emotion. "Before I left, you said I was worse than my mother. But you should know I lied, about that one last thing I said to you—I *didn't* fail to remind you to cast the wards on purpose. I only forgot, exactly like you did. Putting you, and that mundane girl, in that kind of danger . . . that would've been a step too far. Even for someone like me."

"That's good to know," I conceded, feeling an even deeper softening toward her. "That makes . . . a very big difference to me."

"I only said it to make things easier on you, after I left. But you were right about one thing—I do want to be better. I want to be a real person; the person I was supposed to be, would maybe even have become if I hadn't grown up the way I did. Someone with a full-fledged conscience, inconvenient as I hear those can be. And I suspect . . ." Her eyes fastened on mine, alight with yearning. "I suspect you know a thing or two about being good. If you'd be willing to teach me."

"Is this a *Wizard of Oz* thing? You want me to show you where to find your heart?"

"Oh, I already know where it is. What I need is help putting it to better use."

"How about this," I said, holding my free hand out to her. "I'm willing to *consider* becoming your Dorothy."

She grinned at me, bold and rakish, taking my hand in both of hers. "That's more than enough, for starters. More than I deserve." She cast me a coy look, a slow, feline blink with those silky, dark lashes casting shadows on the hollows under her eyes. "What would you say about sealing this joint undertaking with a kiss?"

I shook my head, though it took everything I had to turn her down, with the heat of her hands enclosing mine, that wildflower scent of her swimming giddy in my head.

"The next time I kiss you, I want to know I'm kissing the real Cat," I said, tugging her just a step closer to me. "Not some illusion, some amalgam pieced together just to entice me. When it does happen, I want to know it's because you care about me—I don't want ulterior motives to even cross my mind. And I have a feeling that getting there, feeling any kind of safe with you, is going to take some time."

She rubbed those cerise lips together, her face falling just a little, but she rallied almost as quickly. "But you're saying it might happen? Down the line?"

"The odds are favorable, cat sith," I teased, drawing her down the path with me, ranks of yellow flowers swaying softly in the wind that had kicked up, bringing with it a bracing tinge of smoke and fallen leaves, the very first harbingers of the coming fall. "And I'm not done collecting these flowers. I have some extra garden shears you can use, if you want to help. And if you like, maybe we could even consider this our first real date."

The sunflowers around us reached their angsty chorus, wailing beautifully about kryptonite. Cat arched an eyebrow at them, amused.

"I mean, they certainly seem to think it is," she said, with that silvery laugh. "Even if I have some pressing questions about their taste in early-aughts angst-boy rock."

"Everybody does," I assured her, lacing my fingers through

hers. "It's allegedly part of their charm. So far, they've never in-flicted Maroon 5 on us, so whoever cast this animating spell ex-hibits at least a baseline level of decency."

Cat gave a theatrical shudder, falling into step with me. "Thank fuck for small mercies."

"But here's the thing." I let myself lean just a little closer to her, my robes sliding against the warm, bare skin of her arm. "They don't sing for normie tourists, as a rule. So I think you can con-sider this your official Thistle Grove welcoming committee."

A bright, wide smile broke over her face, earnest and open, no withholding shadows concealing anything dangerous. "Are you saying they like me?"

"They do," I assured her, giving her hand a squeeze. "And—unless you screw things up again—you have at least one local ready to vouch for you."

Acknowledgments

>))) ● (((

Each of the Thistle Grove books has had a theme that felt intensely personal to me: complicated homecomings in *Payback*, anxiety and panic in *Cursed*, familial and generational trauma in *Spell*. But I usually didn't recognize the emotional journey for what it would become until the story had already gotten well underway. Not the case with *In Charm's Way*, which has been Delilah's Book of Rage since its inception. But I still wasn't prepared for how much of my own rage and helplessness would make it onto the page—though mine might have been rooted in a different context, there's a commonality to that overwhelming sense of fury and entrapment, the exhausting anger many of us have endured at our own inability to change our circumstances—and how deeply I would feel for Delilah every step of the way. Surly and damaged and stubborn as she is, I hope you enjoyed Delilah's company as much as I did, even when her decisions weren't necessarily . . . the most palatable. (Unless you're into catharsis by way of blood spells in haunted forests, which, hey, might be just the thing for these trying times!)

ACKNOWLEDGMENTS

At the very least, I hope you understood her; and, if you're in any similar circumstance, maybe felt a glimmer of hope for better days to come.

As always, I'm indebted to my unflagging team at Berkley. Cindy, Angela, Hannah, Elisha, Stephanie, Katie, and everyone else involved in copyediting, design, and production—thank you for your tireless efforts in making yet more Thistle Grove magic. To the Root Literary team, you are and have always been a dream. Taylor, thank you for these books, and for your gentle handling of my sanity. Jasmine, thank you for all the administrative wrangling you do on my behalf, and for the emails, especially the salty ones.

To my critique group ladies, a huge thanks for all the hand-holding and insightful critiques of the first half of this book. Your edits were wise and kind, and reading your work has only ever made me want to be better.

To my family, thank you for standing by me through every stage of every storm. I would be at sea without you, maybe literally.

To Thistle Grove readers, thank you for reading, and for sharing your thoughts and emotions with me so generously. Hearing from you is always my very favorite part.

In Charm's
Way

LANA HARPER

Questions for Discussion

))) ● (((

1. When we first meet Delilah, she's experiencing feelings of utter helplessness and panic in the aftermath of the lingering oblivion glamour—a sense that she can't trust her own memory. Have you ever felt similar frustration or fear when it came to your mind or body? Can you identify with Delilah's reaction to her predicament?

2. Another pervasive theme in Delilah's story is rage—fueled by her circumstances, her reliance on Ivy, and especially by Nina and her presence at Tomes & Omens. Did you find Delilah's anger and refusal to forgive Nina relatable? Did your perspective toward her behavior change throughout the story?

3. How did you feel about Delilah's decision to cast the baneful blood spell? Was it reckless, or reasonable under the circumstances?

4. What did you think of Delilah's headstrong insistence on handling the aftermath of the blood spell on her own, instead of going to Uncle James and Emmy immediately?

5. What did you think of Ivy and Delilah's friendship? Do you think Delilah's abrasiveness and self-reliance are forms of selfishness, as Ivy believes, or a defense mechanism? Or a bit of both?

6. In many ways, Cat straddles two worlds and feels pulled in opposing directions. How did you respond to her moral ambiguity? Did you understand why Delilah might have found her so attractive?

7. Which of the cryptids did you find the most terrifying? The most compelling?

8. If you were to bond a familiar, what animal would it be? What would you name them?

9. What did you think about inner Tomes? If you were to travel into your own mind as Delilah and Cat are able to do, what do you think Inner You would look like?

10. Which spell cast in the story would you most like to see?

Keep reading for a preview of the next book in
The Witches of Thistle Grove series by *New York Times*
bestselling author Lana Harper,

Rise and Divine

From Berkley Romance.

The Pretender

EATING DEVILS IS thirsty work.

Much more than the magic itself, it was the savagery of my thirst that always took them by surprise, along with the unexpected normalcy of my hydration arsenal. Thistle Grove normies and witches alike, most of those who called on me came fully primed to find me using occult accessories of, let's say, a more ominous bent. Pungent curls of henbane smoke wisping from a tarnished censer, clusters of crystal shards bundled with dried herbs and feathers, arcane mutterings. (To be fair, I was more than game for the odd bit of arcane muttering when the exorcism called for it, or when an occasion seemed to demand a certain sense of heightened drama. Even an outlier like me couldn't quite resist the Avramov family flair for the theatrical.)

It barely even fazed me now, the way their apprehension clouded over into bewilderment when I unzipped my entirely mundane black Patagonia backpack to pull out my hefty water bottle, lined with cheerful imperatives to HYDRATE YOUR-SELF! in two-hour increments. Then came the parade of organic apple juice boxes more appropriate for a middle-schooler's back-pack, followed by strawberry Pedialyte, just in case the ritual threw my electrolytes too far out of whack. And, as a last resort, those miniature liquor bottles you usually found tucked away in hotel room minibars like guilty secrets.

It didn't help with the thirst, but with some of the nastier spec-imens I came across, nothing burned away the aftertaste quite like a fiery slug of Wild Turkey, tossed back sharp.

But today, this client's unusual composure was throwing me. When I'd arrived at the Arcane Emporium and quietly drawn back the burgundy velvet curtain that veiled this divination enclo-sure, secluding it from the rest of the occult store and the series of identical nooks on either side, she'd been sitting across the table from Amrita in a posture I knew well. Head bowed, tendons standing out like steel cables in her neck, thin hands clasped on the tabletop so tightly the knuckles had paled into skeletal knobs.

Fear made flesh.

But the appraising glance she'd shot me when I slipped in, a keenly scrutinizing, clear-eyed sweep of my entire person, had been shrouded by only the faintest film of uncertainty. Nothing like my normal clients.

"Hello," I said, setting my sloshing backpack down with a clink and extending my hand. I'd found that a courteously detached demeanor, the kind of brisk professionalism you'd get from a doctor, served me better than any cultivated aura of mystique when it came to setting them at ease. The thoroughly petrified wanted to feel that they were in capable, experienced hands. "Good to meet you. I'm Daria Avramov, Amrita's colleague. Dasha, if you like."

"Right," the woman said, with a crisp bob of the head that made her glossy cap of chin-length brown hair sway, its fastidious caramel highlights glinting in the candlelight. She looked to be in her mid-to-late thirties, a handful of years older than me. Not my type, but a bland and fresh-faced pretty, with the kind of dewy skin that indicated either premium genes or the budget for regular Botox, fillers, and serums. Her handshake was cool but surprisingly firm; I was accustomed to a much clammier and more tremulous greeting experience. "The . . . the specialist. I'm Emily Duhamel, but just Emily's fine."

I withdrew my hand, considering her more closely. Anyone who required my niche services tended to show up beside themselves with terror—and unsure of whether they should be more afraid of whatever it was that plagued them or me, yon fearsome exorcist witch. A "cure worse than the disease" type paradox. Given the breakdown of Thistle Grove's normie population, they were also often the love-and-light types who drove me batty; the low-effort, high-commitment kind who outsourced their chakra cleansings and indiscriminately flung cash at the spiritual life coaches they invariably found through social media.

Unfortunately, this insufferable subgroup came with the territory. Many Thistle Grove transplants were drawn here by the allure of living in a town steeped in witchy history, as if simply paying property taxes in a place ostensibly founded by four witch families might awaken some dormant, deeply buried psychic talents of their own. Even the Arcane Emporium's pervasive herb-and-incense fragrance wasn't enough to mask the patchouli scent they seemed to emanate with their actual souls. The irony of it was, when something sly and eldritch *did* come creeping in at their open-ended invitation, it often turned out that these were definitively not the vibes they'd been looking for. That was when they came running to Avramov diviners at the Arcane Emporium, as the only game in town that cut their teeth on shadows, specialized in dealing with manifestations from the other side of the veil.

But this woman wasn't so easily rattled, and I didn't catch so much as a whiff of figurative patchouli drifting off her; only the sweet floral notes of some top-shelf perfume. Something like Vera Wang, probably, not that I had the first fucking clue how to identify designer scents. But that one at least sounded like something I'd heard of wealthy people wearing, at any rate.

"Thank you for coming out for this, especially on a weekend," she added, with a light laugh and a semi-incredulous shake of her head, as if the patent absurdity of her circumstances—the fact that the "specialist" in question was an alleged witch, with the alleged power to banish whatever monster it was that lurked under her bed—hadn't escaped her. "I, uh, I'm looking forward to your expert opinion."

"Glad to hear it," I said, even more taken aback. Though I maintained a rigorous facade of respect and decorum with my clients, even when I found them slightly ridiculous as people—the last thing anyone needed while already at their wits' end and seeking help was to feel slighted or dismissed—they rarely rivaled me in equanimity. For one of the haunted, this Emily had her shit impressively together, I decided, revising my estimate of her upward by several more notches. Despite the deceptively soft, flower-embroidered cashmere sweater over a preppy collared shirt and prettily distressed jeans, I suspected she did something high-powered in her weekday life. Demanding work that left her encased in an enamel shell that never really chipped off. "And happy to help with . . . your problem, of course. I assume Amrita has discussed our rates with you?"

"Oh, yes." She suppressed a tiny smile, as if she found our hourly rate laughably low but didn't want to offend. I felt a twinge of annoyance with her; whatever it was she did, not all of us were in the business of fleecing people by overcharging for essential services. "It won't be a problem."

"Perfect."

I looked over at Amrita, who, though her everyday role was store manager, was bedecked in the clichéd fortune-teller regalia we wore for the tourists' benefit during our divination shifts— plummy lipstick, a layered cascade of gauzy maroon shawls shot through with silver thread, coin medallion earrings, stacked rings on every slim finger. With her huge, thickly kohled dark eyes and lacquered spill of black hair coursing loose over her shoulders, my half sister looked like my polar opposite, like the entire palette of decadent color that should've been split between us had somehow ended up hers. Her hair inky dark to my white-blond; skin a warm golden brown to my year-round pallor; clothes a bright riot of color to the black cowl-neck sweater, black jeans, and black knee-high suede boots that comprised my fall uniform.

Compared to her, sometimes I thought I looked like a shade myself, a living ghost.

Appropriately enough, maybe.

Unlike me, Amrita blended seamlessly into the divination en-closure décor. We kept the interiors suitably arcane but also fairly simple. Three wooden chairs, and a small round table covered with a silky altar cloth styled after the tarot deck we all grew up using, the one that had been designed by Oksana Avramov two centuries ago. On it sat an ornate silver platter that held a gray pillar candle with a high-licking flame, anchored by a dried pool of its own wax, along with an onyx scrying plate, a bowl of black salt, and a scattering of winking crystals more for appearances than use. A maroon damask canopy swooped over the tops of all the cubicles in the divination area, to blot out the Emporium's brighter overhead lighting. In here there was only candlelight, and the soft bluish glow of a Turkish mosaic spiral lamp tucked into one corner, its turquoise glass-chip globes swaying slightly on their brass chains every time one of us shifted in our chair. It made for a very mundanely achieved yet otherworldly effect.

"Catch me up on the details?" I said to Amrita. She'd summoned me by text once she realized Emily had a problem more in my wheelhouse than hers, but the information she'd sent had been unusually vague.

My sister nodded smoothly, though I caught the familiar flicker of concern that flitted across her delicate features, the same disquiet I often saw in the mirror. Sometimes her expressions were uncanny replicas of mine; a side effect of us both having inherited our father's face. "This is the tainted object," she said, sliding a velvet jewelry pouch to me across the table. I noticed the gingerly way she touched it, as if she'd have liked to limit contact with it even while moving it toward me. "I believe it's the locus for whatever it is that's attached itself to Emily."

"So it's definitely an entity, not a curse?" I asked. Sometimes our clients came into possession of heirlooms that had, either by accident or ill intent, become infused with malign spellwork that affected the wearer. The effects could appear similar to a haunting, but unpicking that kind of snarly working was a completely different undertaking, and not my forte.

"An infestation for sure," Amrita confirmed, with a shudder so faint that someone less familiar with my sister's graceful poise wouldn't even have caught it. "A pestilential one, too, by the feel of it."

"There's no need to put it that way," Emily cut in with a startling edge of reproach to her tone, a flash of temper flaring in her lightly mascaraed hazel eyes. Under closer scrutiny, she looked a little worn out beneath that tasteful makeup, the flesh under her eyes the tender, predawn hue of purple that came from more than one restless night. Something was disturbing her sleep. "So crudely. Like she's *evil*. An affliction. I told you, it isn't like that. I'm not afraid of her."

She, I noted. *Her.* So Emily thought she already knew what had taken up residence inside her jewelry.

Lana Harper is the *New York Times* bestselling author of the Witches of Thistle Grove series. Writing as Lana Popović, she has also written four YA novels about modern-day witches and historical murderesses. Born in Serbia, Lana grew up in Hungary, Romania, and Bulgaria before moving to the US, where she studied psychology and literature at Yale University, law at Boston University, and publishing at Emerson College. She lives in Chicago, where she spends most of her time plotting witchy stories and equally witchy tattoos.

VISIT LANA HARPER ONLINE

LanaPopovicBooks.com
🐦 LanaPopovicLit
📷 Lanalyte